The Bugman Chronicles
Book 1

The Bugman.

'You never know who's listening...'

By Will Conrad.

Table of contents.

*'Eavesdroppers or such as listen
under walls or windows,
or the eaves of a house, to
hearken after discourse, and there-
upon to frame slanderous and
mischievous tales, are a common
nuisance.'*

Commentaries on the Laws of
England (1765-1769)
Sir William Blackstone

1 Monday January 14th 1800 Hours.

The quieter you are, the more you are able to hear.

I'm sitting in the back of the 'Tea Cutter' public house. More like the 'Throat Cutter'. I'm way out back at the table in the corner, out of eye line for most customers at the bar and I have a good view of the door that's far enough away from the toilets not to smell them. This isn't my usual haunt.

A half drunk pint of something ambitiously called bitter sits on the table along with two ragged corpses of peanut packets, glinting brightly to remind me of the debris around my feet.

Hindsight's a wonderful thing. If I knew then what I know now, I would maybe have got up and walked out. Or maybe not. At any rate within the next few days, I'll be behind bars and people will be dead.

My Name's David Quintaña. I've never attached any sentimentality to it. That surname I acquired from my parents, who in turn acquired with it from theirs when they fled Spain following the civil war. The next piece of inaccuracy is my first name which is Buenaventura. Try going to school with that.

It's late afternoon and getting dark outside. Sporadic drops of rain hit the grimy windows to slither down through the layer of dust. At the bar are an old man in a tobacco stained flat cap and ageing lush a long way the wrong side of forty five. The man is reading the racing post and nursing a half like it was the blood of Christ and the lush is knocking back vodka and coke like she had just got the thirty pieces of silver. The barmaid's a skinny kid with red dyed hair trying not to get engaged in conversation while the Lush orders again. Her face turns briefly showing the faded make-up covered bruise on her

6

left cheek as she glances at a male about my age sidling through the doorway. A dirty blue shell suit, all rustling nylon, his eyes momentarily flicker over the open purse the Lush has left laying on the bar. The eyes move away too quickly and barely pausing he comes fully into the pub, the door banging back a little too hard against the stop.

I never forget a face, but names I sometimes have to work for. Jason Connor or Conrad, about my height and build. In fact he must be quite similar to me, because once, several years ago I got mistaken for him. He's slim build, average height with very short dark hair and a goatee. He carries an air of nervous energy about him that's quite wearing to watch, always moving. Jason ignores all of the empty stools and stands at the bar to the side of the Lush, moving back and forth from the bar like a moored fishing boat in a swell. He talks too much and too loud turning to his captive audience dominating the space. I don't like him, but he's a member of a long list

As a pint of watered down lager gets pushed across the bar towards him my attention is diverted by the arrival in the pub of my appointment, the door opens slowly and quietly and Archie Hayes pushes his head in, craning to scan the pub, which he does left to right then back again. The head pulls back like a tortoise going back in it's shell and I can tell Archie is about to leave, until he spots me and oozes around the half open door letting it slip from his fingers and shut quietly behind him. At the bar he buys a house brandy which he pays for with a large amount of small change from a faded leather zip up purse. I can tell it's not his first of the day even before the brandy scented breath hits me across the table as he carefully sets his glass down.

'Hello dear boy.' Archie intones in what he believed for thirty years passed as an Oxbridge accent.

'Archie.' I acknowledge non committally.

7

Archie Hayes. A para-legal parasite. A rep for Morgan, Styles and Brown. Solicitors of choice to every wannabe-be lowlife in town. Styles and Brown are long gone, if they ever existed, and old man Morgan, the dodgiest man to ever practice law hasn't left the office in years. Rumour has it Morgan found a loophole that had somehow been overlooked. It involved empty properties and placing an iron peg in the foundations. I never cared to find the details, but somehow this bizarre ritual allowed Morgan to acquire a large amount of derelict properties in the area.

The result of all this was that Morgan, I presumed, now just counted his money, and while his name was still above the door it was Hayes that handled the, (I hesitate to use the term), "legal" defence of their clients.

Archie sips his brandy and clears his throat. 'It seems we have need,' He leans in closer across the unstable pub table between us, giving me full benefit of his brandy soaked breath and yellow stained teeth, as he lowers his voice with unnecessary theatricality, '...of your services.'

I leaned back, more to get myself out of his face than to lend any more ham theatrics to Archie's already overblown performance. 'What do you need?'

Before you get the wrong idea I'll explain what I do. It involves providing a certain specialised service. Which, while not being strictly illegal could certainly be considered immoral. I don't steal and I've never killed anyone. I produce a certain kind of product and how people use it is up to them. That product is information, for a fee. At one time, in America I would have been called a 'Bugman', someone who plants hidden listening devices and records things the speakers often would rather had stayed private. I suppose Bugman is better than 'Bugger', really not a great name for a trade or profession. Again it's just a name. Some in my field might style themselves 'Technical Surveillance operatives' or even 'Covert Surveillance operators.' but those guys have probably just watched too much T.V. We exist in a legal and moral grey area. While also being the grey man, not standing out, never lingering in memory. The skill set of my profession is as broad as it can be specialised. Work is hard to come by, sporadic and unreliable. The last vestiges of pride I allow myself are in doing the job well and living as far off the grid as possible.

Working for Hayes was not ideal. I had done a couple of small jobs for him in the past, but his sort of clients couldn't really afford what it took to do a proper job. Worse, I didn't really trust the man. But it had been too long since I had last had a decent job that had paid and making my little electronic novelties wasn't cheap and neither was my grubby basement flat. Against all good judgement I had to hear Archie out.

'We are representing a certain local,' He paused before carefully forming the next word as if careful enunciation could somehow launder the word. "businessman." We all knew what he meant. Archie's bloodshot eyes looked up at me from where they had been contemplating the swirling mass of brandy. 'A certain Turkish property owner.'

I nodded, I knew who he was referring to. Mr. Ali. Loan shark and slum landlord and suspected importer of certain chemicals. Also clearly a very poor businessman as most operations he started had a habit of burning to the ground a few months in, much to the insurance company's chagrin. 'And how can I help this model of free enterprise?' I asked.

'Well, he seems to have found himself in a little difficulty.' Archie downed the last of his brandy as if to give himself the courage to go on. 'One of his properties unfortunately burned down last week. Most tragically killing some poor unfortunate who happened to be in the shop at the time.'

I recalled the news headline. I didn't realise it was one of Ali's buildings, but it wasn't that surprising. 'So how can I be of any help?'

'Ah, you see, my client's misfortune didn't stop there dear boy. It appears that some of Mr, er, my clients former employees were caught on CCTV doing things they shouldn't have with cans of petroleum.'

'And?'

'Well that would be one thing, but these ingrates have, it seems made certain scandalous accusations against my client.'

'I take it then, that these ex-employees are not also your clients.'

Archie smiled a long slow thin smile like an overweight shark. 'Ah, yes, dear boy, you see the point. No they are not our clients, conflict of interest in legal terms. You see my client has been arrested and is currently being held on a seventy two hour extension at the local nick. If we were representing all parties I would not need to speak to you now. But we fear these two ex-employees, motivated entirely by malice, are making some very serious allegations against our client.'

I was following what Archie was saying, but not quite getting how all this applied to me and my very particular skill set. 'So where do I come into all this?'

'Um.' Was all Archie said with an overacted grimace that wouldn't have been out of place in a pantomime. 'Another drink dear boy?' I got the impression Dear old Archie needed a hiatus to figure out how best to put this proposal to me so I nodded in affirmation and gestured to my now quarter of a pint. Archie nodded in response and hefted himself from his chair and stalked towards the bar with an air of half cut gravitas.

Seeking respite from Archie Hayes performance I breathed out slowly and let my gaze widen to encompass the pub from its golden yellow stained wallpaper to maroon velvet curtains. Jason was still at the bar almost bouncing off it as he tried to engage the stick thin barmaid in conversation while she wearily tried to divide her attention between Archie's order and Jason's desire for acknowledgement. The lush was seemingly oblivious to all but the glass of vodka she was pouring down her lined throat, maybe I detected a slight pique that she was not the centre of attention. The old man had now taken a seat by the window and was intermittently nodding off.

Jason's constant motion is wearing my patience, as he turns, now between Archie, the barmaid and the lush. His head never still. Then I see the telegraph, the eyes down to the open purse then away to a random, distant corner of the room. Way too obvious for me, but no one else has noticed it. I feel the old familiar tingle I get from knowing things no one else does. I gaze ostensibly at the door, but the periphery of my vision is now on Jason. The barmaid turns with Archie's brandy glass and she pushes it up into the optic, bubbles glugging up the bottle as first one then two measures trickle into the glass.

Jason glances at the first dose dropping into the glass, turns back to the Lush and makes a comment rather too loudly, which is followed up with a nudge of her shoulder. The lush pretends to smile in response to the comment and looks away, she thinks, demurely.

As all that happens Jason loudly demands another lager waving his glass in his left hand while his right pulls a ten pound note from the Lush's purse. No one sees it apart from me. The Lush, quite drunk now, was looking away with the studied demure look, the barmaid her back turned and Archie probably focused on his drink being poured. Should any of the assembled cast have looked the right way their eyes would have been drawn to Jason's glass being waved at eye level and not the purse.

11

The barmaid turns back round and hands Archie his drink. Jason passes her his glass and the ten pounds together.

Nicely done. The money concealed in plain view all along. I wonder where Jason learned that trick or whether it's just an innate criminal reflex.

In my mind I chalk that one onto Jason's account as Archie sits back down passing over a pint of beer, spilling a little on the beer mat as he does so.

I thank Archie and he settles into his chair like he were about to lay an egg. 'Now where were we dear boy?'

'I think you were telling me where I fit into your clients problems.'

'Ah, yes. Well I was rather hoping you could fit into our clients solutions.' He tried a half hearted chuckle, but it came up short and fooled no one. 'You see, the problem is, these two, shall we say ex associates of our client are, we presume, potentially making some outlandish claims against the businessman.'

'and?'

'and he would find it rather convenient to know exactly what he is being accused of.'

'Surely he will find that out in court.' I added knowing how redundant it must have sounded to Archie.

'David, David. I credit you with more intelligence than that. In court it will be a little too late. He needs to know what they are saying to the police. Now if we were representing all parties we would naturally be present in the interviews, but as we are only representing the one party..' He let it trail.

'I suppose you have no way to get it from their legal representatives?'

Archie sighed deeply. 'Sadly not. For some absolutely inexplicable reason the two have chosen not to exercise their right to legal council. I fear the pair are not too bright and may well have been offered some sort of inducement from unscrupulous police officers.'

'If as you fear, there are unscrupulous police officers involved, surely your businessman could come to some kind of arrangement?'

'Perish the thought dear boy, apart from being highly unethical these are from the major crime department, not local. Unfortunately again for our client once people die the police tend to bring in the big boys from out of town.'

A bit rich for Archie to be someone to bring up ethics, but I let that pass. 'So let me get this straight. You, or rather your client, would like me to record what two people are saying in a police interview. A police interview taking place in the custody area of a police station. A police station full of, not to mention of police, but major crime detectives investigating a murder?' I leaned back confident I had made my point.

'Exactly, I think you have understood the brief.' Archie took a hard swallow of some brandy and looked away.

I slowly sipped my beer, carefully placing it back on the damp beer mat for effect. 'No way. First it's impossible and second, even if it weren't neither you nor your client could afford the fee to do it.'

Archie stammered out, 'my, my client has considerable resources.' His fake Oxbridge accent slipping towards south London faster than a Northern line tube train.

'And, how long do I have to do this?' I was guessing, it wouldn't be long. Police normally only have twenty four hours to hold someone, and can get an extension for another seventy two.

'You have less than seventy two hours.'

'I thought as much. Well Archie it's completely impossible. You know how long I need. Weeks if possible. There's the information gathering, the reconnaissance and then building the devices. A job this risky would need months to do properly. Even if I were stupid enough to take the job and your client was wealthy enough to pay, I would effectively be walking into a prison cell and locking the door myself.'

Archie ran cracked nails through his thinning grey hair. He was starting to really show stress and the point that was stressing him was my refusal. There was clearly some pressure on him. 'David, dear boy, I'm sure a man of your talents can find a way to do this, name your price.'

I must admit, my mind, despite myself was running away, spinning and churning up permutations and combinations of ways to achieve the impossible. I thought I'd throw out a figure, but one hopefully large enough to end the conversation and let me get on with my evening without the thought of bugging a police station. 'O.K. Archie, if I were to consider it the fee will be one hundred grand. Ten percent up front.'

I'd never charged anything approaching that for a single job. Even so it wouldn't be an unreasonable price. I'd always tended to sell myself too cheap, particularly with local small local gigs like I had previously done for Archie. In response he nearly choked on the last of his brandy. He gulped it down a small trickle glistening on his jowls. He coughed. 'Dear boy, get another round in would you, I need to make a phone call.' He put his glass down in front of me and pulled an ancient and battered Nokia from his waistcoat pocket and began the process of hoisting himself up from the chair.

Archie slipped out the front door with a fluidity that was surprising, and I went up to the bar. I chose the corner of the bar, both to be as far from everyone else as possible and also to keep half an eye on Archie Hayes through the grimy front windows as he paced back and forth talking into his obsolete mobile phone. The barmaid was at the other corner of the bar and looked to be studying her nails. Despite having no other customers demanding her attention she didn't seem no notice me. I leaned against the bar holding out a handful of change.

I had noticed long ago, when I had started frequenting pubs, that I seemed to turn invisible when I approached a bar wanting a drink. This inexplicable vanishing act puzzled and perplexed me for some years as I often sought in vain to get anywhere near drunk in a crowded pub. It wasn't until I fell into my current occupation that I fully appreciated the art of invisibility. Nowadays I try to channel this when I need to work unnoticed. None of that however was getting me served. I temporarily switched my relaxed but alert mindset off and tried to channel a roaring lion. It seemed to work and the barmaid glanced up, saw the outstretched hand of change and reluctantly stalked to my end of the bar. In my mind I stopped roaring and ordered Archie another brandy, the cheapest the barmaid could find.

I sat back down. I wanted to watch Archie when he returned, confident I would be able to get a good read on him in the time it took him to get back to the table. As it happened it wasn't a hard read at all. Archie slipped back in the door like a Shakespearian assassin with the weight of an corpse on his shoulders. His cheeks were ruddy with the veins on them showing as vivid as the ones on the tip of his nose. He shoved the Nokia back in the waistcoat pocket and then unconsciously wiped his hand on his trousers. He dropped slowly into the chair without saying anything and took a sip of the drink giving an almost imperceptible nod of thanks and not a small measure of regret.

Part of me is surprised and pleased that Archie Hayes Legal Rep. Actually seems to have some kind of conscience, but another part of me was noting his weakness and obvious discomfort and looking for a way to exploit it. 'You've been told it's way too much and they want the job done for much less.' I offered.

15

'Sort of.' He conceded taking another sip.

I found myself frowning. 'Go on.'

'You are right Dear Boy, it's far too much for what our client is willing to pay. However I have been instructed to make another offer. You realise I'm only the conduit, so to speak, acting on behalf of another...' He let that trail, clearly trying to distance himself from what came next. '...our client will pay ten thousand and no more and suggests quite earnestly that you accept the, er, commission.'

I began to shake my head with a very slow and smug 'No. Is your client aiming for an insanity plea?'

'Far from it. I've been instructed to remind you of that little job you did last July.' I cast my mind back, it wasn't hard, I hadn't had that many jobs in the last couple of years and I hadn't done more than two involving Archie bloody Hayes et. al. It had been some kind of messy divorce with restraining orders and accusations from both parties of domestic violence. Normal for round here, but what wasn't normal was some property worth money was tied up in the whole deal. As I recall it was a simple series tap on the land-line. Five minutes work inside one of B.T's magic green boxes that sit at the end of most streets. 'I remember the job.' I said flatly.

'Well, it seems my client would like you to know that he has film of you tampering with British Telecom equipment. I admit, hardly the crime of century, but the law is particularly strict with things of that nature, it all goes back to when B.T. was the GPO. It's still really thought of as Government property.'

I allowed a moment to curse myself for being so bloody careless. I'd never ever treat a job as simple again. I let that self recrimination boil over into a flash of anger. 'Don't lecture me on the law Archie. You don't even have a law degree.' I saw Archie start to flinch reflexively as I jabbed a finger towards his paunch to punctuate my statements and puncture his pride, if he had any left. His discomfort only spurred me on. 'Oh, Archie don't think I don't know you. You went to a local Grammar school which you were spectacularly mediocre at before working at the counter of a local bank until you took a correspondence course to become a solicitors rep. You're not a lawyer, you're not much more than a pimp for failed criminals.' He sat stock still and silent while I continued my quiet onslaught. 'Your penchant for drink and horses have left you alone in the world and with a credit rating, last time I checked, of shall we say, sub prime.'

When I'd finished Archie sat quietly and took a sip to console himself. I considered the implications of what he had just said. The damage was probably not too serious. With no other evidence I doubted the recording, no matter how good, would be enough to land me inside. However I didn't know what else might be lurking. I'd recovered the recording equipment, the only things they could reasonably hold were the recordings themselves. However, the point was, regardless of the legal consequences, any official interest into my activities could severely limit my usefulness in the illicit information gathering world.

I'd never been arrested. I didn't exist as far as the police were concerned. They had neither my DNA nor my fingerprints. My own carefulness, or as others might say, paranoia, had left me off of as many databases and lists as possible. I don't live off the grid entirely, but I do inhabit a very dark and dusty corner of it. Exposure could bring me blinking into the light and I didn't relish the thought of that happening.

'Who is this talking Archie, is this Messrs Morgan, Styles and Brown or is this our friendly local Businessman?' The change of pace and tone took Archie a second or two to catch up with, but he answered without thinking on the ramifications.

'I'm afraid it's our client. A reputable law firm would obviously never condone such behaviour.' I wasn't sure who's behaviour he was referring to, his, mine or Mr. Ali. Not that it mattered.

'You realise Archie, that our relationship is now at an end.'

He nodded solemnly. Even Archie must realise that while honour among thieves is a myth there does have to be a minimal level of trust. 'So are you going to accept this commission?' Archie asked as carefully as an afternoon of brandy would allow him.

My mind was turning fast. I sat still. The best thing to do is to just walk away now. The possible threat from the recording was certainly less than the definite peril of a near suicide mission. In my head I was trying to balance risk versus reward and coming up short at every possible spin of the wheel. Every time I came back to the problem I got a cold tingle down the back of my scalp. The sheer impossibility of job appealed to my perverse sense of vanity. This would be one for the record books. My rational mind was screaming "No!" but instead I found myself saying quite calmly and quietly. 'Ten Grand, up front whether I succeed or not and the recording vanishes.'

Archie pulled a bent and creased Manila envelope from his inside pocket and slid it across the table towards me. I picked it up and looked inside. There seemed to be a large number of well used twenties and and fifties totalling about two thousand. There was a piece of paper which I pulled out. On it was written "Mikal Dinko" and "Grigor Malinkova" and "South Street Police Station." Archie stood up 'Dear boy, you have till midday Friday. I hope to hear from you.' He turned and strode away, out of the pub.

As the door swung shut behind him I pulled the digital recorder I had taped under the table free and switched it off. I looked at my watch. I had a maximum of fifty six hours left to achieve the impossible.

2. Monday, January 14th 1930 Hours.

Preparation and planning prevent piss poor performance.

I walked the long way home from the pub. Mainly to get rid of the beer and clear my head for the task at hand, but also because I had always cultivated habits that kept me safe and secure in my paranoid little world. Several loops around several blocks and then into my road casually noting every vehicle and not seeing any that shouldn't be there. I approached the steps down to my front door carefully, alert to anyone in the street that might be loitering in the sodium inspired shadows, key already in my hand to unlock the six pin Yale, pin tumbler lock. I slipped through the outer door into the damp and musty hallway.

I checked the seal I had placed in the corner of the door, and was satisfied it was intact. I unlocked the mortise lock and went in. My flat is three almost subterranean rooms in a nondescript five floor house in a street of nondescript houses. I don't have many visitors and I don't own a sofa or a TV. The room has four desks and a work bench. Computers, radios and tools adorn them. The only other furniture are several high and overstocked book shelves and a mismatched selection of office chairs.

Most of the kit has been acquired by what the Hacking fraternity call dumpster diving or trashing. Although the actual practice refers to the collection of written or electronic intelligence by rooting through a companies bins, there is also a wealth of used computer equipment and furnishings to had by anyone who cares to take a mid-night rummage through a skip. Again, an activity that the powers that be class as technically illegal, I consider it aggressive recycling.

The rest of the flat is fairly normal. A bed room and a kitchen come bathroom. I'm not house proud, dust coats most rooms and I can't remember the last time the toilet was cleaned. But then I don't encourage visitors. I went and sat in the 'executive' office chair in front of the desk with a dual screen set up on it. I tapped the mouse to clear the screen saver and checked the five camera CCTV display on the second monitor. All the cameras were up and running, I quickly reviewed for any event triggers and satisfied my kingdom was intact and unmolested I went down the hall to fire up the espresso machine.

A good double shot of Italian coffee in hand I sat back down at the computer and started thinking. I had two problems to deal with. The first was the job I had been given. The second was the client, I don't like bullies and I don't react too well to being bullied. I'll admit that I'm not the sort of person to stand up to a bully and make a scene. My style is sitting in the shadows and plotting. Due to the time constraints involved I was going to have to deal with the job first. Mr Ali and Archie Hayes would come later. I resolved to put them out of my mind for now.

That had cleared fifty percent of the issues from my mind. The fundamental principle of engineering is to break down a big problem into smaller chunks and deal with those. I began to break down the task at hand. Getting into the custody area would be the main trick of this job. Of course getting into a police custody block is stupidly easy. Just get caught committing a crime, however getting out is not so simple.

I fired up a web browser and began researching arrest and custody procedures. A couple of hours of civil liberties web sites and mind numbingly boring on-line law documents and I had discovered the Police and Criminal Evidence act and had grudgingly gone through it. Beyond the police themselves I had found several other groups of people that get access to the custody area; prisoners, lawyers, appropriate adults, translators and lay custody visitors. One of these might provide my vector inside. Turning away from that aspect of the problem I made some more coffee and started to consider the actual execution of the bug. The problem was that I didn't have any way of visualising the space I was going to have to record. My clean living, never having provided me a view into the workings of a police interview room.

It was getting late. I was pacing, smoking and simultaneously sipping coffee when I caught the sight of someone approaching the front steps on camera one. A figure in the black and white of infra-red paused at the top of steps and then stepped down gracefully, in my opinion, considering how damp and slippery the steps were. The figure resolved into a slim brunette in a impossibly tight black dress. It was Clara. She paused at the hidden camera, pouted at it and tilted her head. I didn't know how, but she always seemed to know when I was in. I hit the button for the electromagnet door release and she pushed the door out of her way.

I don't have many visitors. Almost none apart from Clara. I don't recall exactly how or when she received that level of access, but there was a sort of trust between us. Clara is what is known as an escort or more simply a prostitute. A high end one, no doubt. We had met on a job a couple of years ago when I had been tasked with the covert filming of a married prominent businessman.

Clara is what any man would describe as stunning. Women like Clara just don't meet men like me. If I've learned one thing in life, it's that men with easy access to cash and a difficult access to honesty are the most successful with women.

We had spent a weekend at a very upmarket London hotel while aforementioned businessman was in town for some business talks. My part involved three days cramped into the next room to his installing and operating a variety of hidden cameras while Clara worked her spell on the hapless executive. We had shared a room as we both plied our trade. From my point of view it wasn't an ideal situation, but the net result was that we ended our weekend with all our professional secrets laid uncomfortably bare.

We are quite similar, although while I hide in the shadows she hides, stunningly and beautifully in clear sight. The people she spends time with end up revealing all their innermost intimate secrets without ever learning anything about her and the people I spent time with share all their innermost intimate secrets without even knowing I exist.

I don't know if you could call what we had a relationship. I think we both liked being around someone we didn't have to lie to. Of course I refuse to make any concessions in my lifestyle for her and she seems to find that arrangement acceptable. It doesn't hurt that she's quite easy on the eye.

I got up and let her through the inner door. She walked in wordlessly in a could of expensive perfume and carrying a new fur coat. Her long dark hair was loose and off the shoulder and fell in relaxed curls halfway down her back. She wore a black dress that left just enough to the imagination and probably more material on the cutting room floor than was stitched over her tight curves.

I assumed she had been working. She put the fur coat over the back of one of the office chairs and looked at me, raising an eyebrow quizzically. Clara had a gift with expression, she could go from nought to innocent girl in half a second and then shift the gears all the way up to worldly wise mistress of her fate. In fact mistress of anyone's fate she cared to manipulate.

Maybe she manipulated me, I didn't think too deeply about that. Maybe I didn't care.

'You've got a job on?' She asked. I nodded. I don't know how she could tell. I'd like to think that somewhere in her half Italian, part Persian and part whatever, that she had some kind of psychic intuition. I suspect the truth of it was that her job had made her extremely good at reading people and situations. She plucked the cigarette from my hand and strode off towards the bedroom smoking it. I sat back down at the computer.

Clara came back in a few moments later. She was now wearing one my sweatshirts and tracksuit bottoms and she had removed the make-up from her face. She sat down in the only chair that could be classed as comfortable, a big fake leather executive affair that once may have adorned the office of an overpaid CEO.

'Have you ever been arrested?'

Clara raised that eyebrow at me again and smiling asked 'No, why?'

'I need to know what happens in a police station.'

'You could always get yourself arrested, honey, but don't expect me to bail you out.' I looked at her sitting there in my tracksuit. They never looked that good on me, in fact I never wore them out. The tracksuit was more the kind of thing that someone like Jason Connor wore and the more distance I could put between him and myself the better.

Clara stood up. 'Do you realise the time?' I looked at my watch and saw it was half past two. I now had about fifty hours left.

'It's half two.' I dumbly read the time to Clara.

'Are you planning on staying awake all night?' I considered the question. I needed to find a solution, but if I drank any more coffee I'd probably start throwing up coupled with that my mind had hit a brick wall. I could sense something on the other side but the more I pushed the higher the wall seemed.

'Not sure, I think I'd better sleep on it.' Clara nodded and went through to the bedroom. I jotted down a few notes and joined her.

As I turned out the light I set my mind the task of solving the problem by morning. Despite the coffee I was asleep quickly.

3 Tuesday 15th January 0800 Hours.

Time Spent in reconnaissance is never wasted.

I awoke at eight from a deep untroubled sleep and in the few moments it took to get back to full consciousness I began remembering the mental turmoil of the night before, I was now more aware of there being a solution nearby. At the moment it was a hazy cloud of disparate parts. As I showered and made coffee I tried to focus and allow that cloud to coalesce into something more solid, something starting to resemble a plan.

Before I could do anything else I desperately needed to see inside of the police custody area and I needed to do it soon. I was aware of the ticking clock of my time counting inexorably down. Therefore the first problem was to get in. Applying Occam's razor to the problem, the simplest way in was to get arrested. The answer was so simple I had been discounting it all along. It was Clara who had jokingly suggested the solution and also inspired me in how I would accomplish it.

The clever bit would be how I got in and out without the Police ever being aware of who I was or what I was doing. I had an idea of how I was going to do this, but I would have to work quickly to iron out the few wrinkles. Once I had seen inside the interview rooms, I hoped the rest of the job would solve itself.

I was sitting at the computer skimming through some last details of research when Clara got up. She reached over me a sat a fresh coffee on the desk in front of me.

'Thanks,' I said 'and thanks for last night.'

'What did I do?' Puzzlement in her voice.

'You told me how to get into the Police Station.'

'You're going to get arrested?' Clara caught in quickly.

I turned round to face her, grinning. 'I'm going to walk into a cell and lock the door behind me.' I told her, aware I was telling her exactly what I had told Archie I wouldn't do.

Clara smiled back at me shaking her head. 'I don't understand what you're doing, but I like you when you're like this.'

'Like what?'

She turned away still smiling. 'A twinkle in the eye and solving impossible problems.' Clara walked out heading for the shower and I considered what she had said. Maybe she was getting to know me too well.

I went out to the shops to pick up a few items I'd need for the reconnaissance visit to the Police station. PVA wood glue from the DIY shop. Double sided sticky tape, the mainstay of all home construction projects. Then I went to a sports shop and got myself the most awful baggy, plastic tracksuit they had. I got back and checked the toner in my laser printer.

One last detail to take care of. This was the detail that amused me the most. Not absolutely essential, but there was a kind poetry to it and it involved some cleverness I'd read about and wanted to try.

It was lunchtime as I headed through town to the Tea Cutter public house. As I approached I noted the three people standing on the pavement outside smoking. I was hoping it would be fairly busy as that would make what I planned a little easier. In my left hand I carried a carrier bag, doubled up for strength and with a fresh broadsheet newspaper sitting inside folded in half so that it made a V shape filling the bag.

I opened the door and scanned the bar room. The same bar maid from yesterday was there serving the same day time drinkers with the same air of bored resignation. The old man was back at the bar reading a slightly newer copy of the racing post. Three or four other men all stood, being bored by Jason, who as luck would have it was holding court in the middle of the bar. He was wearing the same tracksuit as yesterday.

I walked in and stood to the right of Jason and hung my carrier bag by one handle on the brass hook under the bar. His back was half turned to me as he spoke at the two men to his left. While I waited for the barmaid to serve me I took a moment to study Jason. His tracksuit, already noted, the gaudy gold bracelet and neck chain. The thin goatee and the almost skin head haircut. I made a mental note of all this and then ordered a beer. A lager this time. The same as Jason's.

I drank my beer in silence. Jason carried on pouring forth to his audience. I tried to block out what he was saying. It was mostly about himself. He turned halfway towards me once or twice, but as it would have meant losing his larger audience to his left he gave up. I finished the first pint and ordered a second. I didn't touch it, but waited.

Jason was in full flow telling his audience about some unfortunate he had beaten up the night before. He was even acting out some of the punches he'd apparently thrown. I was carefully watching the level of his pint of lager descend. When it got to the last third I was ready.

I eventually caught the barmaids eye and ordered a packet of peanuts which were tossed down in front of me. I made a show of rummaging through my jeans pocket for the change, which I took slightly too long over. The barmaid began showing clear signs of impatience so I pulled the the change out rather too quickly, accidentally allowing a pound coin to slip from my hand and roll across the bar top to my left.

I quickly reached to grab the pound before it rolled out of reach, my hand knocking Jason's now almost empty pint, over. Time stopped, everyone jumped back from the spreading pool of beer.

'Ooops sorry.' I quickly said reaching for a nearby bar towel. I lifted Jason's overturned glass out of the way. No one paid any attention to my picking it up with my hand on the inside of the glass. I moved it fast away from the spreading liquid and dropped the bar towel onto the pool mopping it was one hand as I said 'Sorry, Sorry.' With the other hand I dropped the glass into my bag between the V formed by the newspaper. My body in front of the bag all the time, and all eyes watching me mop the bar with the other hand.

Jason had recovered from the shock. 'You spilled my pint.' He glowered. Hardly original, but accurate up to a point.

'I'm sorry my mistake.' I told him as I watched him clearly trying hard to puff himself up and work himself into a state of righteous indignation. Before he could finish that I quickly shifted my untouched pint along the bar in front of him. 'Here, have this as a replacement.' I added as meekly as I could. Jason, looked at the full pint and appeared slightly mollified. 'I'm very sorry, I'm a bit clumsy.' I tried to say, channelling meek and mild even though inside I was patting myself on the back at my sleight of hand.

Head down, apologising like a Japanese businessman I picked up my carrier bag and backed out of the pub. I allowed myself a broad grin as the door closed behind me and I made my way home with Jason's pint glass.

Back in my basement version of Moriarity's Workshop I put on some rubber gloves and carefully pulled the pint glass out, holding it, once again, by placing my fist inside it. I laid the newspaper on my workbench and placed the glass down on it. Next I took a graphite pencil and with a knife I shaved away the wood to expose a length of the grey inner. Into a small dish I scraped away at this producing a small pile of metallic powder. I stole one of Clara's make-up brushes and carefully twiddled the graphite powder onto the top third of the glass. I worked at this for a few minutes making notes as I identified each different fingerprint. When I was sure I had a complete set of Jason's I allowed myself a coffee break.

Suitably refreshed I cut several neat squares of double sided sticky tape. I used these to lift each of the prints and then stuck them all down on some white card. The white card then went into my computer's scanner which I set to monochrome and maximum resolution.

The resulting image I then loaded into an image manipulation program, my choice of graphics software. I ran an edge detect filter to clean up the image and then touched up the images by hand, before running another filter to thicken the lines and improve contrast. I ran a test print onto paper and checked this with a magnifying glass. I was happy with the results so I loaded the laser printer with clear acetate sheet and printed the dabs, running the sheet through multiple times to build a think layer of toner.

The printer toner on the sheet made nice textured ridges. So far so good. I took the PVA wood glue and began spreading a thin, even layer of the sticky white fluid over each print. I left it to dry.

I had wanted to try this technique out for some time. I first heard of this after the Chaos Computer club in Germany copied the finger print of the German interior minister some time back. It was good enough then to fool a fingerprint scanner. I was banking on that still being so.

While the PVA glue dried I spent some time committing to memory all the details of Jason Connor I had managed to glean from a few hours of Internet research. The electoral Roll, provided some address details. A credit check confirmed them and some incautious privacy settings in Facebook allowed me to flesh out the profile until I knew his name, address, Date of birth, national insurance number, mobile number. I knew where he went to school and I knew who his

29

friends were. I knew where he liked to go on a night out. I knew who his favourite band were. More pertinently I inferred he had been arrested more than once, but that he had been keeping his nose clean for a while. All of these made Jason Connor the perfect identity to borrow for a while. Well, that and I figured that fate owed him a small kick in the balls.

I went to the bedroom and using a precarious arrangement of mirrors took a set of clippers to my hair, both head and facial. I took a shower to get rid of those small hairs that always find their way down my neck after a hair cut. Mentally I used to the shower to mark my transition into character. You can forget your Oscar winners. This kind of acting was the most demanding. Self belief, or self delusion was everything. I wasn't sure how long I would have to be Jason, twenty four hours maximum, but I hoped it would be less. Channelling him was going to be very tiring.

As I pulled on the tracksuit I got over the initial revulsion quite quickly and by the time I'd put on the cheap chain store jewellery I found my body movements unconsciously slipping towards Jason's. My neck hunched forward slightly and a began to walk with kind of bandy legged swagger.

Back at the work bench the PVA glue had dried. With tweezers and a thin bladed knife I carefully peeled off each plastic blob. They came up very thin and transparent. I laid them on a sheet of card.

The last stage was the most fiddly and time consuming as I used theatrical spirit gum to stick each of Jason's prints over the correct finger. Being right handed doing the right hand was the most problematic and the thin plastic was difficult to work with. I sat at the work bench waving my hands in the air like I had just painted my nails. I was going to have to be very careful. I didn't know how rugged these prints were going to be and I wouldn't have a chance to reapply them.

I'd lost an hour applying the prints and so didn't have a lot more time to waste. I stuck a pocketful of notes in the ample jacket pockets and headed out. I had a good venue for my "crime" ready worked out. Mr Singh ran a small convenience store a mile or so away from my flat. In the past I'd used his photocopier and fax machine and kept quiet about the counterfeit cigarettes and wine he sold while his son Gianparkash ran occasional errands for me. The shop had the faded air of a business that probably just about broke even, The dirty cracked front windows bearing advertising for a cigarette brand that no longer existed and an over-abundance of rickety shelves inside that made for a narrow, cramped rat run of a store. Bits of cardboard packaging and cut bindings from newspapers littered the floor.

Singh sat on a stool behind the over cluttered counter watching a fuzzy and badly tuned portable TV. The shop was empty of customers so I walked straight up the counter pausing for a second to make an impulse purchase of a three litre bottle of "?Quite Frightening" premium cider. Seven point eight percent and guaranteed never to have been near an apple.

Singh nodded to me swinging round on his stool to one handedly punch in the price. 'How are you today?'

'I'm well Mr Singh. I have a proposition for you.'

'A proposition eh?' He fingered his beard. 'What nature of proposition?'

'How would you like a new window?' I asked him.

The finer points of the deal were negotiated in his cramped stock room. I handed over enough cash to more than cover a new window, knowing full well he'd still claim on the insurance. I made sure he understood the exact part I needed him to play getting him to repeat it all back to me. Then we rewound the CCTV in the shop and I left by the back door.

In the alleyway I opened the bottle of quite frightening. I instantly poured about two of the litres of premium apple like alcohol down a drain. I splashed a little down the front of the tracksuit and swirled some around my mouth. The stuff was vile and I didn't need any excuse to spit the stuff straight out.

I waited in the alley way until I saw a customer go into the shop. I figured that a witness or two would probably help. It was a little old lady with a shopping basket on wheels. I waited to give her enough time to get to the counter then and swaggered in, exaggerating it a bit to give the impression of drunkenness.

Singh was politely counting out change into the gloved hand of the old lady. I barged up the aisle towards the counter bumping the shopping basket as I got near. The old lady turned to me with a flash of annoyance which was quickly averted as she saw the drunken lout. 'Oi mate.' I shouted. 'gimme another of these.' I held up the now almost empty bottle of cider.

I could see Singh was relishing his part as looked from me to the old lady and gave a little shake of his head and a sigh. 'Oh, no sir, I cannot serve you.'

'You what?' I spat out at him.

'No sir, you're quite drunk and the licensing laws clearly prohibit me from serving a drunk person with alcohol.' He shook his head as he said this in the way only sub-continentals can. I had to suppress a grin. I'd never known him worried about licensing laws before.

'You fucking what?' I asked again this time more loudly. The old lady paled slightly, but bolstered on by Singh's resolve she pursed her lips in a show of annoyance.

'I am asking you politely to leave Sir, or I shall be calling the Police.'

'Call the gavvers, you 'aving a fucking laugh.'

The old lady looked on with a grim expression on her face. I turned to her and spat out a 'You what?' Then I added a 'You mugging me off?' towards Singh for good measure.

The old lady pursed her lips harder, adjusted the knitted woollen hat on her head and suddenly spoke. I had expected a disapproving tut. Instead I got a quite clear and prim, 'Why don't you just fuck off.'

I couldn't really come back to that.

Singh sighed again and picked up a cordless phone and proceeded to dial. 'Hello, Police please...' he shook his head sadly as spoke into the phone. I took this as my cue to leave and staggered up the crowded aisle, deliberately knocking a pile of magazines to the floor. As I got outside I shouted a string of obscenities back down the aisle then elbowed the front window as I went past. There was a loud and impressive thump but nothing happened. I shook my head to myself and walked back, this time taking careful aim and putting my weight into the blow. This time the thump became a crunch and the point of impact from my elbow became the centre of a frosted star of cracks.

Satisfied with my work I walked a short way up the street and sat in a bus stop pretending to swig from my bottle while staring out belligerently at passers by.

Some minutes later I heard the distant sound of sirens. I reflected that had I been intent on getting away with my crime I would have had ample time to vanish. However, I just sat at the bus stop and waited as a patrol car flashed past and pulled up outside Singh's shop. Two police officers got out. Pausing to put their hats on and adjust their belts. They walked into the shop. A minute or two later they came back out with Singh who was gesturing towards the window which they appeared to notice for the first time. One took out his notebook and was furiously writing everything Singh was telling him while other made a careful inspection of the damaged glass.

Singh was obviously still enjoying his part and eventually remembered to point up the street in my direction. I ignored this and the fact that the two police were, clearly reluctantly, but inexorably walking up towards me.

I made a very slight show of resistance. The comprised of my standing up, placing my bottle on the ground and swearing a bit. I was mindful of what was glued to my fingers and I didn't really want to test them by getting dragged around the ground. With one copper standing either side of me they quickly cuffed me with a set of rigid handcuffs. It wasn't that comfortable, but I was glad they had chosen to cuff my hands in front of me when they sat me in the back of the patrol car. They shut the door and one stood by the car while the other went back in the shop to talk to Singh.

I was sat there quite a time, while I presumed that Singh was expanding his part in the drama while carefully keeping the officer away from the counterfeit booze and tobacco. I wasn't bored, this was a new experience to me. I used the time to take a good look at the equipment in the car. The radio was a Motorola TETRA. I could hear the inane chattering of a police force going about it's daily business even though the volume was turned down. In the centre console was a fairly cheap touch screen display. On it were details of this call. I read with amusement the description Singh had given of me, if they had tried searching for me using that then they would still be looking for me in ten years time. The most amusing item was I noticed the whole thing was running on a Windows XP desktop. I guessed there was probably an ageing laptop bolted under a seat or something. I filed this all away for a rainy day.

The officer outside the car was past the point of boredom. He paced about and spent more time looking at his mobile phone than me. I started wondering about what avenues of escape I might have. I didn't have any intention of doing so. That would have ruined my plan, but it's the way my mind works. Show me a fence and I have to see what's on the other side. I examined the handcuffs. They were Hiatt Speedcuffs. Not being a connoisseur of restraint equipment I had no idea of how they compared to any other makes. There were two stainless steel bracelets with a section of black plastic in the middle, I assumed concealing a rigid metal bar. Each bracelet clearly fastened by a ratchet which unless unlocked with the key only went one way. I had noticed when they cuffed me they had also depressed two little metal pins. I tested my theory about this and it confirmed they served to double lock the cuffs. This would both to prevent the cuffs tightening and also would prevent me opening the ratchet by inserting something to shim the ratchet. I tested how securely the cuffs were on my wrist. They weren't over tight but they sat between the big bone at the end of my wrist and the hand. There was no way these were coming off without either using the key or my thumb coming off first.

There was still no movement from the shop so I let my mind wander a little further. If the cuffs would only come off with a key I would need to make one or find one. I looked about the car in the hope the police had left one laying about. No such luck.

One thing I do know, is that all handcuff keys are pretty much the same. They are a simple cylinder with a raised section which lifts the ratchet from the teeth. There is no attempt to mortise the lock, they are the simplest lock in common use. I figured it wouldn't be hard to make something that approximated this. I took an inventory of what I had on me. Precious little, some cash and door keys and the cheap jewellery.

I considered the key ring, the metal ring could probably be straightened and then used. I rummaged and managed to pry it a little from my jacket pocket. I had to work one handed due to the rigid cuffs. All I managed to do was break a nail. The metal coil holding the keys was too think to bent. I stuffed the keys back in my pockets and considered the problem. I now had a broken nail and red raw wrists. The door opened and the officer who had been in the shop slid in next to me.

'Not trying to escape are you.' He looked at my slightly contorted wrists.

'Just trying to get comfortable.'

'Good, you wouldn't get far,' He added smugly, 'Child locks on the doors.' I filed away another pointless fact in case it ever came in handy. The other officer got in the drivers seat and we began pulling away. The smug officer reached over and pulled the seat belt across me. 'I am arresting you on suspicion of criminal damage.' He started to caution me. Inwardly I said to myself it was about bloody time. I glanced at my watch, the wrist movement causing a sharp slice of pain. I had about forty six hours left.

The journey to the police station was mercifully short and no one said anything. I had done my research and had an idea what was coming up next, but text book study is one thing. As someone smart had once put it, "no plan survives contact with the enemy."

We arrived at the back gate and drove right up to what I was assuming was the custody entrance. I was led in through a heavy steel door, to a hallway where a set of heavy iron bars formed another barrier. Someone in a white shirt came unlocked the doors with a large complex mortise key. It was too fast to see the detail of key, but I would have loved a closer look.

Into the lions den. I was led into a small holding area next to the high wooden topped custody desk. I was separated from there by a wall of bars, but they didn't shut the door. Smug cop went over to the desk while quiet cop began searching me. He got me to empty out my pockets. Not knowing where to put anything I made a neat pile on the wooden bench which ran the length of two of the walls. A neat, comprehensive list was made of all my possessions and then I was patted down. It wasn't what I would have called a thorough search. Natural embarrassment and caution prevented quiet cop from really searching my groin area, which I had already reasoned was the best natural void to conceal anything.

This was clearly something quiet cop had done many times and I guessed he did it the same way each time. He finished up with a cursory sweep of me with a hand-held metal detector. I felt like just another item on a never ending production line. It allowed me a feeling of detachment, like it wasn't really happening to me. In a sense it wasn't. It was happening to Jason Connor.

I signed a form which I didn't read. It had something to do with my property. I did take care with the two signatures required. I hadn't taken the time to practice a consistent one for Jason. If in doubt keep things simple. So I just wrote "Jason Connor." I'm sure a lot of their customers got away with a "X" and no one read it anyway.

I sat on the bench and waited and watched. Quiet cop fidgeted in the doorway to the holding room, still checking his mobile from time to time. Smug cop stood at the desk talking with the custody sergeant. Smug cop was not tall to begin with. The desk came almost to his chin and the custody sergeant a bull of man in his fifties towered a good foot and half above him. The custody sergeant looked over at me from above the rim of his glasses. He said something to the smug cop and he trudged over to me and said 'Up to the desk.' I followed.

The Sergeant ran a hand through the stubble on his head and pushed his glasses back up his nose a fraction. He examined me for a second with all the curiosity of something that passes along a conveyor-belt by their thousands. 'If you'll just listen to officer while he explains why you are here. You don't need to comment.' I didn't I just nodded once.

Smug cop took out a leather bound note book and took a breath before starting his soliloquy. 'Sergeant, at 1400 hours today we were dispatched to a call of criminal damage in progress at the Stafford street News and Tobacco emporium. There I spoke to a Mr. Singh, the owner, who described a drunk male who had come into his shop and attempted to buy alcohol. On being refused and asked to leave the male left the store and smashed the front window of the shop. On leaving the shop to assess the damage I spotted a male matching the description, attempting to leave the scene. I pursued him and arrested him on suspicion of causing criminal damage. He made no reply to caution sergeant.' Smug cop got that all out in one breath. I reflected he was probably one hell of a didgeridoo player.

I was tempted to correct the one or two inexactitudes in that account. However, it would have only complicated things and I doubt it would have done any good. I think if the journey to the police station had been any longer then smug cop's account would have grown to the proportions "Crime and Punishment."

The sergeant never looked up from where he had been writing this all down and said. 'In that case I'm authorising your detention here so we can investigate the allegation.' He finished writing and looked over at his computer screen, partially hidden from me in the desk. 'I just have to ask you some questions so that we can look after you while you're here.' I nodded again. A barrage of questions were put to me, mostly about my medical and mental health. I had to improvise, while I had my own opinions as to Jason Connor's state of being, I kept my answers as nondescript as possible.

The sergeant hit the "Enter" key one last time and laid an A4 sheet of paper in the desk in front of me. I stood on my tip toes to read it. I needn't have bothered, the sergeant read it all out to me pointing out relevant paragraphs with the tip of a well chewed Biro. 'While you are here you have certain rights and entitlements. You have the right to free and independent legal advice. Do you want a brief? You can name one or have a duty solicitor.'

In my technical planning of this job, I had of course known I would be asked this, but I hadn't given much thought to my answer. I wasn't planning on contesting the charge. What Jason did later would be up to him. Suddenly in the heat of action a beautiful idea occurred to me. A chance I hadn't considered to kill two birds with one stone. I answered. 'Yeah, I'd like Archie Hayes. I usually have him.'

The sergeant nodded. 'All right I'll get him called. Also while you're here,' He moved his pen down a paragraph. 'You have the right to have someone told you have been arrested, do you want anyone told?'

I shook my head.

'You also have the right to consult the codes of practice, a book which governs how we treat you while you are here.' He gestured over to a shelf of books at the far end of the booking desk. I glanced over and saw the 'Police and criminal evidence act 1986 codes of practice.' staring ominously back at me. I had read most of it on-line last night and the thought of doing it again struck me as a cruel and unusual punishment. I shook my head again.

The sergeant turned to smug cop. 'Take him for Livescan and then cell nine.' He looked down again at his computer. I was of no more interest. The item had moved along the production line. I was now the next person's problem.

I was led by the arm by smug cop back past the gate where I came in and past what looked like the interview rooms and into the fingerprint room. Now for the acid test of my bright idea.

I carefully felt my finger tips by rubbing my thumbs gently along them. I could still feel the thin layer of rubber on them. None seemed to have worked loose or frayed at the edges. However without examining them closely and thus drawing attention to them I wouldn't be able to tell if the prints had survived.

The room was a windowless, narrow and harshly lit space. Along one wall was a desk with small brass plates fitted along it. The brass was dulled with age and still coated with thick black ink. I presumed they were still kept in-situ in case of power cuts or computer failure.

Smug cop logged into a large free-standing steel encased computer. The screen bore the logo of Smith's industries. Below the screen was a large glass plate lit red by lasers inside. Smug cop put on some rubber gloves and then wiped the glass plate clean. This was a good sign, through the gloves there was no way he would be able to detect the thin layer of PVA glue stuck to my finger tips. He began to ask me all my, or rather Jason's details for the second time in the space of half an hour and punched them one fingered into the computer. He was still in production line mode. He had done this a hundred times before and it bored him. I guessed he wanted to get back on the street rather than be stuck here in the cells processing me. His air of bored impatience was good for me.

I had always imagined the life of a police officer to be one of excitement. Fighting the bad guys, chasing criminals and dispensing righteous justice. I was fast forming the opinion it was actually a life composed mostly of routine, a never ending succession of minor no account crimes committed by minor no account people. And of course, paperwork.

Standing there in the windowless, air-conditioned fingerprint room, I was starting to feel a little sorry for officer smug. When I go to work, which I admit is not as often as I like, it's a new challenge, a new problem. Each time is different and I look forwards to the challenges I am about to face. The police officer in front of me clearly had nothing to look forward to than the chance every little once in a while, to be smug in front of a dumb criminal.

Smug took my right hand and pulled it over to the glass plate. 'Just relax your hand and let me do this.' He said. He proceeded to take my prints. As he rolled my finger tips over the screen they appeared writ large in black and white on the screen in front. The machine would give a cheerful beep with each successful roll and an angry buzz when it wasn't happy with the quality.

The tension was high for me each time a finger was rolled. I watched the screen carefully for any obvious flaws in the fake prints. I'm sure my heart started pounding faster when I noticed a tear in my left middle finger. However Smug's boredom was working for me and he was going fast. He was letting my fingers slip and slide and I was helping that happen as much as I could without being obvious. I remembered I was also supposed to be drunk so I swayed a little and in general made the job as awkward as I could without actually resisting.

Smug was starting to get a little flustered and red round the cheeks. I hadn't noticed it before, maybe it only came out under stress, but Smug had a slight lisp. 'Stop trying to help. Stay Still.' He almost shouted as the machine gave yet another angry buzz and prompted him to redo a print. Instead he angrily jabbed the override button and forced the machine accept another almost unreadable print.

This was getting to be almost fun and I was starting to relax. That is until something I hadn't planned for happened.

We had finished the finger tips and thumbs. I was the one starting to feel smug by this point. Pride before a fall and all that. The machine changed screens and now prompted for palm prints. I hadn't considered that.

The original demonstration for this technique as done by the Chaos Computer club related to biometric data in ID cards. Obviously, now that I thought it through, that data at most was composed of finger tip prints. Not whole palm prints which by their size must take up a lot of data points.

Shit.

There was nothing to be done now, but go through with it and attempt to make the prints as unreadable as possible. Smug took the prints. I could feel his relief as he sensed the procedure was nearing it's end. He over rode the last of the palm prints and hit the submit button. I guessed now that the data was rushing in a flood of electrons down phone lines all the way to some central fingerprint bureaux. I wondered how long the results would be, soon as Smug made no attempt to leave. He must have sensed my puzzlement and offered an explanation. 'Easier if I do this now rather than come back later.'

I just nodded, stood very still and waited. In some detached way this very interesting. Instant feedback on the success of a plan.

To my ear the ticking of a second hand of the cheap clock on the wall was very loud. The sound was punctuated by the almost rhythmical jabbing of Smug's finger on the refresh button. Then after an age the screen refreshed and it was different. Smug wrote down a reference number and then clicked on an entry. I read it.

"Jason Connor 19/11/1975 CRO 8X/9475B Confidence 57%"

Well, Fifty seven percent confidence. It was much more than I felt a mere couple of seconds ago. However over half. I was quietly pleased. I watched Officer Smug write down the CRO bit and clearly pay no attention to the accuracy figure. He grabbed the paperwork and marched me back to the desk.

Officer Smug was about to walk me past the desk and to my en-suite accommodation when the custody sergeant called him back. This was mildly concerning. Smug wheeled me around and we went back in front of the high desk.

The sergeant looked over his glasses at Smug. 'Andy, did you PNC check him at the scene.'

Smug looked a little downcast at this, like a school boy who hadn't done his homework. 'No, Sergeant I was busy getting the statement from the victim.' The lisp was back with a vengeance.

The sergeant used his forefinger to push his glasses up his nose before continuing. 'I just have. Mr Connor here has an outstanding no bail warrant for common assault. So when he's dealt with here he will need taking to the next court.'

I felt like I had just been hit on the back of the head by a copy of the PACE codes of practice.

4 Tuesday January the 15th 1800 hours.

No Plan survives contact with the enemy.

Forty four hours left. At that point, the Police had either to charge or release the suspects. That meant no more interviews. Nothing for me to record and no information for the client. A reasonable assumption, applying game theory, was that the police would use all the time available. There was even a slim chance that they would go to court for an extension. I couldn't rely on that. So I was aiming for as much time before that deadline. I calculated that the interviews at that end of the process were probably the ones most useful to the client.

Meantime, Mr Ali was sat in another custody block, no doubt very similar to mine, keeping stumm and waiting for whatever bone I could throw him. He had been arrested after the other two, so he had slightly more time to play with. I didn't, what I still needed to do takes time. It was always going to be very very close.

I asked the custody Sergeant. 'What does that mean?'

He lowered his glasses down his nose a fraction, so he could look over them at me. 'It means,' He took a long pause. 'That you stay with us until we have finished our investigation.' He paused again as if willing the strength to explain something so simple to an idiot. '..And then we turn you over to the next available court, whenever that is.'

'And when is the next available court?'

'That will be tomorrow, court transport picks up at eight. If you're dealt with by then you'll go to court, if not then it will be the session after lunch.'

'Why won't I be dealt with by then?'

Wearily he looked at his watch. 'It's gone six now, you've been drinking. I have to give you a rest period and judge you're sober enough to be interviewed. By then we could be in change over to early shift. In which case you probably won't be interviewed till after eight tomorrow morning. I'd say you'll be out by lunchtime. Well off to court anyway.'

Whichever way I did the maths it wasn't looking good. I was guessing court could well run to at least five in the afternoon. Not much later I guessed. It would be Magistrate's and they need time to get off and get changed for the lodge meeting. Maybe I should have gone with a completely false identity. I was about to ask another question when Smug propelled me by the arm down a narrow corridor. Big steel doors were regularly spaced down one side. I could guess where we were headed.

The overriding sense was a smell of disinfectant. The architecture was pure public lavatory. Not the sort we have, or rather don't have now, but old school, Victorian public urinals. The theme was steel, concrete and tiles. Most doors we passed had a rather sorry pair of soiled trainers parked outside.

We passed a half dozen steel doors, went through a couple of other intermediate doors, turned left and faced a door sitting open fully back against the wall. I could see the cell within, all concrete and tiles and harshly lit by fluorescent tubes in the ceiling.

'Ok fella, shoes off.' Said Smug. I sensed the relief in his voice as I was about to become someone else's problem. I kicked the trainers off and prodded them with toes until they were neatly lined up next to the doorway and stepped in. I felt rather than watched the great weight of the door swing smoothly closed behind me. It made no sound hitting the frame, again I assumed reinforced steel. However the catch made a very loud clunk as it caught and deadlocked in the receiver.

I had indeed walked in and had the cell door closed behind me.

I breathed in the heady aroma of cheap industrial disinfectant. I had about six feet by four of floor space. Grey concrete floor, cold to my stockinged feet. It was a poured cast and curved up about four inches till it met the white washed brick. There were four walls of white washed brick broken only by a small aperture of glass bricks about two feet square opposite the door. Even had it been daylight I doubted much would make it's way through.

Along one side was what I could stretch the truth and call a bed. It was a shelf, built a foot above ground level. It was topped with a blue painted hardwood sheet. On that was a blue plastic mattress about the thickness of a cheap paperback novel. Bunched on that was a grey horse blanket. The kind I imagined Napoleon's soldiers retreating from Moscow would have had wrapped around them. Looking at the one in front of me I suspected it had been to Moscow and back at least once.

At the foot of the bed was a shiny brushed steel toilet pan. No seat I noted. I paced the floor my unshod feet leaving sweaty footprints as I went. I turned and faced the door. More blue painted steel. Riveted, not screwed. In the middle about two thirds up was a small hatch. I believe this is what's known as a Judas hatch. Above it was a spy hole. There was another in the wall near the toilet.

In one of the apex corners, by the door, encased in thick wire was video camera. Even here Big Brother was watching. There is truly no escape from him.

Glancing upwards, the lighting was a double tube fluorescent inset into the ceiling behind very think perspex. Spray painted in crude stencil around it was the ironic warning. "ANYONE CAUGHT WRITING ON THE WALLS OR DAMAGING THE CELLS WILL BE CHARGED."

I lay down and gazed up at the authoritarian pronouncement above me. It was comfortably warm. It was quiet. The bed was O.K.. I took a moment to relax until I was brought back with a start as the Judas hatch opened with fearsome clang. A chubby face appeared at the opening.

' 'ello, I'm the gaoler. Do you want a drink?' Northern accent. My guess Leeds. Pleasant enough.

'I'd love a coffee, no sugar.'

'Right ho.' He replied. With another earth shaking clang the hatch went up. It dropped again a few moments later and a rather poor instant coffee was handed through to me. 'Watch out, it's 'ot.' He said as he passed it through the slit. 'I'll be back in a while to take your order for dinner.' Clang. And he was gone.

I sat on the bed and sipped at the drink. The coffee wouldn't pass muster in my house, but there was no reason to complain. I ate a very poor microwave meal brought to me by the cheerful gaoler and laid on the bed and waited. This time of day seemed quite a busy time for the custody block. I listened to boots tramping up and down the corridors and cell doors closing with their distinctive clunk as the very expensive locks engaged. I pondered if I was hearing the movements of the two suspects I was here to record.

About hourly either the Judas hatch would clang down or I would hear the shuffling of steps and an eye would appear at the spy hole. The steps would shuffle from cell to cell repeating the process. I'd had two visits, not counting the food and drink when shortly after the second I heard the footsteps of the gaoler return. The eye appeared at the the spy-hole then I heard the jingle of keys and the

47

lock clanked twice and the door swung open. The gaoler stood in the doorway. He was shorter in real life.

'Your Brief's here. Do you want to put your shoes on and go down and consult with him?'

Consult indeed, the right word should be conspire. I got up from the bed and went out into the corridor and slipped my trainers on. I followed the gaoler back down the corridor towards the booking desk. We passed through there and down towards the fingerprint room but before we reached it we turned left into a tiny cupboard of a room. The gaoler left me standing at the doorway and returned to his duties.

The room was barely an arms width wide and the same deep. In the middle taking up most of the floor space was a wooden table. It was bolted to the floor as were two chairs positioned facing each other. Archie Hayes sat overflowing in the one facing me. His head was bowed and his brow furrowed in the concentration as he filled in a form.

I took the seat opposite Archie. He still didn't look up. He was wearing the same suit as yesterday. It had once been a good suit, I imagined it was now the only suit Archie owned. I could smell the brandy coming off him from my side of the table. My call had probably interrupted an extended afternoon session in the pub or the bookies or maybe both. Clearly the paperwork he was doing was more important than his client. I glanced down at it. It was an expenses claim for the call out to the police station.

I coughed. 'Hello Archie.'

Archie paused. Then he looked up quickly, the surprise registering slowly as his eyes took time to focus on me.

'I, er, um. David dear boy.' He stammered, his brain was trying to catch up with his mouth.

48

'Good evening Archie.' I smiled at him. An attempt to put him at ease, but by the reaction in his eyes I think it had the opposite effect.

'David, David, dear boy what are you doing here?'

'I believe the military types call it "Reconnaissance" Archie.'

'But, but,' Archie squinted hard at the paperwork on a clip board in front of him. 'But, there must be some mistake. I'm supposed to see a Jason, Jason,?' He ran a yellow stained finger down the top sheet on the clipboard. 'a Jason Connor.'

'And you are. Archie, you are. As far as anyone will ever know.' I added as ominously as possible. That also fell flat, I was having too much fun with pudgy old Archie-Bloody-Hayes.

There was a slow look of dawning realisation viscously spreading itself across Archie's veined and ruddy face. 'What have you done? I mean how have you done. I mean, don't tell me. I don't want to know.' He looked down at the expenses form and sighed. 'I can't be a party to this. I shall have to withdraw.' He looked up at me through his bleary eyes. 'I'll cite a conflict of interest and you, or Jason, or whoever you are will have to find alternate representation.'

'Archie, you can't withdraw. Time is short.'

'David, dear boy, you must realise that this could easily be construed as perverting the course of justice. As an officer of the court I simply can't be involved.' Archie was doing a good job of talking himself out of this. 'David, they would throw away the key.'

'First off Archie. It's Jason. Get that through your grape addled head. Second, you hired me to do a job. I'm doing it. Do you think these recordings make themselves?'

Archie sat back as far as the cramped bolted down furniture would allow. 'I merely act as a trusted intermediary for our clients. How you do, whatever you do, is not my concern.' He began to fiddle with the cheap Biro on the desk.

'You've been lucky up to now Archie, you've managed to keep things at arms length. I can understand that now you're involved you may be getting a little squeamish. But, Archie, involved you damn well are.'

'I am-' He started to say, but I cut him off.

'You are involved, what do you think you hired me to do? How would what I am attempting, be, as you put it, construed, Archie?'

'Well I-'

'It would be construed Archie, for what it is. It's a painfully late and underfunded attempt to pervert the course of justice. You are involved Archie, right the way up to your double chins.' Archie just sat there. I had no idea a man with such a ruddy complexion could look so pale, but right then Archie was a ghostly white. 'It's time to play your part Archie. If this plan goes south, I'm the one stands to lose the most here. Which is why it's not going to. But, Archie, if it were to go wrong for me here, either due to your actions or inactions, then the recording I made of you hiring me yesterday will most certainly get played in court.'

Archie sat there in a stony silence, barely daring to breathe. He seemed to consider the issue for a long time, then at last he spoke, a barely voiced whisper forced out through clenched teeth. 'David, you are so unfair.' With that he seemed to deflate. I could almost visualise the fight seeping away from him and pooling on the floor under the bolted down desk.

Hook, line and sinker. I had Archie in way over his comb over. I didn't think I ever had to worry about him pulling any stunts like he had down in the Tea Cutter. Archie now had his hands bloodied and

I think he finally got the point that if I went down, he would fall far further and far harder than me.

'Ok, Archie. To business. As you have hopefully realised, I am, for the moment Jason Connor. Time is short, so work your magic and get Jason out of here as quickly as possible.' This seemed to jolt Archie from his state of shock. He instantly took refuge in the familiar and began to scrutinise the custody record with a practised eye. No matter what I thought about Archie's character failings I also knew that drunk or sober there was probably no better man in town to have represent you in a police station.

We sat in silence while Archie read the statements and Jason's criminal record. Mid way through we were interrupted by a quiet knock on the door. It was the ever cheerful gaoler coming to ask if we required drinks. I ordered another instant coffee and Archie a tea.

The gaoler returned quickly and deposited the drinks on the desk, then left carefully closing the door behind him. Archie was still reading, his lips moving as he read the spidery handwriting of Officer Smug. I went to reach for my coffee. Without looking up Archie wagged a finger before delving into a hip pocket of his jacket. He came up with a battered silver hip flask. Without looking he uncapped it one handed and poured a generous measure of brandy into each paper up. I caught a quick glimpse of engraving as he deftly tucked it back into his pocket.

"Archie, all my love Gwen." Was inscribed.

Archie put down the papers and took a sip of his laced tea. 'Well, Dav- I mean, Jason Dear boy.' He swallowed another gulp and squinted over the desk at me. 'It's all quite straightforward. However, you have two problems, only one of which I can do anything about. The criminal damage is quite simple. You'll be interviewed. Jason, isn't eligible for a caution so it will be a straight charge and bailed to court. Which brings me to the court part. Very unfortunate choice on your part, dear boy.'

Archie allowed himself a thin smile. 'Jason has a warrant issued by the court for failing to appear at trial. It seems there is a little assault allegation going back a few months and Jason didn't bother turning up.'

'What does that mean for me?'

'It's a court warrant. You have to be kept in custody and taken before the next court. Which should be tomorrow. Just be thankful that this isn't Saturday night, or you'd find yourself incarcerated here Until Monday morning.'

'So how do we speed things up.'

'As I said, the warrant is in the hands of the court, neither I nor the police can do anything about that. What I can attempt to do is expedite the criminal damage part. If we waive your rest period and I persuade the custody sergeant you are fit for interview then we can get all that dealt with tonight. I'll then get to court early tomorrow and do what I can to speed things up at that end.'

'What's going to happen tomorrow?'

'Oh, the court will almost certainly bail Jason again. Unless you do something ill advised like attack the magistrates.'

'Tempting as that may be, you can guarantee I won't do that. Tell me Archie, can Jason enter a plea on the assault charge?'

'Of course, dear boy, the accused can always change their plea.' I could at least take some comfort that the time wouldn't be a total loss.

'Just out of interest Archie, if the court are just going to bail me tomorrow, what's the whole point in this warrant business?'

Archie took a generous sip of his drink. 'No idea, but it keeps me in fees and gives all those green grocers and carpet salesmen in the Magistrates something to feel important about.'

'Back to tonight. I am here to see how I am going to bug the interview rooms. How many are there?'

'There are two, there are also two consultation rooms, of which this is one.'

I took a closer look around the room. There wasn't much to it. The bolted down furnishings and the walls were covered with a fabric topped pasteboard, I presumed for some kind of soundproofing. The light was another faded fluorescent inset into a suspended ceiling. The light switch was on the wall next to me. I admired the attention to detail. Every screw head in the custody block was a security screw with odd heads that only expensive and hard to obtain screwdrivers would open. These heads had the star shaped pattern of the security Torx.

Set further up in the wall into a cut out section of the pasteboard was a speaker. I stood up and took a closer look. Again more security Torx screws holding the yellowed plastic over in place.

'What's this?' I asked Archie as my fingers tested the cover.

'Oh, that, it's the tannoy system. Not been used for years and years. I believe they now do it through these digital phones they have now.'

'Is there one in every room?'

'I believe so, or at least there was, back in the days when they let us smoke in here. Not been used in years, once taped recorded interviews came in the tannoy kept interrupting the flow, so to speak.'

'And where was the other end, the microphone end?'

'Oh, that was the front counter desk. Back in those days there used to someone there at all times. Cut backs, and all that.' Archie added wistfully.

I had the tingle of an idea forming. A look at the insides of the speaker would prove very helpful. However the cover was fixed tight, in part by the glue of age and the Torx screws. It was frustrating, at home in my tool kit was just about every type and size of screwdriver known to man. Even had I thought to bring any I wouldn't have got them past the search.

Time to improvise. I snatched the Biro from Archie's hand. He looked up in surprise. I shushed him with a finger to my lips. 'Archie, do you have a lighter on you?' He nodded and rummaged through an inside pocket before coming up with a blue disposable lighter. 'Right, Archie, keep an eye on the door, make sure we're not disturbed.' Archie started to protest so I shushed him again and climbed onto the table, thankful now that it was bolted to the floor.

Archie laboriously squeezed round the table to position himself at the door. For the first time in knowing him I had found an advantage to his bulk. Anyone coming to the door would be unlikely to see past him. I prized the blue plug out of the end of the Biro and discarded it. Then I took the lighter and heated the end of the pen. I was careful not to let it burn, but still a faint smell of burning plastic filled the room.

'Whatever are you doing?' Whispered Archie. I ignored him and carried on the heating the end of the pen. Once the plastic had softened enough I quickly and firmly pressed the end into the head of one of the security Torx screws. I let it harden in place for a few seconds then I began to carefully turn the pen anti-clockwise. It was tedious work, only enlivened by the prospect of discovery.

The process took some time. I had to re-melt the pen end many times for each screw. The pen was half its length by the time I finished. I used the writing end to prize the cover from the layer of dust and grime holding it in place. The cover came off and I let it hang by the red and black wires fastened to a cheap four ohm speaker. The wires disappeared into a conduit in the wall. The whole thing was full of dust. I noted what I needed and then replaced the cover.

I sat down and Archie fought his way back behind the desk while I brushed away the covering of dust that had fallen.

'Happy now?' Archie asked.

'I have the dim beginnings of a plan. I need to see in the interview rooms now.'

'Right, I'll go and talk to the custody Sergeant, but before I do that I need to give you the legal advice I'm paid for.'

'Which is?'

'When we get into interview, you answer "No comment" to every question.'

'Why?'

'Dear boy, let's assume this is for real and you are really Jason Connor. The advice I would give him is exactly the same. The Police have good evidence, there is no use denying the offence, however there is nothing to be gained by directly admitting it at this stage.'

'Wouldn't I, or rather Jason get a lighter sentence for admitting it?'

'Makes, no difference. At court you could still plead guilty and get the reduction of tariff. However, why make the police's job easy. It's best to make them actually work with the evidence. You'd be surprised how often they mess up. Besides, it's the best way to get this wrapped up and over with. The police will take your silence as effectively a guilty plea, you'll be charged and bailed to court, which is the result we want. In addition it will keep the interview short and hopefully prevent you getting either of us in any deeper than we already are.' Archie gathered up the paperwork and began the task of unsticking himself from the chair. 'I'll go and see if I can hurry up the interview.'

As Archie reached the door he turned back to me. 'Remember, "No Comment." is all you say.'

'Just how much do you get paid for this advice?' I asked Archie's departing back, but he was already out of ear shot.

I used the time I was left alone in the consultation room to go through the developing plan in my mind. There were gaps I still needed to cross, but the simplicity of the approach was enticing. Given the amount of time I had left I doubted I could come up with a better solution, there was going to be no plan B. Either I could make this work or the job would fail.

5 Tuesday January 15th 2130 Hours.

Abuse of Process.

I spent the best part of another hour sitting in the consultation room, going slowly insane with boredom. Eventually Archie and a police officer came and got me and we walked the short distance to the interview room. This police officer was not one of the ones that had arrested me. She was a she for a start. She was uniformed but she didn't have any of the paramilitary type kit strung all over her. Instead she carried a pile of blue folders.

The interview room was very similar to the consultation room, except that it was about three times the size. The same wooden desk bolted to the floor and a bench one end, obviously where I was meant to sit, and three other similar chairs all bolted to the floor no doubt at positions carefully worked out for maximum psychological effect.

I slid along the bench and made myself comfortable. Archie took the chair by the door. The petite blond officer fussed about getting paperwork in order. I looked the room over. In all respects a larger version of the room I had just been in. The main difference here was that the light was noticeably brighter. I hadn't noticed before that all the rooms and the cell had been in relative gloom. The light here seemed oppressive in comparison.

The other difference that got my attention was a large blue metal box in the corner. In it's front were two DVD drives identical to the sort you would find in a desktop computer. It had a few buttons on the front and a small LCD display showing me, sat in my corner. I looked at the walls. There were two camera's, one right in front of me and one in the opposite corner. On the wall between the police officer and myself was a single black microphone affixed to the fabric covered pasteboard.

I noted with satisfaction the faded yellow plastic cover to the old tannoy system, sitting gathering dust, long forgotten in the wall above the Police officer's head. I pondered briefly the prospect of taking an audio and possibly a video feed direct from the recording equipment. It would have been an elegant solution, but it was a sealed unit and I worried that any extra devices attached to it might attract attention. I tried to spot a makers logo or identifying mark on the unit so I could research it later, all I could find was a small green portable appliance testing sticker. It was in date, just. At least no one would be getting electrocuted.

The police officer placed two blank DVDs in the machine. It whirred and hummed for a few moments and then she pressed a red button.

'It's Twenty one thirty seven hours, on Tuesday the fifteenth of January. We are in an interview room at the police station. I am Police Constable Anderson.' She looked over to me for the first time and smiled. It was a nice smile. 'Could you state your full name and date of birth?'

I gave her Jason's details followed by his current address. She nodded as I answered and wrote in the notebook in front of her. I began to feel like I was in some kind of test.

'Jason, you've been arrested for criminal damage. Do you understand what that means.' I nodded and she smiled again. 'Right, Jason I have to caution you again. You do not have to say anything, but it may harm your defence if you fail to mention something that you later rely on in your defence.' I nodded again and she smiled again. It was still a nice smile. 'What that means, Jason, is that you do not have to say anything to me today. But if you don't say anything or you go "no comment" it may cause the court not to believe something you later say to them.'

I wondered if she guessed what I was going to say, or rather not say. I nodded again. She smiled again. 'So Jason, do you have to talk to me today?'

'Um, no.'

'What might happen if you don't answer my questions today, but you do in court, later?'

'The court might think I'm lying?'

This time she nodded and I smiled. 'OK. I think you understand the caution,' She looked over her shoulder towards Archie who sat there mute, but watching the proceedings with an experienced air of detachment. 'Are you happy to begin?'

Archie nodded and she smiled. Quite a collection of Police I was amassing, first Smug and now Smiler, but I knew which of the two I preferred. She turned to me her face now a little more serious, but still the traces of the smile lingered. 'Jason can you tell me where you were at two O'clock this afternoon?'

Seven and half hours ago it seemed like last year. As I looked at the ghost of the smile on her face I answered as Archie had directed. 'No Comment.'

She froze for a fraction of a second. 'Oh-k.' She said slowly as she used the pause the phrase gave her to look down at her notes. Clearly this was not an unexpected development. It probably happened in a lot of interviews, but still it looked like she was changing tactic. 'So,' another pause word. 'You were at the Stafford Street News and Tobacco as at least two people have provided statements describing you there. Had you been drinking this afternoon?'

'No comment.' I said. I almost wished I could give her some kind of answer, if only to bring the smile back, but I could sense Archie watching me like an alcoholic owl. Police Constable Anderson, previously the smiling Officer Anderson went through the questions, her interest dwindling away as each enquiry was met with a 'No Comment.'

The interview crawled to an anticlimactic halt. The questions just petered out. No clever probing and unravelling of my refusal to talk. The smile had gone for good to be replaced by the weary air of bored resignation I was getting very used to. Anderson shuffled up her papers and we all got up to leave.

We walked down the corridor in file, Anderson leading the way. Archie tapped me on the shoulder and put his brandy soaked breath up to my ear.

'That should have done the trick. You'll be charged with the criminal damage. I'll see you at court in the morning. Try and stay out of trouble.' Archie stopped at the custody desk. Anderson lead me down the corridor to cell number nine. I left my shoes outside and she pushed the door shut. No final smile as the door closed.

I laid on the bed. It was about ten O'clock. To mark the time I tore a strip into an empty paper cup each time the eye appeared at my spy-hole. Just after midnight the cheerful Gaoler appeared at the Judas hatch to tell me he was soon going off duty and offer me food and drink. I accepted a cup of water and tried to get some sleep.

The lights were kept on, but it was fairly restful until about two O'clock when I heard a commotion. From what I could hear at my end of the block it sounded as though some drunk had been brought in. There was shouting and then a thundering of feet on the concrete floor as the drunk was dragged down to my end. There was more shouting then a loud slam as a cell door was closed with some force.

The drunk began banging on his cell door and rattling the hatch almost as soon as the booted feet retreated up the corridor. The bare concrete of the cell clearly made an excellent amplifier. Whoever it was had some stamina and patience. The banging carried on with only short breaks throughout the night. After an hour or so I managed to get some sleep, though oddly enough I was still woken by the quiet shuffling of my hourly checks through the spy hole.

A different gaoler woke me around seven and brought me a microwaved all day breakfast and a coffee. I was offered a shower before court which I declined. I paced the cell to get some blood flowing again and the door opened soon after. The new gaoler was tough looking man in his twenties. He had perfected the production line indifference. Without him saying a word I put my shoes on and followed him down to the custody desk.

There were two men in white shirts with long key chains on their belts waiting. A new custody sergeant was behind the desk. This one was younger and thickset with the build of a rugby player. The area was busy at this time of the morning with cleaners moping corridors and cheap suited detectives bustling about with arms full of files. The conveyor belt ran on.

A uniformed officer appeared at the desk next to me and the charge of criminal damage was read out. I signed some more papers as Jason Connor and then I was signed over to the white shirted men. I was searched again, handcuffed and lead back out through the gate I had arrived at.

A large white van waited outside. Tinted perspex windows looked unpityingly down at me and I could just make out faces staring vacantly out from some of them. I was locked in a small cell about the size of a Portaloo and we were off to court.

The drive to court was short. There the whole process was reversed and I found myself back in a similar cell to the police station. I sat down to wait. I estimated it was probably about nine. I hoped court would be starting soon.

Some time later, I had no cup to mark time on so I couldn't be sure how much later, a court gaoler came and fetched me to what I took to be a consultation room. This was even more bare than the one at the police station.

Archie walked in. Same suit, different tie. For court he pushed the boat out and wore a bow tie. It was tied a little lop sided. Whether that was to prove he tied it himself or because his hands shook in the mornings, I didn't want to guess.

'Good morning Dear boy. I hope you passed a restful night.'

'Very peaceful Archie. Now clock's still ticking. What's happening?'

'I've had a stroke of luck. I had to tell a bit of a fib, but I've made progress.'

'You seem to be catching on fast Archie. Now what's happening?'

'I have told the court that your mother's sick, which is, incidentally, why you couldn't make your last court appearance. I've laid it on a bit thick, but the prosecutor is in agreement. You, or rather Jason's to be re-bailed to a later court date. The best stroke of luck is their worships have agreed to hear your case before lunch.'

I didn't see why they couldn't rush me through and get me out sooner, but before lunch was better than after lunch. 'Well done Archie.' Then I'd almost forgotten. 'Can I enter a guilty plea, will that delay things?'

'Why would you want to do that?'

'Karma Archie, Karma.'

'No it won't delay things. I'll let the prosecutor know.'

It wasn't that long a wait before I was marched up some back stairs and let into the dock. It was a wooden box, but larger than I imagined. Four people would have fitted into it comfortably. It was also surrounded by toughened glass with narrow strips to let the sound through.

The courtroom itself was much smaller than I imagined and far less grand. No ornate wood and church like atmosphere. This room had all the charm of a modern open plan office block. At one end sat three stout burghers in their Sunday suits and golf club ties. Before them a sea of desks with various people sitting at them. I spotted Archie sitting at desk not far from my box, he didn't acknowledge me.

A woman in a business suit sat in front of the Magistrates handed them a sheet of paper. The Magistrate in the middle turned to me and spoke into a microphone. His voice came out of a speaker behind me.

'Could you confirm your name?'

'Jason Connor.'

'Well Mr Connor. You're representative has made us aware of your personal circumstances and while we understand them, we would like to make it quite clear that your disregard of the court can not go unpunished.' He was wearing half moon spectacles and he looked sternly over them at me. 'However on this occasion and this occasion only we shall give you the benefit of the doubt.' He paused for effect. 'If you were to come before this court again for a similar transgression then I warn you we will be forced to give you the severest punishment we can.' He finished speaking but held his gaze on me for some time. At last he turned to the desk in front of him.

A man in a double breasted suit with dyed hair sitting a few seats to side of Archie suddenly stood up. 'Your worships, my colleague here,' he made an expansive hand gesture towards Archie. 'Has informed me that the defendant wished to change his plea.'

The Magistrate turned to Archie. 'Is this correct?'

Archie rose, nodded and sat back down again.

The Magistrate turned back to me. 'In that case, what is your plea?'

I cleared my throat. 'I plead guilty to the charge your worships.' I had to stop myself tugging my forelock as I spoke.

The magistrate leaned over his desk and spoke to the woman in front of him. There was nodding of heads and the woman turned to a computer for a moment before handing a sheet of paper to the Magistrate. He read the paper and turned to me.

'You are bailed with the same conditions as before to return here in the twenty eighth for sentencing. Please make sure you attend promptly.' He turned back to Archie. 'Make sure your client is well aware of the date and time of his next appearance.'

Archie rose, nodded and sat back down.

'You may be released from the court.' The magistrate pronounced in my general direction.

Pompous fool I thought to myself, but I kept my mouth shut. I reasoned that Jason's Karma was just about back to equilibrium, or it would be when all this caught up with him.

I was quite quickly let out of the box and handed back my property. Having not come in the front door I had to be shown the way out by a helpful security guard. I emerged blinking into the sunlight. I couldn't allow myself the luxury of enjoying the moment. I had a lot left to do and very little time left to do it.

First order of the day, however, was to get out of this awful tracksuit.

6 Wednesday 16th January 1200 Hours .

Can you help me?

Twenty six hours left. I took a taxi home. My flat was barely above freezing, I hadn't left any heating on when I left yesterday afternoon. I switched my one electric heater on and put some food down for my cat "Brill". I had my first decent cup of coffee in almost twenty four hours and checked my phone for messages while cleaning the remains of the false prints from my fingers with surgical spirit.

Clara had left a couple of messages throughout the night. The first read "Don't pick up the soap." The next read "Gone up town for work, see you tomorrow. X"

I stripped off the tracksuit and stuffed it straight into a bin liner. It was too damn cold to take a shower in my flat so I put on jeans and a couple of sweatshirts and sent Clara a message asking to use her shower. She, or more likely an admirer, rented a flat two streets away from mine. Unlike mine it was a modern conversion with double glazing and central heating.

I hurried round there through the cold. I didn't have a key but her door was easily carded with thin sheet of mica. I had been on at her for months to let me fit better locks. They wouldn't have stopped me either, but they would have slowed me down.

Clara's flat was the antithesis of mine. Where mine was cluttered and dingy hers was spacious and light. Large windows with blinds let the light in and central heating kept it warm despite the wood flooring. The flat was sparse and almost completely devoid of personal effects. I think that was why I was never really comfortable there. It might also explain why Clara spent so much time at my flat, either that or she liked slumming it.

I set her coffee machine going and took a shower. I spent longer in the shower than I planned but when I came out I was warm and had washed the last traces of the cells and Jason away. I padded around wearing a towel while I fixed more coffee. The next twenty four hours were going to need plenty of stimulants to get through at the top of my game.

While I sipped at the thick dark coffee and felt the caffeine start to liven me up I heard a key in the lock and Clara slid in through the door wearing a long black coat and high heels so sharp they could have slit throats.

'I see you got parole.' She said mischievously. I could tell she was slightly tipsy, which was about as drunk as I had ever seen her. She was a girl who never lost control.

'The plan worked, so far. Have you been working?'

She grinned. 'Let me show you.' She dropped the long black coat to the floor. Underneath she wore stockings and a black corset pulled in tight to exaggerate her curves. She wore little else.

'I guess you have.' Was all I could think of as a response. She pulled the coffee mug from my hand and put it down on a worktop. While I pondered this she had quickly pulled the towel from my waist then flicked it back with snap of wrist that would have put a tennis player to shame. I reeled in sudden pain. I don't really do physical confrontation.

Before I could react to any this I was dimly aware of some kind of arm lock and I found myself propelled into the bedroom and onto the bed with Clara straddling me, pinning me down. I tended to forget she took martial arts classes twice a week.

'I thought prison might have toughened you up, turned you into a bad boy.' She said.

'I'm neither good, nor bad.' I don't know why, but with a tipsy Clara pinning me naked to her bed, I reflected on my own morality. 'I'm something else.' I added not sure what I meant.

'I see, so you could be bad if you tried?' I half attempted to struggle but she just waggled her way to a better grip and pinned my wrists down on the bed. Her lips were next to my left ear and she whispered. 'Want to know about my day in the office, honey?'

'OK.' was what I intended to say, but it came out as a squeak as her searching fingers found some kind of nerve point at my left wrist and electric pain shot up my arm.

She continued to whisper seductively in my ear while searching for and pressing very painful nerve points up my arm. 'I spent the night with a millionaire.' She squeezed me harder with her thighs. '...who paid me just to make out with another girl.' She sat up and a finger traced its way up my neck to press a point just below my ear where my jaw bone met my skull. I thought my head would explode. 'And do you know what?' She stopped inflicting pain and paused. 'he can't get it up.' She laughed, 'I can tell it's not a problem you have.' She grinned a lop sided grin and kissed me. 'It just proves money can't buy you everything.'

I burned up a half an hour of time I could ill afford to lose. However she wasn't giving me a lot of choice in the matter. My coffee was cold by the time I got back to it. It's an imperfect world. I got dressed and headed back to my flat. I had wasted time, but Clara had cleared my head. Maybe she did know me too well.

My reconnaissance had been useful and provided the inspiration for a plan. Getting in and out of a custody block was possible as I had just proved. But it was also a real pain and not something I could keep doing.

In electronics there is a device called a transducer. It simply means a device that converts some physical property into an electrical signal or vice versa. A microphone is one such device. It converts changes in air pressure into an electrical signal. A speaker is very similar as it converts an electrical signal into changes in air pressure, or sound. What many people don't realise is that these two devices are very similar and in some situations can be used interchangeably.

Sitting in every interview room there was a microphone with wires running out of the custody block. If I could get to the end of these wires I could record everything going on in the custody area without ever having to go back there.

With time this short it was a simple and viable plan. The hardware would be quick to make. The trick would be getting into the police station again. One of the key skills of anyone in my line of work is "social engineering." It's the dark art of manipulating people. We all do it all the time anyway. Put a little thought and creativity into it and it becomes a very powerful tool.

To achieve a successful social engineering attack I needed some preparation. I started by searching out the public web site of the Police force. I used a script called Metagoofil to search the whole web domain for documents of interest to me, by searching through the meta-data buried in them. It very quickly pulled up a myriad of documents including most helpfully an internal telephone directory. I'm always surprised at the amount of classified documents left sitting on public web servers.

Using Skype, with an anonymous account paid for from a heavily laundered Paypal account I called the facilities management department at Police headquarters. A very helpful secretary there with a chirpy voice told me the company that the portable appliance testing was out-sourced to. She also told me the name of her boss who was unfortunately off work that day. I hoped that Gavin Turnbull-Jones was having a good day at the golf course or wherever he was. People in large organisations are usually pre-programmed to be helpful. This is the crack that the wedge of social engineering can be driven through.

I now found the web site for Parkway Electrical. Provider of electricians and P.A.T testing. I saved a copy of their logo onto my computer. Using Metagoofil again I found a few memos with names and details of a handful of employees. One man's stupidity is another man's key to the door.

I used a graphics program to make up an I.D card for Parkway Electrical in the name of Stan Harrison. I had no idea what an ID for Parkway would look like or even if they used them, but I could safely assume no one else would either. I used a special tray for my ink-jet printer to print directly onto a plastic ID card. When it had dried I added a hologram sticker for added authenticity.

While the ID card dried I looked up the user manual for a Cisco IP phone, which I noticed were in widespread use at the Police station. It was a short but interesting read.

I next called another minor functionary in Facilities management. I put on a loop of busy office sounds playing on the surround sound system as background noise. This time a male answered the phone. I told him I was from the I.T. Department and that I had been trying to reach Mr Turnbull-Jones. I was told he wasn't in the office, but I could talk to his secretary. I didn't want to do that, she would surely recognise my voice so soon after my last call.

'Look, I was supposed to come and sort out your boss's phone yesterday.' I told him.

'Well, he isn't in the office today.' Trying to pass the problem on.

'I realise that, but to be honest I messed up and my line manager is furious, but I've been pulled away onto an urgent server upgrade.' I paused to let this sink in. 'I'm not going to get down to you and reconfigure your boss's phone today.' I was playing two of the most powerful social engineering cards, fear of the boss and a desire to help out a fellow working stiff. 'Look, sorry what's your name?'

'Nathan.'

'Ok. Nathan. Sorry to use up your time, but if I don't change the settings on your bosses phone he's going to be furious when he comes in and finds it's not been done. It's going to make your day difficult and really mess up mine.'

'OK?' I could almost hear Nathan thinking this one through.

'Could you do me a really big favour?' The co-worker "favour" gambit. Rarely ever fails.

'Um, I suppose.'

'Nathan, what I need you to do is simply go and press a couple of buttons on your bosses phone and everything will be sorted.'

'Well, I don't really...'

I cut him off. 'It's simple and will take you twenty seconds and will mean your boss is in a far better mood tomorrow, oh and I won't get a really huge bollocking from mine.'

A slight sight I took as a non verbal tic caused by Nathan's resistance crumbling. 'Well, Ok, I guess.'

'Got a pen, fine, write this down. Lift the receiver then press the button marked "CFWD" then type in 0913341 on the keypad. Got that.'

'Yes, I think so.'

'Read it back to me.' He did. 'Nathan, thanks so much. You've saved me a roasting from my boss. I owe you one. I'll check the line when I've hung up from you, but if you don't hear from me then its gone ok. Thanks again Nathan.' I hung up.

I had just got Nathan to set up call forwarding on his bosses phone. Now when I dialled in using the direct dial number the call would automatically be forwarded to the front counter phone at South street Police station. On their display it would appear as if the call

70

originated from the Facilities management department. As a bonus if they called the phone themselves they would get an engaged tone.

I had a another coffee and waited a couple of moments before calling Gavin Turnbull-Jones's phone. The phone rang straight through to the front counter at the Police station. From the voice a middle aged woman answered. I had the office sounds playing in the background again.

'Hello is that front counter South Street?'

'Yes, it is. How and I help you?'

'Hi, this is Gavin Turnbull-Jones from Facilities management. This is just a quick call, because I haven't had a response from my email about the PAT testing. Did you receive the message my secretary sent about ten days ago?' Another good social engineering technique, make them feel like they messed up.

'No, I don't recall seeing one.'

'Damn, that's what I thought, you people must really check your mail more often. Well if you want a job done properly and all that. Look it's just to let you know you've got someone coming down this afternoon from Parkway Electrical to do some testing and look at the equipment you've got behind the front counter.'

'Oh, Ok.'

'Can you make sure he's got the necessary passes and give him room to work, his name is, hang on let me find the works order. It's a Stan Harrison. I think he'll get to your station about mid afternoon, shouldn't be there too long. I'll forward the works order in the internal post.'

'No, problem Mr. Turnbull-Jones, I'll see to it.'

'Thank you very much.' I hung up. A couple of calls and I had the keys to the castle. The bigger an organisation is, the easier it is to subvert.

I called Nathan back straight away. I couldn't have calls for Mr Turnbull-Jones going through to the front counter all afternoon. They might get suspicious.

'Hi Nathan, it's me again.' Always easier the second time round. "Somethings not quite worked. You did do exactly as I said?'

'Um, yes exactly as you told me.'

'No problem Nathan. We can fix your mistake together. Go back to the phone and lift the receiver and press the "CFWD" button again.'

Nathan went off the line for a moment. He came back breathless like he had run. 'I've done it.'

'Ok, let me check my display. Yes. That looks fine. I think you've done it this time, well done Nathan and thanks again and Nathan, I owe you but probably best not to mention the cock up to anyone.' I hung up. Call forwarding disabled. Tracks covered.

Now for the technical part. The signal generated by the speakers will be weak and full of noise. The long cable run would be picking up every piece of electrical noise in the neighbourhood. I fired up a CAD program on my computer. In this line of work you tend to use a lot of circuits over and over again. I loaded up a filter and pre-amp circuit and modified a couple of values to what I thought the audio signal would look like by the time it reached the front counter.

I had two interview rooms to bug, but I knew there were more speakers around than that so for good measure I would bug four of them, the interview rooms and the consultation rooms. I cut and pasted the filter/pre-amp circuit four times. Then I added a simple FM transmitter circuit. It was nothing fancy, a low power simple circuit that transmitted just out of the FM broadcast band. There was no time for anything complex. I copied and pasted that four times, changing the values of each so I had a reasonable amount of channel separation. Each transmitter had a vox circuit fed from the AGC turning on the output only when the audio level got above a certain threshold. I would have to adjust that manually for background levels when I installed the unit.

I checked the circuits for obvious mistakes, I was confident there shouldn't be any as I'd used these circuits in various guises many times over the years. I then printed the circuit board layout onto some etch resist copper sheet.

I must confess to not using my iron very often to put creases in clothes. Most of my apparel finds enough creases all on its own. However the iron gets regular outings ironing etch resist onto copper clad circuit board. Managing not to burn my fingers this time, I got the backing peeled off and the board etching away in a warm bath of ferric chloride. I gently sloshed the tray as the chemical went to work eating away at the exposed copper.

When that was done I washed the board, dried it and began syringing solder paste onto the pads on the circuit board before using a magnifier and vacuum pen to place the components down onto the tacky solder paste. When all the tiny rectangles were stuck in place I loaded the board into an infra-red oven and set it off baking the circuit.

I avoided coffee for a my next little break in my work and went with some orange juice. Much more coffee and my hands would start shaking. I lit a cigarette and called my friendly mechanic Duncan.

My paranoid nature makes owning vehicles difficult. You have to appear on a lot of databases just to drive one. A driving licence is first and unavoidable, but also the vehicle has to be registered to someone and then it has to be insured. The insurance is the biggest security hole in the act of driving a car. For a start they run a credit check on you before they even give you insurance and of course they keep a record of your insurance which links you to the vehicle.

Outside of my professional work I have little need for a car. I like the anonymity of public transport. I also like bicycles. Very few people realise that a push bike is the hardest vehicle on which to follow someone covertly.

However, for professional purposes I sometimes need a fast but nondescript car and an anonymous van. This is where my friendly mechanic Duncan Mcleish comes in. I help him out with vehicle electrics, and he helps me out with transport.

Duncan was ex Royal Corps of Transport and a magician with any kind of internal combustion engine. He runs a small garage on a bleak industrial estate on the edge of town. He charges very reasonable prices and in return for my occasional services with cars that arrive without the proper keys he keeps me on his trade insurance policy. I have an old white Ford Escort van that I paid him a few hundred pounds for. He stores it at his yard for me and keeps it registered to his garage. In addition he allows me to borrow cars when I need to. All in all it's a very useful relationship for me. Being on a trade policy means that should the police run the number plate of the car it won't be registered to me either through the vehicle or the insurance. It's a trick I learned from the local drug dealers who all drive under trade policies.

'Hello Pal.' Barked Duncan. I imagined him wiping the grease off of his hands as he cradled the phone in his shoulder.

'Duncan, I need the van for a day or two.'

'Aye, nay problem pal, I've got a few spare parts in the back. I'll clear them out just now and leave the van round the front of the yard.'

'Cheers Duncan, I'll come see you when this job is finished.' I hung up as the oven beeped to tell me the circuit board was cooked.

I tested the board out and it worked as I expected. It wouldn't win any awards for audio quality and would be discovered by the most basic of bug detection sweeps but it would do the job it was designed for. I boxed it up in an old metal box and added a power supply with a lead and a plug. The antennas for the FM transmitters were simple helical rubber ducks. They would stand out like a proverbial sore thumb. I was planning on hiding the box out of the way and relying on the fact people don't tend to mess with electrical equipment they don't understand. For good measure I put a couple of "Danger High Voltage" stickers around the case. Last task was a complete wipe and clean inside and out with isopropylene alcohol. This would dissolve the grease that left fingerprints and sterilise any DNA I had inadvertently left while constructing the unit.

I loaded up several plastic storage boxes with the equipment for the job and cycled round to Duncan's. The exercise was good for burning off some of the excess caffeine. Using my set of van keys I stuck the bike in the back and drove to my flat. I loaded the kit and then changed into a blue boiler suit, hi vis vest, baseball cap and my Stan Harrison ID card. I stuck a few screwdrivers and pens in the top pocket and put on a pair of thick rimmed glasses with clear lenses. I hoped that would be enough of a disguise should anyone encounter me from last night. I reckoned there should be a different shift on duty now.

7 Wednesday 16th January 1830 Hours.

The Prisoner's dilemma.

As I pulled up and parked the van a hundred yards away from the Police station I had about nineteen and half hours left. For an impossible mission things were going quite well. I took out two large tool boxes and locked the van and walked to the front counter of the police station. I passed through the automatic sliding front door and joined the line of people reporting lost dogs. The queue moved slowly. A middle aged woman with tightly permed battleship-grey hair sat behind the counter alternately answering the phone and fielding enquiries. We all shuffled forwards with painful slowness.

Eventually it got to be my turn at the front of the queue. The grey haired lady looked up at me with the police issue air of bored resignation. I tilted the ID card hanging round my next towards her, but didn't offer it over. Rule number one with fake ID, don't invite close inspection.

'Parkway's love, come to PAT test your stuff.'

The lady brightened a little the variety from the usual lost dog and bail returns. 'Oh, yes, we're expecting you. I thought you'd be here earlier.'

'So did I, you should have seen the state of the last station I was at. Still your front counter looks a look cleaner and tidier.'

From her ID badge she was Marion and Marion patted her hair self consciously 'Well, we do try and run a tight ship here.'

For effect I pulled a clipboard from one of the tool boxes. I had printed out a fake works order with the Parkways logo on top. 'Let's see, yes I'm to PAT test the front counter electrical equipment and check the general state of all electrical items.'

'Yes, so I've been told.' She passed over a clipboard of her own. On it was a combined signing sheet and visitors badge. I filled in the relevant parts and she tore off the badge part which she slipped into a plastic wallet with a clip. I clipped this to my top pocket. 'I'll buzz you through, use the door to your right.'

I carried my tool boxes through the access door and met her at the rear of the counter. 'I'll be working here.' I said. 'I'll try to work round you, but if I need to move things around I may need a few minutes alone.'

'That's fine. If you can keep the disruption to a minimum, as you can see we're quite busy today. You'll be OK working here, but if you need to go anywhere else I'll have to ring through for an escort.' The mention of an escort made me think briefly of Clara, but I put the thought aside and focused on the job.

I started off by really PAT testing all the portable electrical equipment I could find. I carried a reel of little green stickers which I duly signed off and stuck on each piece when I had finished it. When I had been working long enough to become invisible to Marion I started rooting around for the tannoy system wires. It took me some time to find the cables as they had been painted over many times but I could see they led into a stationary cupboard at the back. I worked my way round to that checking sockets and light switches as I made my way. I finally reached the cupboard and opened it to find on the bottom shelf an actual vintage tannoy system. It was dust covered and had a fabric covering to the lid and on the front proudly bore the label "All Solid State construction."

I turned to Marion. 'Ere how long's this been here?'

Slightly irritated at the interruption Marion span in her chair towards where I was kneeling on the floor. 'Oh, that. I don't even know what that is, but it's been here since before I joined.'

'Looks it love, it's from the ark. Very unsafe too. Something that old, you could have been given a nasty shock. I'll have to remove it and make the connections safe.'

Marion paled slightly at the notion of her possible electrical demise. 'Oh, thank you it's a good job you came and checked I suppose.'

'Don't worry, I'll have it done in no time, but this old stuff often has some nasty high voltages. I'll just need a few minutes to clear the area.'

Marion looked doubtful for a second but then made up her mind. 'Well, I shall just be outside if you need me.' She walked out of the area and shut the door behind her.

I quickly pulled the tannoy amplifier out. It wasn't even plugged in. I ran a multimeter across all the speaker sockets in the wall checking for shorts or open circuits. The resistance across all of them was about the same, within the range I was expecting. I then traced back which ones led towards the custody area. This was tricky again because of the accumulation of decades of paint and dirt.

I got my unit out of the second tool box and plugged it into a handy socket. I put a PAT test sticker on the plug and wrote in a long date on the sticker. I also stuck a red "Do not unplug" sticker. I opened the unit and clipped some headphones to test points on the circuit board. I listened to each input to check I had the right rooms and to set the circuits up for the correct levels. Satisfied the audio part of the system was working I plugged in the antennas and switched the transmitters on. I used a hand-held scanning receiver to check the FM transmitters.

All was working. I screwed on the lid and then piled reams of papers and pads of tickets and crime prevention leaflets in front of the unit to conceal it. I closed the cupboard and busied myself PAT testing anything that didn't move.

Marion hesitantly put her head round the door. 'Is it safe to come in yet?'

'Yes, it's safe as houses now. I'm nearly done.' I got my clipboard out again. 'Could you just sign here to prove I've been here and I'll get out of your way.'

Marion signed my fake works order and helped me out of the door with my toolboxes and tannoy system. I walked back to my van and stuck my tool boxes with my new trophy into the back. I got in the front seat just in case anyone was watching and then locked the doors and climbed over into the rear.

The van has slight modifications. Nothing fancy, no smoke screens or ejector seats. The main modification is that the rear compartment has been boarded out with cheap plywood and that has had old carpet stapled onto it. Between the wood panelling and the metal walls of the van old cardboard boxes have been stuffed in. This is to soundproof the back and the little insulation it provides is also welcome.

Some thick curtains separate the two front seats from the rear and the back windows have a film stuck across them to make them one way glass. Inside I have a very warm sleeping bag that I sit in and a wide necked bottle to pee into.

It gets cold in the van. I can't run any heating, that would be a dead give away and I have to keep the van well ventilated to stop it steaming up which would also give me away. There's a rotary vent in the van roof above my head, through that snakes the coaxial cable going to the magnetically mounted antenna on the roof.

I've fitted a second large capacity car battery which sits in the rear and via an inverter powers whatever equipment I am using. On this occasion I'm using a laptop with a software defined radio. This little box is made from a converted USB digital TV stick. It now functions as a wide band communications receiver. I had brought along a scanning receiver as a back up, but the SDR is ideal. The laptop screen showed a spectrum display of the band where my transmitters were located. Should any of them turn on I'd see a peak appear in the screen and can tune in on any or all of them at the click of my mouse. The radio software was set to record automatically as an MP3 file.

I put the headphones on, poured coffee from my flask and sat back to wait. I had just under nineteen hours left and I was in position. I flicked through the four channels listening to the background noise of the custody area. A moment of the buggers pride warmed me as I sat, unseen and unknown listening in upon the unsuspecting.

I'm used to not smoking while I work. Apart from the risks it would give my location away, when you've spent two days in the cramped rear of a van you really do stink if you smoke. My first initiation into the world of surveillance had been sitting in a car in small village waiting for the heir to wealthy family of stationary manufacturers to come out. I spent eighteen hours sitting in the car, the last twelve of which were desperately fighting the urge to pee. After so long I think my body started sweating to the fluids out, despite the temperatures outside being around freezing. I'll never forget how badly I stunk at the end of that job.

I listened bored to some minor criminal having a consultation with his solicitor. The advice he got was the same Archie had given me. Money for old rope. Then some activity started in one of the interview rooms. I heard movement, sounds of papers being moved and a brief bit of chatter as someone walked down the corridor. I stayed on that audio feed, watching the screen for any activity in the other rooms.

The footsteps came back, at least two sets this time. There was some idle chit chat, a female voice, Eastern European and a male English voice. I was betting this was a translator. Things were looking good. Then more footsteps and the chit chat stopped. Two more sets and another male English voice telling someone where to sit. The female voice translated, it sounded Eastern European, possibly Czech, but not speaking any Eastern European languages I was guessing.

I noted all this down in my log alongside the time. This would make it easier to find the relevant sections of recordings later. There's not much worse than having to go through ten hours of audio to find the few minutes you require for the pay day.

The door closed. This improved the quality of the audio I was getting somewhat. Then I heard the first English male voice start speaking. I recognised the start of the interview, it was almost identical to mine a day earlier. Everything that was said was translated by the female. The interviewee confirmed his name as Dinko then there were guttural grunts as responses which she didn't bother to translate. Nevertheless the whole procedure was frustratingly slow.

The main English voice speaking introduced himself as DC Jenkins. Jenkins then did me a big favour and began to recap the previous interviews. This was surveillance gold, a chance to catch up on all I had missed.

It seems our pair of hapless Eastern Europeans had been caught coming out the rear of a shop carrying cans of petrol and had been grabbed none to gently by the first fire crews on the scene. They had initially tried claiming they were moving the cans away from the blaze. This was all very funny right up until someone died. Well, several people. The family that lived in the flat above the shop all dead from smoke inhalation. At this point Dinko and Malinkova realising the gravity of the situation had offered the roll over and drop the boss in it.

None of this came as a surprise. I had gathered as much from the little Archie Hayes had told me. That the shop was owned by infamous local businessman Mr. Ali didn't come as a revelation either and therefore it followed that the fire was started by or on behalf of Mr. Ali sure as a hangover follows a night's drinking.

Jenkins recapped the earlier interviews. The pair had gone with the Nuremberg defence. The one where they say they are just minor functionaries following orders. It didn't work in forty five, it wasn't working now. So as the days of interviews wore on the pair had entered a kind of bidding war on out doing each other to provide information relating to Mr. Ali's entrepreneurial activities.

The situation Dinko, Malinkova and Mr. Ali were in was one I recognised. In game theory it's called "the prisoner's dilemma". True to the theory the former two were confessing hoping for a lighter sentence. Perverting the theory was Ali, cheating by using me.

Now Jenkins' recap got more interesting and I forgot the cold as I sat huddled in my sleeping bag in the back of my van on a cold winters night. Jenkins began going through one by one all the gossip and information Dinko had provided about Mr. Ali's operations. He was getting Dinko to confirm each piece. I could guess what Jenkins was up to. He must have had a similar list from the interviews with Malinkova, he would be correlating the two to sort the wheat from the chaff.

After an hour or so of working through this list they took a break in the interview. I poured myself another coffee from my flask while backing up the audio I had recorded so far to a USB stick. When they reconvened Jenkins changed his tone to a much harsher one and began going back through certain items in the list and challenging Dinko for more specifics. It was easy to work out these were the items that didn't match the Malinkova list.

82

Even through the medium of an interpreter I could hear in Dinko's voice a large amount of stress as he was challenged on points he had made up in his eagerness to get a lighter sentence. I doubted any reduction in sentence would really make a great deal of difference. From the stories I was hearing about Ali's business operation I doubted either Malinkova or Dinko would be in prison very long. They'd be leaving feet first.

Another hour and I was wondering how late in the night the police would continue interviewing. They were up against a clock so maybe they would carry on as long as it took. The interview with Dinko wound up and they stopped the disks and marched him back to his cell. Jenkins and the silent detective stopped to chat in the corridor. They must have been outside the second interview room because the audio feed from that room showed some activity.

They were going to charge both with manslaughter and then go to work on Mr. Ali. Malinkova was next up for a final run through like Dinko had just endured. I settled in for a few more hours of eavesdropping.

My eyes shut and my mind became lost in the aural world of the interview rooms. The vibrating of the phone in my pocket startled me. Annoyed I pulled it from my pocket. It was Archie-Bloody-Hayes. More annoyed now I rejected the call. He knows the rules. You don't call me when I'm working. If you must you text me, which is what Archie did next. I was tempted to ignore it purely out of annoyance but curiosity got the better of me.

"Job's off. Call me." Was all it said. This was a new one, the job was very much on. I was doing it. I left the equipment recording the empty interview room and climbed into the front of the van with difficulty as my legs had seized up. I let myself out the drivers door and walked to the next street lighting a cigarette and calling Archie back as I went.

'Archie, what the bloody hell is going on?'

'David, David, new instructions from the client, the job is off.' He slurred down the phone.

'What do you mean the job's off, I'm in the middle of doing it.'

'I don't have the details, but I believe the situation has changed somehow. Call me tomorrow to arrange the balance of your fee.' Sounds of a pub in the background and Archie hung up.

I'd never had a job cancelled in full flow like that. Especially when it was going so well. Puzzled I walked back to the van.

I stopped the recording and packed up the laptop then I walked a circuit around the van, one street out to check for any counter-surveillance on the van. Satisfied no one was interested in it I drove off taking a long and meandering drive home.

I unloaded the van and dropped it back at Duncan's. It was eleven O'clock. The job was done and I might just make last orders if I hurried.

8 Thursday 17th January 1030 Hours.

Boxes within boxes.

Daylight. Cautiously opening one eye I looked around battlefield of my bedroom thinking I must get round to tidying up at some point this year. My mouth felt like the inside of an old man's pocket. I grimly reflected on the four pints I had managed throw down my neck before I had been ushered out the door of the Engineer's Thumb way past closing time.

I was dehydrated. Sitting long hours in vans drinking nothing but strong coffee and pissing in a bottle will do that to you. Four pints of "Old Bedsocks" or whatever it was, hadn't helped the situation. Neither had the bloody kebab as I plodded my way into the kitchen and noticed the empty container gaping accusingly up at me. I downed a litre carton of orange juice straight from the box the fluid spilling out the corners of my mouth and running in cold rivulets down my neck.

I switched the espresso machine on and put down some food for Brill. He was probably out chasing tail some place. A shower and caffeine and the world started to fall into some semblance of order I could cope with.

There were several messages from Archie Hayes asking me to call him. Not a bad idea. The balance was eight thousand. I was already considering which new toys I'd treat myself to and I needed to put in an order for components to replenish my stock. I called Archie back.

'David, I'm glad you called.' He answered quickly. The pubs weren't open yet.

'Archie, I'll be glad for the eight grand.'

'David, yes, that's what I called about.' Some hesitancy in his voice. I really hoped he wasn't about to try and screw me over.

'Before we arrange my payment, what the hell happened last night?' Yes. The money was important but my curiosity overrode that.

'I really don't know David, The client was released without charge last night. A stroke of luck, and a good result, but I'm at a lost to explain why.'

'Archie, you're representing him, you must know why.'

'David, all I know is the Magistrate refused to extend his detention, it seems the Police didn't feel they had enough evidence to charge so they let him walk.'

Stranger and stranger. From what I'd heard of Dinko's interview they must have enough to charge Mr. Ali with something, if not manslaughter then some other crime. 'So, Archie, my money?'

'Yes, your money. That's what I've been calling about. Mr. Ali would like to pay you in person and thank you for the work you did.' It sounded hollow even coming from Archie Hayes.

'The eight grand will be thanks enough and you know my rules. I never meet the client directly. That's how come you get to earn your cut.' Another one of my rules and another Archie should have known full well was inviolate.

There are many good reasons to never meet the client. Most of the people that use services like mine are not nice people. There is a risk I might decide I dislike them too much to do the job if I met them in person. A couple of very practical reasons also exist. I don't like the client knowing what I look like. During surveillance the client can often be with the subject and there's a huge risk the client will inadvertently betray me if they recognise me. Also this weeks client is often next weeks subject.

'I'm sorry David. I know you don't like to meet your clients, but Mr. Ali has insisted, it seems he may have some more work for you. He'd like you to bring all recordings and all copies with you when you come. Shall we say four O'clock at my office?'

I hung up the phone without committing to anything. I had a bad feeling about Mr. Ali. He hadn't endeared himself to me by putting the squeeze on me to take the job. Then there was the matter of cancelling the job in full swing and his mysterious release from police custody. I particularly didn't like the comment about bringing all the recordings.

Clearly I was going to give him the recordings. It's what I'm paid to do. I was going to burn them onto a nice shiny CD that he could listen to in glorious high fidelity at his leisure. However asking for all copies was a bit redundant and I didn't figure Mr. Ali for being that stupid. In this digital age audio, photos and video could all be copied ad infinitum. Like lending someone your door key you would never know how many copies existed or where they were. The genie can never be put back in the bottle. That's why I'm a little like a doctor or lawyer. Only my professional code of conduct prevents me revealing all the secrets I pick up as part of my work. There has to be a level of trust or people won't hire me.

My reasons for being suspicious of Ali were ignoring the fact that I now knew him to be an arsonist and killer, my customers don't tend to be very nice people. I exist as an observer of life, I don't participate. I had the feeling now that Ali was trying to involve me as an actor in his little drama and I didn't like it. I was going to have to do something to convince him to forget all about me. At this point he seemed a little untouchable. Whatever I was going to do would be a lot easier with a cold eight thousand in my pocket.

I got dressed in nondescript street clothes and then packed a small shoulder bag with a few of my electronic toys.

The office of Morgan, Styles and Brown was in the middle of a small street running parallel to the High Street. It was one of the older roads in town and was filled with solid brick and stone four story buildings. Several of the buildings housed solicitors firms. It was a legacy from when a local police station stood a street away. That station had long since been sold off and was now a designer crèche for designer children. From the proceeds they had built the South Street station located just out of town which I was now intimately familiar with.

The rest of the buildings had undergone conversions into flats with varying degrees of success. As I looked along the row some still appeared smart and comfortable while others decayed bit by bit as absentee landlords bled the architectural lifeblood of the town to pay for expensive Range Rovers with blacked out windows which they used to visit their "portfolio" once a year.

The Morgan office had two short but solid steps worn into a graceful curve by a hundred and twenty years of shoes. A solid oak door with blackened iron studs stood guard and a half dozen sash windows stared blankly at the twenty first century. I walked past the office two and a half hours early for the appointment.

Parking meters lined the kerb like anorexic soldiers on some forlorn parade. I glanced at each as I passed to see how long they had left. I turned at the end of the street looking for an alley way to the rear of the properties. Past town planners had clearly understood the value of space and would have left an alleyway between the rows of houses to bring coal in and mistresses out. I found the entrance mid way down the parallel road. I threaded my way past dustbins, used nappies and dog shit. The rear of the office was recognisable by its lack of washing hanging from its windows. The rear windows were obviously considered an extravagance and had been left dusty and cracked. An iron fire escape, now mostly rust, made its angular way up the rear of the building broken by the cracked and peeling exteriors of the doors.

There were no curtains or blinds on the windows this side. I stood in the alleyway and watched trying to identify which rooms were used for which. I sketched a plan of the layout in my notebook.

I left the stench of the alley and walked through town towards Singh's shop. I was greeted by a shiny new window. Singh had worked fast getting that replaced. Singh himself sat in his usual place behind the counter avidly watching his poorly tuned portable T.V. He Greeted me enthusiastically and insisted on giving me a tour of the notable features of his new window. I asked him where Gianparkash, his middle son, was. Singh disappeared into the bowls of the shop to look for him.

Gianparkash, eighteen years old and considered runt of the family. I had been using Singh's shop for several years. The place functioned as a cut out address for me. I had mail, packages and faxes sent there to provide me another layer of anonymity.

While Mr. Singh could never be considered a particularly devout Sikh he did cling on to the traditions and rituals of his native faith. Gianparkash or Kash as I called him, had never seen the relevance of the old ways, or his ancestral land and had grown up embracing the Western world and all it's faults. Much like me, all that Kash had left school with was a deep mistrust of authority and a fascination with computers. Against my wishes and best judgement Kash had begun, unasked for, running errands for me. After a while he wore me down and I had began repairing the damage the education system had done to him, first off teaching him maths and then when I felt he'd the logical foundations I'd started him on the path to the dark arts of computing.

Thin and wiry like the rest of family, but with a edge of softness probably from the burgers snuck down his neck when his strictly vegetarian mother wasn't looking. He kept his hair uncovered and shoulder length in an untidy mess and dressed in black jeans and a black hooded top bearing the logo "2600". He came bounding past the counter.

'What's up Bugman?' He asked using a nickname I used on certain Internet relay chat rooms.

'Kash, what did I tell you about discretion?' I chided him. 'What am I always telling you?'

He looked crestfallen, I'd just knocked some wind from his sails. 'Oh, yeah. Compartmentalise.' He shuffled on the spot his hands thrust into the deep front pockets of his top.

'Have you finished the project I gave you?'

'Yeah man, that was easy. A few lines of code was all it took.'

'Good man. A ping scan is a useful tool, but not very stealthy. Next time we'll look at a syn-ack scan.' I was slowly teaching him to program and in the process getting him to write his own custom hacking toolbox.

'Oh, Chatar,' Kash suddenly remembered, using the Sikh name his father had sarcastically given me. 'I had some replies from the universities.' We had Kash registered to sit A-levels as a private student and he was busy applying for universities. He was desperate not to end up working in a corner shop the rest of his life.

'That's good, it's your decision Kash. Now I've got a little job for you. Lets walk and I'll brief you.'

Kash brightened at that. Once again he'd been wearing me down over a period of months to involve him in one of my jobs. I'd been reluctant to. Clara and I inhabited a world of lies and deceit for as long as we could remember. Our daily grind was to observe humanities greed, weakness and cruelty. Without those elements of human nature we'd never be able to ply either of our trades, but you can't unsee things. The moment you went through that door, stepped into the shadows, a part of you could never come out again. Every walk down the street is now past abusers, embezzlers, cheats and thieves. Hidden glances, secret exchanges and petty deceptions become as clear as day to your seasoned gaze. The sky is still above you, the ground below and the trees there, but you don't notice them any more. Your world becomes the arena of human failings and you can never go back to ignorance.

A part of me wanted to delay Kash's loss of innocence as long as possible, but I felt deep down that one way or another he would find a way into the murky world of shadows all by himself, if he was going to go there he may as well have an experienced guide.

We walked to a nearby park. We sat on a bench in a large area of open space. I could see anyone approaching for a hundred yards.

'Right, Kash.' I tried to marshal my thoughts. 'Here's the deal. I need a small job done. There may be some risk. This is serious stuff.'

Kash nodded thoughtfully.

'We're moving up a big step with this, we're going beyond cool tricks to impress people with. If you decide to do this then everything I've told you about never letting people know what you know, is the rule from now on. You have to do things for their own sake, because if you do them well no one but you will ever know what you've done no matter how brilliant it was.' I watched Kash carefully, I had to be sure he was ready. If he carried any of the pride or arrogance of youth along with him on this journey it would be a short one.

Kash met my gaze, smart enough to say nothing.

'This job may seem a small one, but every job you do has big ramifications for someone, somewhere. If you don't keep your stuff together then that someone will be you.'

Kash nodded again.

'This has to be all your own free choice. I won't think any differently of you either way. Take a minute and consider what I've said.' I shut up. I was talking too much.

Kash sat in silence, almost in a meditation. I wasn't sure if I was doing the right thing, but using Kash made sense tactically. He was an asset I could use up on this small task leaving some of my other cards for later if required.

He came to a decision. Without saying anything he removed his wallet from his jeans and put it on the bench between us. Next he took out his mobile phone. He prised off the back cover, removed the battery and the SIM card and laid them on the bench. He was doing as I had taught him, readying himself to go operational.

'OK then, here goes.' I said dropping Kash's personal effects into my satchel. I handed him back another mobile. A disposable phone I called them. Cheap twenty quid phones bought from a supermarket using cash and fitted with an anonymous prepaid SIM. 'Relevant numbers are pre-programmed.' I told him. Then I fished out a fairly expensive looking divers watch with a black rubber strap. 'This is a video camera, 4 gigabytes of memory. Sixty quid from China via Ebay.' I handed it over.

Kash turned the watch over in his hands like it was a rare Rolex.

I pointed to the buttons on the case. 'At two O'clock here, this button puts it on standby. The indicator LED goes blue.'

Kash pressed the button.

'And here at seven O'clock, one press for video, two for audio only and three for still pictures. With video selected the light will go red for five seconds and then go out. Press standby to stop it.'

Kash tested the process and put the watch on.

I handed Kash a rape alarm next. 'If everything goes wrong pull the pin on the top. It makes a lot of noise and flashing lights. Leave it in your pocket and I can find you.'

Kash deposited that into his pocket. 'OK, Chatar, what's the plan?'

I passed over a CD. 'You are going to a meeting at a solicitors office. All you have to do is hand over this and receive eight thousand pounds in cash.'

'So, what's the catch?'

'I think the people you will be meeting may intend me harm. At the very least I don't want them to know what I look like.'

'I guess they're not expecting me.'

'No. If anything goes wrong. If anything happens that you're not happy about then you get out straight away.' I opened my notebook on the bench and pointed to the sketch map. 'If you can just walk out the front door normally, do that. If you can't what I want you to do is go upwards. There are four floors. They won't expect you to do that. At the top of every flight of stairs is a fire escape leading to the rear. Use one of those. I'll be waiting in the alley.'

Kash studied the drawing. I turned the page to show another sketch of the surrounding streets. 'Which ever way you leave I want you to follow this route. The only difference will be the speed you are going. Do you understand?'

Kash nodded.

'OK then repeat the plan back to me.'

We walked back into town. I took Kash to the end of the street and showed him the front of the offices. Then we took a long looping walk to the alleyway. We gingerly threaded our way down the detritus strewn walk and I pointed out the rear of the building and all the possible escape routes. It was now three O'clock. The meeting was at set for four. I instructed Kash to walk into the office at ten past.

I sent Kash to get himself a sneaky burger a looked for a convenient place to watch the street from. The van would have been handy now, but I didn't have time to go and get it and it was another card I didn't want to expose too soon. Some rooting round in the back alleys and I opened a side gate to a neighbouring property giving me easy access to front and rear. The only downside was the view to the front of Morgan's offices was a very oblique one. I slipped a small round mirror from my wallet. I carried the mirrored circle from a budgie mirror and had sprayed the back of it matte black, it was an invaluable, yet inexpensive surveillance tool I was rarely without. By pulling the gate almost to I could stand with my back against the wall of the alley and exposing only a sliver of an arc of mirror I could watch the front of the office.

I settled in to wait. It was starting to get dark and street lights were flickering into life at random locations. The sky was heavy with the threat of rain. Perfect conditions.

At twenty to four a large dark old style Mercedes pulled up abruptly outside the office and two large men in dark coats climbed out, glanced up and down the street before striding into the offices. Through the limited field of view in the mirror I couldn't see a lot of detail but the pair looked heavy in every sense of the word.

If I were having recriminations about sending Kash in, then now was the time to abort my scheme. I decided to let things run on a little more.

I was just starting to feel the cold when I saw Kash walk by on the other side of the street. It was seven minutes past. Pretty good timing. Without hesitation Kash crossed the road and pushed his way through the heavy wood door his small frame leaning in with the effort. I pocketed the mirror and ducked through the alley to the rear.

Lights had come on in some of the offices and I could see clearly into the ones on the ground and first floors. I could partially see the room that would have been on the right as you walked in the front door. It had a desk and a coat stand with one coat hanging from it. The room looked empty but filling cabinets and a corner of wall blocked my view. The room on the left was clearer. This looked to be Archie's office. A large and weighty desk littered with bundles of papers and files sat haphazardly in the corner. The two large men stood by the desk, one half sitting on the edge of it. I couldn't see any sign of Archie.

From this distance I still couldn't make out much from the pair. I took out a small pair of binoculars from my satchel. Brought a little closer I couldn't see much more to tell this pair apart. Very short crew cuts, clean shaven, dark coats and large bodies. The way they moved suggested bulk rather than muscle. They waited calmly barely moving and not appearing to talk. Then both of them looked up at the door unhurriedly.

Kash came through the door first, ushered in by Archie who then backed out closing the door behind him. I watched intently. The pair looked over at Kash without getting up. I could see Kash talking, then he proffered the disk with one hand and held out the other palm up. He must have been asking for the eight thousand. The man on the edge of desk laughed while the other stared silently at Kash. I could see a moments indecision in Kash's movements as he pondered what to do next. He thrust the disk back in his pocket, turned and walked out the door. Neither man moved for a few seconds then the one on the edge of the desk shrugged and pulled out a mobile.

I made my way quickly back to the side gate. I was in time to see Kash walk past heading towards the end of the road. I slipped the mirror out of the gate a small amount. I could see Kash disappearing down the road in my peripheral vision and a slice of the office front in the mirror. As Kash reached the end of the road I saw the two men leave the office. One started up the road towards me, the other seemed to be heading for the car.

As the one on foot passed my hiding spot I gently pushed the gate closed a fraction more. Once he had passed I slipped the mirror out and caught the car doing a hasty three point turn. The male on foot turned left as I hoped Kash had. I waited for the car to reach the end of the road before I emerged onto the pavement and joined the procession.

Having one person on foot doing a follow is amateur night. I was also following alone, but I had the advantage of knowing the route in advance. The car might have helped them, but I had given Kash a route to follow full of alleys and one way streets. I was going to enjoy this, not eight grands worth of enjoyment, but a start.

As I turned left I emerged onto a long straight road with a slight uphill gradient. I could see Kash quite far into the distance. On the same side of the road about a hundred yards ahead was the large male. I slowed my pace to let our separation increase then I crossed the road.

My main reason for giving Kash the route to walk was to throw off any attempt to follow him back to me. As a bonus I was now going to get a chance to see how efficient Mr. Ali's people were. So far I wasn't impressed. I was also keeping half an eye on Kash. This was his first time and if he could get through the whole route without looking back once I would be very impressed. If he did or didn't ultimately wouldn't make much difference as in a while the pair following would have to be pretty dumb to not realise they were being strung along.

I crossed the road keeping myself at angle off the right shoulder of my subject. People tend to have a blind spot right about the same place it is when driving a car. I was out of his peripheral vision and not directly behind him if he were to suddenly turn round. My one concern was the car. They surely couldn't be that stupid to have the car crawling along at a walking pace. It would most likely be driving ahead and waiting.

Kash made the two left turns as planned and I watched his tail speed up and close the gap, no doubt worried Kash would make another turn before he got round the junction. I kept my pace, I knew where all this was leading and I didn't want to risk walking past the car if it were waiting round the next corner.

I turned wide, keeping on the right hand side of the road giving me the maximum amount of view and warning as to what lay in the next street. As I sliced round the corner I saw the male way ahead, but Kash was already gone from view. Then the Mercedes pulled out from between some parked cars ahead and drove round the corner, no doubt to park up again ahead of Kash and wait.

Kash should be coming up to the park soon. This was where we'd start to shake the tail. There were four exits and two of them were alleys. We'd be saying goodbye to the car if things went to plan. I called the mobile I'd given Kash.

'Don't look round, but you're doing well.'

'OK man, this is kinda fun.'

'You've got a car and a man on foot following you. We're going to shake off the car first.'

'Got it.'

'But first I've had an idea. As you get into the park I want you to speed up like you're nervous.'

'Man, I am nervous.'

'Good, this should be easy then. As you speed up, accidentally drop the CD. Don't look back whatever you do, but speed up as fast as you can go without running and follow the rest of the route. Got it?'

'OK boss, got it.'

I put the phone away and sped up. I'd need to close the gap to the safest minimum for this to work. In the distance I could see Kash approaching the entrance to the park, a wide gap in the fence with a bollard in the middle to stop cars getting in. On the other side of the road right in front of the entrance was the car. They weren't completely stupid. It would wait there till the foot follower knew which exit Kash was taking.

I could see the foot follow. He'd let the gap get larger between him and Kash again. No doubt because of the long straight road they were on. He'd be trying to close it again as they got to the park. I lengthened my stride to increase my speed without seeming to hurry.

The male on foot had his phone out and pressed to his ear. He would be giving the guy in the car a commentary. I crossed the street and stopped with a parked van giving me cover from the car. Kash entered the park and ten seconds behind him was the male. I watched the parked car through the windows of the van.

Kash should have dropped the disk by now. I was hoping the pair would have some magpie in them and go for the shiny bait. The male in the car sat with his head turned to the side watching his colleague progress across the park and listening to the large mobile pressed to his ear. He suddenly dropped the mobile onto the dashboard and jumped from the car with surprising speed and bolted across the road into the park.

I had no definite plan in getting Kash to drop the disk. I hoped to create some kind of opportunity. I ran from behind the parked van. Bad road safety, but I probably had only seconds. I opened the drivers door. He hadn't closed it fully. I scanned the interior for anything useful.

There wasn't much to get my interest. Some kind of religious ornament hung from the rear view mirror, a half empty pack of Turkish cigarettes and the phone. Then my eyes caught the dull black shape in the drivers door. I didn't touch it but crammed in among empty cigarette packets was the cold metal of an automatic pistol. It didn't occur to me to look at it to see if it was real, time was very short.

Instead I took the phone and ran. I got back behind the parked van as the male emerged from the park. He was walking now and proudly carrying the disk. I hoped he liked country music. The disk contained forty three minutes of the greatest hits of Johnny Cash. I thought it poetic to send in Kash, with Cash to exchange for cash.

The driver slammed his door and started the engine. He pulled the nose out into the road then the nose dipped as he hit the brakes. Through the two layers of the vans windows I watched him feel round on the dash looking for the phone. He scratched his head then started poking around in the foot well. While he did this I removed the back cover of the phone and pocketed the battery.

The driver gave up looking for the phone and pulled out. He was going to try and make the best of the job and carry on. Very commendable. I walked back the way I had come and turned down an alley. More rubbish and shit to avoid. I waited, at any moment now Kash should have doubled back and would be here.

Slightly breathless, but grinning a wide grin Kash jogged up the alley way. I said nothing, but pushed open a rickety wooden gate and ushered him in. Not that you could really tell from the alley but this was the overgrown and neglected garden of a small backstreet pub. Kash followed me in the back door and through to the games room. He sat getting his breath back while I got him a lemonade and myself a pint of old bedsocks.

'So tell me how it went down.' I asked.

'Man, that was cool. I went to the office when you said and some fat old guy led me in.'

'Did he say anything?'

Kash thought for a second then shook his head. 'Not really, maybe just "Follow me." or something like that.'

Strange for Archie to be so taciturn. 'So then what happened?'

'I went into this, like, office and there were these two huge fellas in jackets. They were foreign like Greek or something. One didn't say nothing, but just sorta stared at me like he was trying to be the mean dude or something. The other one, well he seemed a little pissed off at me and asked me for the disk, so I asked him to show me the money. The guy just laughed at me, which I thought was a bit freaky so I left.'

'Ok, go on.'

'I left just like you said, turned, left, left and left again. I never looked back but I could kind of feel them there. I cut across the park and then dropped the CD like you asked. Then I cut down the alleys and I think I lost them at that point.'

'Nice work Kash. That went as smoothly as I hoped.' I handed him back his personal effects and he in turn passed across what I had issued him. 'Now, it's not over yet. What you need to do is head home keeping off of the main streets as much as possible. Take a wide rambling route home and make sure no one follows you. I suggest you lay low for a few days. Stay home and work on your projects. I'll call you when I need you next.'

9. Thursday 17th January 2130 Hours.

Open source.

The night time economy. Another attempt to use words to sanitise what goes on at the strip of bars just off the main drag in town. At the one end they start as upmarket coffee shops that serve champagne for those that don't care for espresso. As you progress towards the far end the bars get progressively larger, louder and stay open later and the champagne becomes Cava about half way before ending up as vomit in the gutter at the far end. The street has bars on one side only. The neon lights and blank looking doormen face the park that runs the length of the other side and that looks back on the world of men with a casual indifference.

I had taken a seat on the edge of the greenery about half way down. The sighs of the wind ruffling the bare branches making a soothing contrast to the revelry on the opposite side of the road. I was slumped back on the hard bench with the air of someone taking a break from having too much of a good time on the strip. Thursday is the new Friday.

It had been a busy evening. After leaving Kash I'd followed my own advice and taken a leisurely walk in ever decreasing circles. I doubted that Mr. Ali had any extra manpower to call upon at such short notice and I equally doubted he had access to the kind of team that he'd need to follow me unnoticed, but it pays to be careful.

On the way Archie had sent me a text asking 'what the hell I was playing at.' I might well have asked him the same thing. Archie Hayes was playing both ends against his ample middle. When Archie tries to keep the peace between people I'm sure the motivation is not some trace of morality but economic imperative.

I had managed to become a threat to Ali. That was a problem. I could have lived with another drop of doubt in the ocean of my paranoia, but the fool had sent thugs with guns to greet me. I doubted he was going to let things be until he'd eradicated the doubt that I personified.

My greatest advantage was that Ali knew nothing about me. Assuming Archie had one way or another been persuaded to tell everything he knew about me, and that process would be as simple as a bottle of cheap brandy, then all Ali could possibly have was a generic description and a mobile phone number. On the other hand my trade was finding things out about people. Know your enemy. I didn't doubt that there was something to find that at the very least would force Ali into some kind of détente.

Earlier in the evening I had carefully crafted an espresso with a strong Italian grind and sat at my computers and begun an open source search. This had led me several hours later to a park bench over looking a row of bars in the freezing cold while young professionals with ruddy cheeks and cheap business suits hanging off their inebriated frames rushing past me to piss and vomit in the park amid similarly disarrayed couples furtively stealing into the trees to attempt a sub zero copulation against the trunk of an oak tree ten times their combined ages.

I sat slightly lolling to one side with the glazed vacant expression of the drunk while I pretended not to feel the cold and watched the Vista Bar. A bar I was sure had close links to Ali and was equally sure was named for the stunning view of the park with its trees, shrubs, used condoms and discarded bottles.

An open source search is a method of research using only publicly accessible sources of information, in the hacking world we called it doxing. Some of these are obvious; the phone book, the electoral roll, the press, the ubiquitous Google search. Then there are the lesser known and more technical things like web domain registrars, companies house and social networks.

I already knew Ali's full name. He was fairly well known in certain circles and pub talk had given me a couple of starting points along with a few horror stories and urban legends that I couldn't readily verify. I knew he was "Ali Mehmet" a Turkish national. I also knew he owned a Turkish barbers in Town and a hand car wash not far out of town. He was in his late forties and drove an upmarket Mercedes with a personal plate.

I used the Barbers as an entry point and took a virtual walk with Google street view and found the premises and the address. I then web searched the business and got a yellow pages entry. Each piece of information I entered into a database in a piece of intelligence processing software, called "Maltego", which as the items of information built up connections would become visible between disparate elements in a diagram reminiscent of a crazy spiders web. The yellow pages entry was interesting as it still held an record for a previous business at the same address, a travel agents that must have closed down a year ago. I did a search on that and found it had a website that still lurked on the Internet like some ghost of a company that refused to go away. The site gave me nothing but the DNS records gave me the details of person who had registered the domain name.

I had found Ali's first mistake. Whoever had designed and set up the web site, I didn't peg Ali as a part time web coder, had used Ali's real details. In a stroke I had his full home address and landline number. I took a quick tour of his neighbourhood courtesy of Google Earth and found a large detached property on a private estate backing onto a golf course. Nice.

Next I paid a visit to the Land Registry web site and for a small fee I got a copy of the deeds including a plan of the house and how much was paid for it. I wasn't surprised to find out that the house wasn't in his name, but had been bought by a company. So now onto companies house. Things got more interesting here. No surprise Ali was a director of the company that owned his house also no surprise he was or had been a director of quite a few companies, most of which were dissolved prior to having to submit mandatory accounts. I added all these into the database along with names of the various co-directors.

I trawled through each registered business culling news items and where a web site still existed I leached phone numbers, names and address from each along with DNS registration details. I fed this all into my ever growing database carefully connecting each element as I found links between them all.

Last of all I went through the the social networks. Again nothing I wouldn't expect. Ali didn't have a Facebook account or a Twitter feed and who has a Myspace account these days? However he did have a Linkedin account. Dormant for a a while, but with a slack handful of connections which I duly fed into Maltego.

The connection diagram did indeed look like something made by a drug crazed arachnid. There must have been over a hundred pieces of information. I ran what the software calls a transform and some further points were added and then began panning around the diagram twisting and rotating the seemingly random mass of connections. I was looking for a nexus,a convergent point within the mass of entropy.

A couple presented themselves. So I picked the one with the most recent links. The Vista bar and it's nominal owner or at least manager fronting for Ali Mehmet was a Nico Constantinou. I looked up the name and it looked to be Greek Cypriot. Interesting. I went to the Vista bar web site again. Nothing much to note but a few nice photos of the interior. I saved these and noted the layout for later. The website linked to a Facebook fan page. I set up a counterfeit Facebook profile and became a fan.

The fan page had a huge number of photo albums, some submitted from camera phone wielding carousers and others clearly done by a club photographer. I found the opening night album and started to browse. Amidst the short skirted drunk girls which clearly the photographer had been biased to snap, were the bar staff. I quickly identified Constantinou and focused on pictures with him in easily disregarding the pictures of drunk girls in various states intoxication with half closed eyes and increasingly dishevelled hair as the night wore on.

I was looking for a picture of Ali Mehmet. I found a few snaps of a suited man, normally back turned to the camera or just managing to get out of shot. Then I found one that had clearly slipped through. Mistake number two. The picture was taken towards the end of the evening. Nico Constantinou was standing proudly behind the bar raising a glass to the camera. Next to him his arm round Nico's shoulder also raising a toast was, I was pretty sure, Ali Mehmet. Hard to refuse a toast to your new business. Hard to refuse without looking churlish or odd. Difficult to avoid particularly after a few drinks.

The picture showed a Mediterranean looking man in his forties. His jet black hair starting to be speckled with grey at the temples but neatly cut, combed back at the top but short at the back and sides. The advantage of owning a barbers. Clean shaven. Square jawed. Clearly fit and on the muscled side, although going to fat with the start of middle aged spread. He was wearing a tailored black suit and blue shirt open collared. All in all the picture of a successful, handsome businessman. Until you looked in the brown eyes, even after drinking, they were hard and focused. Boring through the camera, not happy with being photographed.

So hello Mr Ali Mehmet. This isn't getting to know each other. This is me getting to know you. This is me crawling into your life. Open source search done. Now I get under your skin, in your walls, under your bed and into your head till I know you better than you know yourself. The best part is you'll never see me coming.

I decided to take a look at Vista and see what leads I could develop from there. I called up Clara and invited her for a drink at ten. I changed and headed straight out. I wanted a couple of hours watching the place before Clara arrived.

The hour and half on the bench had chilled me. I was wearing a shirt and a lightweight jacket. Casual enough to be an evening drinker, but not smart enough that anyone would notice me. I glanced up at the night sky and noted the clouds were thinning out and it was going to be another cold one.

Vista had been empty till about nine O'clock. I had seen Constantinou come out and fussily arrange a few of the stainless steel chairs and tables arranged outside. The bar was about a third of the way down the strip. Not quite Moet et Chandon but not yet into the snakebite and pitcher of cocktail territory. There was a rope partition held up by shiny metal posts around the outside area of the bar doing nothing except attempt to create an air of exclusivity for the tables and the patio heaters.

I could see all the way in through the floor to ceiling glass at the front. It looked like they might fold away to leave the place open plan in the summer. Just after Nine they dimmed the lights and I felt rather than heard the subdued bass beat of music joining the background of the strip. Barmaids leaned listlessly on the bar waiting for the rush that might never come.

Once Constantinou came out went to an old looking silver BMW. I could see the indicators flash orange as he locked and unlocked the car with a fob. So far nothing to pique my interest. I suppressed a shiver and looked at my watch willing Clara to hurry up so I could get warmed up.

The time wasn't a total waste. I was starting to tune into the rhythm of the street. Middle aged couples dinning out had come to the bars at the top end for a postprandial drink and were now mostly leaving in taxis two by two like animals fleeing the coming flood. The rising tide of that flood was beginning with younger drinkers arriving mostly in single sex twos and threes. Some going to the first bars and others jumping straight into the middle of the strip. The progression was almost entirely one way down the road. The only exceptions to these were the hardcore daytime drinkers now heading back up the road weaving in a drunken amble amidst the still sober night shift coming the other way.

It was getting close to the time I was due to meet Clara. There was no way for her to contact me. I was carrying an operational phone. One of the mobiles I owned, that while not quite disposable, contained no personal information on it, but still a functional smart phone unlike my disposable mobiles. Apart from some cash and my keys the only other item I carried was a hidden camera disguised as a disposable lighter, just in case an opportunity presented itself.

I got up stiff from the bone chilling cold. My jerky walk and stretching fitted in perfectly with the performance of a tipsy drinker without my having to make any effort. By the time I got to the corner of the road I had started to limber up and my act had sobered up. I found a doorway to stand in at the large edifice at the end of the strip. I think it used to be a bank, but had long been a restaurant but now it's shutters had been pulled down ahead of the coming tide.

I leaned back comfortably into the door. A mere nine inches from the street, but a world away. Out of eye-line of the bustling pavement and if you stand still no one notices you. I've always considered humans almost unique among mammals. We're both hunters and prey. It's largely a matter of choice which you want to be. While most of us have good forward vision we also have excellent peripheral coverage. The thing to bear in mind is that peripheral vision is movement sensitive. Therefore standing still and just off of the shoulder one can quite literally disappear.

The street was getting busier with drinkers pre-empting the pubs closing and heading down to the strip. Groups of girls in party frocks clacked past on heels while jeans and T-shirt wearing groups of young males passed by all talking too loudly. Out of the passing traffic I picked out the sound of a diesel engine idling as a taxi pulled into the kerb in front of me.

The door opened and with perfect poise a pair of black stilettos followed by stockinged ankles and slim calves emerged. Closely behind the rest of Clara flowed onto the pavement, the passing throng automatically flowing seamlessly around her. I stayed leaning casually in the doorway enjoying the scene. Clara wore a close fitting black roll neck sweater and a figure hugging skirt that came down to her knees. Her long dark hair was loose down her back. The contrast between her and the scantily clad girls showing more flesh than a butchers shop, was remarkable.

Clara could wear a mini skirt, I could vouch for that. But in her own demure way she was sexier than hell the less she revealed. She, of course, knew where I'd be standing and as the taxi pulled away into the traffic behind her our eyes met. I looked into the oil like blackness of her eyes and couldn't help but grin, but still didn't move.

Clara took the two steps across the pavement into my doorway. Which was what I wanted. Before we ventured into the fray I needed a word. She stepped up to me. 'You're early.' She said putting a hand to my neck and kissing me. 'And you're freezing.' She wrinkled her nose. 'What have you been doing?'

Ignoring the question. "You look good tonight."

She looked down at herself as if noticing for the first time what she was wearing. 'Oh, this. I've got a client tonight.'

I tried not to let it sting that she hadn't dressed up for my benefit. I almost succeeded. 'How long can I have you for?'

Clara reached down and took my left wrist in her slender right hand. I inwardly winced remembering her viscous wrist locks, but she just pulled my arm up to look at my watch. 'Just under two hours honey. Then I must look good on the arm of a very wealthy man while he does his best to make himself progressively less wealthy at the casino.'

'Then what?' Mentally kicking myself for transgressing our boundary.

She dropped my arm. 'Who knows.' She replied coolly. Always in total control she shifted tack, her eyebrow arching and a trace of smile playing on those full red lips. 'So what antics are we up to now.' She turned the full force of her liquid clear dark eyes on me. 'I thought you'd finished the job.'

Those eyes could melt me and she knew how to use them as the world's best lie detector. 'It's sort of finished.' I added as the eyes glistened in front of me. 'There's an issue with the client. I think he might want me dead.'

'So.'

'So, I'm taking a look at a club he owns and I thought you might like to come along to protect me from all those half naked young girls.'

'You mean I might like to come along and divert all attention from you.'

'I think it's best we each keep within our skill sets, yes.' I wanted to kiss her just for being a better player of the game than I could ever be. I almost did, but only the thought that I would be admitting total defeat stopped me.

'Then I think you can buy me a drink.' She turned her face back to the playful half smile so full of improper suggestion. Her game face. 'An expensive one.'

She took my arm in hers and walked out into the stream. The flow of people parting for Clara like the red sea for the Israelites. We went to the first bar on the strip where it was a certainty the drinks would be most expensive. I wanted us to fit the pattern I had observed for

109

the strip. We were just a couple out for the evening, we'd probably had a nice meal of small food on large plates and now cocktails at a classy bar. Then we'd progress down the strip maybe for a bit of dancing before a taxi home to screw like rabbits.

In another life maybe. I held the door for Clara like the gentleman I'd never be. While I held the door I used the pause to scan the interior for anything untoward like big Turks with guns. I followed her in knowing all eyes would be on her while I trailed in her wake.

The place was fairly empty I guessed it would be closing in an hour or so as those people intent on staying out headed further down the road. The bar ran the length of the right hand wall and we headed to the far side where I took the stool so I could sit with my back to the rear wall. To anyone looking on it would appear that I was being polite and not giving my shoulder to Clara. However it gave me view of the whole bar and anyone entering would see only Clara. I would just be the lucky guy with the beautiful girl, half hidden in the corner.

Clara had a hand mixed Martini extra dirty. I opted for an overpriced bottle of Italian beer. We waited in silence for the drinks to arrive both appraising the room and everyone there in our own ways. The drinks arrived and we both took a sip and turned toward each other. Neither saying anything. It wasn't an awkward moment. We don't do small talk. Clara can and she does it very well. It's her job. I just can't. I have nothing small to say that could interest anyone at all. We both laughed. Clara put her glass down.

'That's what I like about you.'

'What, my ineptitude in social situations?'

'No. When there's nothing to say you don't say anything.'

I couldn't say anything to that.

'How are you going to deal with your situation.' She asked.

'Run amok with a sub machine gun and kill everyone while wearing a sweaty vest.' I said as deadpan as I could.

Clara laughed again. 'That I'd love to see, but it's not your style. You're much more subtle.'

'To be honest I'm not entirely sure right now. I've worked for some pretty rough people over the years, but I always keep them at arms length and never get involved in their stupid squabbles. I'm not really comfortable being involved.'

'You're scared?'

'Damn right I'm scared. More scared of what I'll do when I'm cornered than anything else.'

Clara took a sip of the Martini and I could see her mind working. 'Look honey, don't worry too much. At heart these people are just businessmen and everything comes down to profit in the long run. Find a way to make it better business sense to leave you alone and they will.'

I considered what she had said and on an intellectual level it made perfect sense. At the visceral, people after you with guns level it was still a mess of hormones and unhelpful emotions. Deep down I hated bullies and particularly rich ones who feel money entitles them to whatever to whoever they want. I looked at my watch. I didn't have Clara for much longer and I needed to have a nose around Vista. 'We'd better hustle and try another bar.'

Clara delicately bit the olive from the end of the cocktail stick. 'Ready when you are honey.'

10 Thursday 17th January 2240 Hours.

Getting the boot.

Back on the street we skipped the couple of bars in between and casually ambled towards the Vista bar. The patio heaters emitted a dull red glow like inefficient beacons that I couldn't decide if they were warning me off or beckoning me in. A couple sat at one of the tables and a doorman now stood at the entrance to the rope barrier. The doorman barely glanced at me as we passed him. I didn't need to look, all his attention would be focused on Clara. I scanned the interior through the glass front. The Vista bar was more crowded than when I had left my bench. The bar itself was two deep with mostly young males and hugging the walls were small groups of girls and couples all trying hard to have what they assumed was a good time. Another twenty or so either danced or flitted about from group to group having shouted conversations.

I dislike crowds. With all the to-ing and fro-ing and dancing inside you'd never be able to tell who was behind you or next to you. That makes me uncomfortable. That and the noise of the music preventing any reliable communication, other than semaphore, made me choose a table outside. I selected a corner table up against the front windows. To the doorman's rear and with a good view of the entrance. Clara took a seat, smoothed down her skirt and lighted a cigarette. I headed inside to get drinks.

I pushed through the doors having got a good look at what might be waiting on the other side. Inside the music was deafening rendering my ears insensitive to anything but the booming bass. I threaded through the throng skirting around gaggles of girls with orange tans and groups of young men all dressed roughly the same in jeans and a checked short sleeve shirts. The toilet was my destination. Not so much for a call of nature but as an excuse to get a good look around.

I scanned the bar as I passed, peering between and over the shoulders of the incumbents doggedly resisting being jostled out of their place in the queue. I was looking for Nico Constantinou, but only saw two barmaids about the same age as most of the clientèle and both displaying an impressive array of belly button piercings.

The bar area occupied a large part of the far left hand corner of the club. A door at the far end obviously led through to the staff area. Next to that door but on the customer side of the bar was the door marked toilets. I went through and as the door closed behind felt nothing but relief as the volume of the music was attenuated. Like almost every other dive like this the glitz and shine is applied only to the front and I found myself in a dingy corridor. To my right doors marked gents and ladies. In front of me a large double door with a push bar and faintly illuminated fire escape sign. To my left was another door marked "Staff Only" which clearly lead to the same place the door behind the bar did. It was protected by a Simplex 1000 series lock.

The Simplex 1000 lock has vertical row of five unmarked push buttons above a rotary knob. Not very secure but that's offset by the convenience for the user. I looked around and saw no obvious CCTV in the corridor. I had counted six cameras in the bar area. Three above the tills and optics behind the bar and three covering the room.

I turned left and went into the gents. I doubted I'd have the five minutes I'd need to get through that lock without being disturbed either by staff or someone heading to the toilet. I used the facilities and headed back into the club. There was a momentary space at the end of the bar nearest the door so I slid quickly into the space. With my track record of getting ignored by bar staff I prepared myself of a long wait. Oddly enough I think the fact I wasn't jockeying for position and clamouring for attention caused one of the girls to notice me quickly and come over. I doubted this place would run to hand mixed Martinis and dreaded the thought of trying to communicate that one through the fog of noise. Using a mixture of shouting and hand signals I think I ordered to two gin and tonics.

The bar seemed to be staffed with the two bar girls, a pimply faced boy glass collecting, the ubiquitous D.J., the doorman and whoever was through the staff door which I assumed led to an upstairs.

It's an observable fact that as a group of people get drunker their volume gets louder in a kind of sonic arms race. I noted that in an environment as loud as this people's non verbal communication also got louder with the hand signals, mouthed words and gesticulations getting ever more expansive and frenetic. The bumping, poking and jostling I was getting just trying to hold my position at the bar was evidence enough of that and it irritated me a lot.

I watched the bar girl as she prepared our drinks, with an air of studied carelessness, in my periphery I caught Nico Constantinou emerging through the staff door. I avoided looking at him directly but the bright brown hair which I guessed was either a bad dye job or an even worse hairpiece, confirmed my identification of him.

Nico wore a white long sleeved shirt unbuttoned far to low for man probably in his early fifties. He got the attention of the second bar girl and put his face close up to her ear to give some kind of instruction. I feared for a moment that he might get his head caught in the oversized hooped ear rings she wore. He didn't and after giving his instructions he backed up a few steps to the doorway.

My drinks were dropped onto the soaked bar top in front of me. There was no way on earth I was going to be able to hear what I owed so I fished out the largest note I had and mutely passed it over. My bar girl walked over to the till activating it by waving a small fob over it like some miniature magic wand before punching in the order by hitting small icons representing whatever it was she assumed I'd asked for. I kept half an eye on the other girl. She slammed a measure of whisky into a highball glass and then splashed coke over the top. She then rummaged a bit and came up with a brandy glass which she dropped two full measures into. My change was dropped on the bar top next to the drinks and I struggled to pick the cash from the puddles of nameless sticky drinks while girl number two handed Constantinou his drinks which he vanished out back with.

Using my elbows as deflector shields and a certain amount of agility I weaved my way to the entrance without spilling a drop from either glass. I sank into the seat next to Clara, stole one of her cigarettes and lighted it, exhaling in a sigh of relief to be in the cold but relative calm of outside.

The other tables had filled up with small groups and couples so I leaned in close to Clara to talk, smelling her hair and getting a good angle on her smooth legs as I did. 'I think I'm out of my comfort zone.'

Her gaze followed mine down to her legs. 'Not entirely.' She replied sardonically.

I averted my gaze slightly, not that Clara minded for a second me looking, but I wanted Clara badly at that point. Maybe it was a reaction to the stress of having people actively out to do me harm or maybe it was the beer. Drinking and working don't mix, but to sit here and drink lemonade would have been slightly suspicious and I wanted to stay well under the Radar.

We sipped our drinks. Vodka and tonic. Not quite what I ordered but close enough. My mind wandered back to the staff door. Picking a Simplex lock is not at all complicated. There are five buttons and each can be used only once. In addition the code can be entered in any order. This leaves one thousand and eighty two possible combinations. Not a large key space in the great scheme of things but more that I'd have time to go through between customers coming past to use the toilets. Rather than brute forcing the combination I could pick the lock. Like all picking I could use the minor imperfections found in all mechanical manufacturing to subvert the device to my will. Turn the knob while feeling for the button with the most resistance. That would be button one of the combination. Then reset the lock hit that button and find the second. Repeat until open. I estimated the process should take me around five minutes. Again longer than I'd have undisturbed.

While not a secure lock the Simplex 1000 series was clearly the right choice for that location. Ease of use for the staff while being sufficiently time consuming to bypass when you took into account the frequency of passing traffic. Therefore I'd have to manipulate or negate the passing traffic. I considered seeing if Clara would provide some kind of diversion sufficient to keep everyone's attention for at least five minutes and to bring down Constantinou and whoever was up there with him. Then I could slip upstairs and work my dark magic.

I felt Clara looking at me. 'Hey, wake up.' She nudged my leg with the black pointed tip of her high heels. 'I've got to go soon.' She said fishing in her handbag for a slim mobile phone.

'Do you really have to?' The words out before I'd really considered what I was saying.

Clara gave me "The Look." 'This is work honey and I thought we didn't interfere in each other's careers?'

'It's just,' I started to say realising there was no point continuing. She was right. The basis of our relationship was that we kept our secret lives separate, our time together an island away from the deceit and subterfuge that made up our working world. Now I was mixing things up and starting to confuse the issue. What was I thinking anyway, using Clara for a diversion, compromising her and to achieve what? I had no clear plan on what I was doing here. I was winging it, hoping to find what? A stash of heroin worth the national debt of small country? A smoking gun to beat Ali Mehmet round the head with?

I had come in here without an objective. One thing I always stipulate to clients is that they give me a specific piece if information they are interested in. No random fishing trips. It's unprofessional, a waste of the clients money and of my time. Yet here I was randomly casting my line into a murky pool not sure what I'd drag up. I was feeling vulnerable and if I wasn't careful I'd make a mistake.

I turned to Clara putting my hand on her arm. 'Clara, people are trying to get to me.'

Her face softened for a second and I thought I detected some level of concern. 'I know, you said. Look, you've been at it all day. Go home get some sleep, you'll think of something tomorrow. You always do.'

Not really what I wanted to hear. It was very close to someone telling you to pull yourself together. 'I need to do something.' I said.

Clara's phone buzzed and she glanced down at it then across to the road. 'My taxi's here. A girls got to earn a living.' Her game face back on.

I snapped in my own quiet way and leaned back in my seat, resigned and in a low voice spoke. 'Go on then, go fuck your rich, fat old businessman.' I regretted saying it even before the words had finished dripping from my mouth, but I'd set the program running and run it would, till all the words had dropped out, leaden, flat and full of bile onto the ground between us.

Clara could have slapped me. I wouldn't have blamed her. Other women would have. Maybe they'd have shouted and ranted or stormed off. Clara just turned her face to me and looked at me. Not so much angry. More pity and maybe a dash of sadness. She held the look for what felt like a hundred years. Then she silently stood, gathered her bag and flowed out to the taxi.

As she went I stared at the curves of her departing rear with a profound sense of longing.

I downed my drink and picked up Clara's unfinished one. I considered what I had achieved tonight and felt incredibly stupid. I'm not a stand up and fight kind of man. I lurk and watch and most of all listen, but here I was flailing around in the dark like some punch drunk brawler. I raised Clara's glass preparing to gulp that down and head off with my tail between my legs, but from the corner of my eye a dark blue flash of movement arrested my attention.

A dark Blue Mercedes S 600 pulled up next to the silver Merc belonging to Constantinou. It double parked right outside of Vista not even bothering to put it's hazard lights on, the universal cloaking device for illegally parked vehicles the world over. A tall dark haired figure climbed out, locked the doors and walked round. There was no room for doubt, it was Ali Mehmet.

He walked with an air of absolute confidence as if he owned the place, which from my research at companies house, he did. The doorman advanced half a step holding out an obsequious hand which Ali shook barely glancing at him. The doorman did an almost comic fast shuffle to get to the main doors and hold them open allowing Mehmet to stride in without breaking step.

It looked like I was going to have to stay a little longer. Holding the half finished drink I slowly sauntered inside. No one knew who I was or what I looked like so I decided a closer look at the proceedings were in order. I threaded my way to the opposite side of the bar from the rear door and found a space at the corner. I leaned casually on the bar sipping the drink and with my eyes towards the young women on the dance floor I widened my gaze and watched Ali Mehmet from the side.

Just as in the photo Mehmet was immaculately turned out. A black suit this time with a light pin stripe. A pink shirt again open at the collar. He had reached the opposite corner of the bar when Constantinou emerged from the door to the club area. Either Ali had called in advance or more likely Nico had seen him arrive on the CCTV, which meant either he was expected or someone was watching the CCTV carefully. They shook hands and then Ali bent to Constantinou's ear and I saw Nico nodding in response. There was more of this and Nico stretched up to say something to Ali's ear. Then Mehmet slapped Constantinou on the back in a paternal kind of way and strode out, the crowd parting for him an unconscious act of deference.

What was it Machiavelli said, something about it being better to feared than loved? So I had met the infamous Mr Ali. It hadn't really added to my growing store of knowledge about him. I now knew how he moved and that might assist me in any following I might do. Apart from that all I had done was confirm my suspicions about the link between Ali, Constantinou and the Vista bar. I saw his car pull away from the edge of my vision.

My head had been turned toward the centre of the bar all the while Mehmet was there, never looking at him directly. I suddenly became aware I must have appeared to be drunkenly fixating on a group of girls dancing several meters into my eye line. I shifted focus to them to check if I'd freaked them out and thus drawn undue attention to myself. A petite blond smiled at me.

I turned back to the bar and went through the ordeal of ordering and paying for another drink. Receiving it I turned and lent back against the bar. A far safer way to stand in a crowded place like this. I mulled over what to do next. I was starting to get a little fuzzy headed from the drink and really should have just gone home, slept and attacked the problem with a clear head tomorrow. Trouble was, that was exactly what Clara had suggested. I decided to stay and see what opportunities might develop.

I became aware of someone next to me, far too close to my personal space for my liking. I used the reflection in the front windows to check the intrusion out. It was the little blond from the group on the dance floor. She was leaning over the bar her feet inches from the floor as she leaned across using the bar edge as a fulcrum, obviously trying to impart a complex drink order. She came back down to earth with a dainty bounce holding her prize, a vivid red coloured bottle of something. She bumped into me as she recovered her balance. I turned my head in annoyance. She took a swig and grinned up at me. I killed the *"go-away"* expression from my face before it had a chance to form.

Blondie stayed put swigging her drink with her right side pressed against my left as we both leaned back against the bar. Her straw coloured pony tailed head coming to just above my shoulder level. I observed her reflection in the windows more closely. She looked about nineteen, very slim to the point of almost being bony. She wore a very short and very tight sliver mini skirt and a short sleeved blouse unbuttoned but tied in a large knot just below the hint of cleavage. Not in Clara's league, but very pretty in a way that was the antithesis of Clara's dark beauty.

Another flash of annoyance passed through me. All the while I was thinking about Clara I wasn't concentrating on the job in hand. I wasn't concentrating period. I was aware on one level that the drink was now thinking for me but I managed to ignore it on every other level. Mentally I gave myself the night off and decided another drink was the way forward. I turned back to the bar accidentally brushing against Blondie who was bopping away to herself next to me. I made to apologise and bent to her ear. She shook her head and pointed with her free hand to her ear and shrugged. I could understand that. She smiled at me revealing an ever so slightly buck tooth row of white enamel which the alcohol in me found endearing along with her pale blue eyes, overly large false eyelashes and a slight upturned nose. I was staring so I grinned an apology, clearly starting to get the hang of mute conversation.

Obtaining a drink was getting easier the more I did it. I now just had to gesture with my empty vessel and a replacement would be dropped down in front of me a few moments later. I fished in my pocket feeling brave enough to try and pay the right amount with coinage when the bar maid waved me off I shrugged and pulled what I believed was a quizzical expression and the barmaid pointed to Blondie who smiled impishly while swigging on her bottle. She backed off to the dance floor and her group of friends looking back at me as she went.

I loitered at the bar idly watching Blondie and her friends dancing. I sipped at my drink admiring the tight sinuosity of Blondie as she gyrated, the tight mini skirt barely covering the cleft of her buttocks. She studiously ignored me while I let my mind wander over what I'd like to do with her.

The bar was thinning out now and I had no idea what the time was, the effort of looking at my watch too much to bother with. Blondie danced over to me trying to look serious before failing in that and giving into a fit of the giggles. She danced right up to my face before spinning on her toes to put her back to me pressing into me as she writhed to the music. Her pony tail flicked my in the face. I savoured it's sting. I was sure I was being led along by a girl half my age, but equally I didn't care. Right then I felt I deserved the attention of being teased even though it would lead nowhere.

Blondie stayed pressed against me one hand idly brushing my thigh while she swigged her bottle. From the recesses of my brain I began self-justifying everything I hoped to do crossing off objections like an out of date to do list. All logic stopped when Blondie gave my buttock a playful squeeze and looked up at me biting her lower lip with her cute buck toothed teeth. She put her bottle onto the bar top and mouthed "Follow me" and took my hand and pulled me through the bar. I just watched her backside shimmering in the silver mini skirt as it wiggled just in front of my like a hypnotists watch.

I had no idea where we were going or why, but I had plenty of hope on both those subjects. She pulled me through the door at the rear of the bar and as the door closed behind us she leaned in putting her lips up to my ear. 'Just give a minute or two and then come in.' she whispered breathlessly. She flashed a mischievous gap toothed grin and skipped off through the Ladies toilets door.

I wasn't sure what the etiquette was in a situation like this, I'd never had a spur of the moment assignation in a bar toilet before, but I pretty sure that was what was on offer. I paced the empty corridor trying to work out just how long I should give Blondie before furtively sliding into the ladies bathroom.

I was about to walk in when the fire escape doors opened in front of me. I froze like a guilty schoolboy mentally preparing an excuse as to why I was hanging around outside the toilets. Then it dawned upon me that two figures barely fitting side by side in the double doorway, were the two Turkish heavies from earlier in the day. I think I controlled my face enough to stop the shock of recognition leaking over it, after all they had no idea who I was.

'Women,' I started with an air of frustration and a shrug. 'they take forever.' Gesturing towards the toilet door. There was no reaction from the five hundred pounds of fat and muscle in front of me. It occurred to me they might not speak English. 'I'd better go and check she's OK.' I added turning to the door.

I saw stars. It's true you really do. Though it's more like a blinding flash of blackness. Sound stops and reappears as light. Vision went for a moment too and my mind stuck itself in an infinite loop screaming "He's just hit you." indignantly over and over again, yet offering nothing constructive. I think I was knocked back into the wall, but nothing was really very clear at that point. My vision returned as a narrow tunnel of a two dimensional, black and white version of what was happening. A large dark shape loomed in front of me and a blow to my stomach knocked the wind from me.

All my mind's effort was put to trying to suck in and hold a lungful of oxygen as my legs buckled and the two Turks generously supported me either side and walked me out the back. I think I was more dragged than walked as I saw the open boot of yet another old model Mercedes. I was tossed like a rag doll into the back as I heard the fire escape doors slammed shut and a click as my hands were handcuffed behind my back. The initial shock was wearing off as adrenaline flooded my system far too late now to be anything other than a hindrance.

One of the Turks leaned over me his face inches from mine and air of garlic and foreign aftershave pervaded my perceptions like an unwanted house guest. He began rummaging through my pockets eventually pulling out my smart phone. 'This is for taking my phone.' He spat at me while pocketing it. The other Turk took over and masking tape was roughly pulled over my mouth and then the world went dark as the boot slammed shut above me.

Deep shit.

Right over my head and I'd dived in. I felt the car pull away and panic enveloped me. They were taking me to the secondary crime scene. Everything I'd ever read said never let them take you to the secondary crime scene. That's where you died. A jumble of thoughts raced through my mind looking for somewhere to go like a panicked crowd: How had they found me? how did they recognise me? Why had I been so stupid?

I forced those thoughts aside for now. I wriggled around a bit. The boot was lined with plastic. Not a good sign. I think the best I could hope for was that they'd kill me quick when we got where we were going. More likely they were going to torture me first. I shut down that unhelpful train of thought and got my head working something close to normal. First things first, engineering principles, break down the problem into manageable steps.

Issue one was the handcuffs. I had no idea how long this journey was going to take. At least out of the cuffs I'd have a chance of fighting or more likely running. I'd also need rid of them if I were going to find a way out of this car. I turned onto my side and blood started to flow back into my hands. I could feel these weren't the same as the police handcuffs used on me recently. These had no rigid bar, but were fixed together by a short link of chain. This was a good sign. I brought my knees together and tried to relax. Slowly with the metal bracelets cutting into my wrists I inched my hands down and my legs up until at last I had the chain snagged against my shoes. I let out a long breath willed myself to relax more and managed to slip the chain past my feet. Thank God for the alcohol, I doubted I'd have managed the gymnastics completely sober.

I lay back panting and sweating while ruefully conceding this wasn't how I'd planned the evening to pan out. At least now my hands were in front of me. I needed some kind of light. My wristwatch lit up with a dull green glow if you pressed a button on the side. It wasn't much but I quickly identified the cuffs as a standard pair of chain linked ones. I cursed myself for not getting hold of a handcuff key following my last time wearing a pair, but it was far too late to worry about that now.

The watch was OK, but I needed some light source that kept my hands free. I removed the masking tape from my face and then began pulling up the plastic lining beneath me. Behind that was the fabric covered cardboard lining of the boot. I pulled a section of that away from behind the offside light cluster and a red glow brightened my potential coffin.

An idea struck me that the lights might prove more useful in attracting some attention to the car carrying me to my uncertain fate. I ripped away the covering of the nearside light cluster. I briefly considered attempting some form of signalling with the lights. I opted instead to pull the spade connectors from the back of the bulb. With a light out there was a chance, admittedly a very slim one, that a passing police car might pull the Mercedes for the faulty running light and afford me an opportunity to attract their attention.

I put my focus back on the cuffs. The adrenaline dump had at least sobered me up. A little too late to avoid trouble, but I fervently hoped in time to keep me alive. My last ruminations upon escaping from handcuffs had been academic and a lot more leisurely. The promise of imminent peril focuses the mind, or at least I hoped it was so. Any second now the car might pull to a halt and I would have to face whatever horror the Turks had planned for me.

I couldn't tell how long I'd been travelling. Time was disjointed. The physical attack on me probably only lasted a matter of seconds, but felt like hours. My time in the boot conversely felt like seconds but had probably been much much longer. A funeral cortège threading it's way inexorably to my bitter end. I cursed myself for my stupidly and I cursed myself for Clara and the things I'd said and never done. I stopped that train of thought quickly, as those are the thoughts of the victim, not the hunter. I hunt and I hunt people. I don't kill my prey, but that didn't mean fate owed me any favours.

The keys I still had weren't going to help with the cuffs. Neither would the change in my pocket. I looked about the boot. It was empty. I pulled up the the lining above the spare wheel. A jack, a wrench for the wheel nuts and of course a spare wheel. Nothing helpful there. I glanced at my watch. The leather strap had a buckle, the pin in that was a small rectangular piece of stamped metal. That might do. I used my teeth to pull the leather strap through the buckle and free it. I picked it up from where it had dropped. In rigid cuffs none of this would have been possible. I thanked Hiatt for their policy of only selling to law enforcement. I flicked the pin away from the buckle and inserted it into the keyway of the left cuff, I pushed it in about a third of the way down and then levered it against the edge of the steel keyway. I got a good ninety degree bend. I pushed it a little way further down and did the same again.

A little experimentation and some jiggling and my approximation of a handcuff key opened the ratchet with click sweeter than the sound of the pearly gates being unlocked for open day. I repeated the process on the right a little surer this time on how to position the makeshift key in the hole.

Free of the cuffs I started to feel a lot more like my old self and much less like the fool I'd been for the past few hours. Next step now was to get out of the boot and as far away from the two goons as I could and do it as quickly as I could.

I examined the boot locking mechanism. It wasn't that complicated. A latch stuck out into a small metal U shape. I tried pushing the latch in. Clearly the boot was locked as it didn't budge. I briefly considered the possibility of going through the back of the seats that formed one wall of my prison, but then I would have to face two large Turks who had nothing good to say about me whatsoever.

Some more gymnastics and pulling up of the lining of the boot and I freed the jack from its compartment with the spare wheel. I held it by the latch and began to wind it up. It quickly began to buckle the boot lid and I guessed it would eventually punch through. It'd give me some nice ventilation but wasn't what I had in mind. I lowered the jack and ripped up some of the cardboard and fabric lining and folded a thick pad which I put on top of the jack.

I raised the jack till I could feel the latch being pulled hard against the bottom of the U holding it in place. With the system under sufficient tension I used the pointed end of the now open handcuff ratchet to start to lever the latch back. I locked the other end of the handcuffs through the U. With a pop the latch slipped back enough to permit the boot to open. The boot lid jumped up and stopped as I was still holding the other end of the handcuffs.

The last thing I'd wanted was for the boot to fly open in full view of the rear view mirror and alert my terminal chauffeurs. I peeked through the gap at the road receding behind us. We were on a country lane, hedgerows at either side and no other traffic in sight. I couldn't be sure where we were but we were remote enough for it not to be good news for my health and welfare.

The only thing I could do now was wait for the car to stop or slow enough for me to exit gracefully. We slowed once for a turn but getting out then would have mangled me a bit and avoiding bodily harm was now the single aim of my evening out. The lanes we were traversing were becoming increasingly narrower. I guessed we were nearing some remote destination were a persons dying screams wouldn't be heard.

I felt the brakes come on and the force of deceleration pull me towards the front of the car. I got a leg over the side in readiness and jammed the free end of the cuffs under the lip of the boot to hopefully prevent it springing up when I got out. I saw the indicator next to me come on for a turn. A pointless act as there was no other traffic, but I supposed when carrying someone to their death you try not to make mistakes that may attract the attentions of the law.

The car came almost to a stop for a hard left turn. I judged it was probably now or never and relaxed and rolled out the back. For the second time tonight the wind was knocked from me as I hit the road like a sack of potatoes. Fighting for breath I stayed still as the car turned right and accelerated away, my eyes following the dim red glow of the one working tail light.

My left arm was numb and breathing hurt like hell. I figured I'd maybe broken a rib or two. I couldn't risk staying on the road and so dragged myself up and plunged through the hedgerow barely noticing the thorns as I pretty much swam through the foliage to fall to the frozen ground the other side. I lay still and listened for any signs of immediate pursuit and everything was silent. Once I'd got

my wind back I pushed myself to my feet using my one good arm
and then began running.

I had no idea where I was or where I was going, but I kept on going
in less of a run and more of stumbling meander, but I wanted to put
a couple of fields between where I got out of the car and myself.

11 Friday 18th January 0234 Hours.

Exchange is no robbery.

I had rolled myself in to a dry culvert at the edge of a field and rested. The feeling of the sweat starting to freeze around me spurred me into movement. At the very best the Turks would discover my escape when they reached their destination. At worst the handcuff would come loose and the boot would fly up much sooner. Either way, in their position I would have to start the search for me at that point and work outwards. With only two men in the dark that wouldn't be an easy task. Therefore I had a reasonable head start.

I dragged myself to my feet again and walked out over the frozen furrows. I span around a full circle looking carefully. I could make out a main road in the distance from the occasional passing car's headlights and began to walk in that direction. It was most definitely below freezing so come what may I had to keep moving. I feared if I lay down to rest then morning would find me in a similar position to that which Ali Mehmet intended for me.

My left arm was loosening up but breathing still hurt with a sharp stabbing pain at each inhalation. Several fences and ditches later and I crouched behind a gate. I recognised the road and estimated I was probably about three miles from town. I was going to have to keep off the road. At some point the Turks were going to work out my only choice would be to head to town and I'd be easy prey on the road. I began crossing the fields parallel to the road. Often having to deviate a field or two over to find gates through hedges and to cross streams. It was slow painful going but I passed the time trying to work out what had gone wrong.

Stupidity, alcohol and thinking from below the waist had got me into that corridor. That wasn't a bizarre coincidence so it was obviously a set up. Not a bad set up considering no one knew I would be at Vista in advance. The one thing I couldn't explain was how they knew who I was. I hadn't done anything in the time there to arouse any suspicions. True Archie could have given them my description, but I'm a very generic looking person. It's one of the reasons I've ended up in the business I'm in. Further to that I'd shaved my hair off to impersonate Jason since I'd last seen Archie.

Something wasn't quite adding up and the annoyance of not knowing was helping to keep me stumbling on field after field with the lights of the town getting slowly closer. Conan Doyle once had Holmes say "Eliminate the impossible, the whatever is left, however improbable, is the truth."

Fact. They didn't know what I looked like. Therefore the only explanation was that someone was there who did. That person could only be Archie Hayes, but why would he have been there? It was clear from my observation of the failed exchange at his offices that Mehmet had set the Turks on him. After that little plan failed it's reasonable to assume they kept hold of Archie to try something else. Why wouldn't that something else be them anticipating my next move?

Just like the Vista bar had stood out to me as an obvious starting point it would also have for Mehmet. Not a bad theory. Drag Archie-Bloody-Hayes up to the Vista to ID me. Was there anything else to support that? I thought back to the hazy time at Vista. There was Constantinou coming down and collecting two drinks one of which was a double brandy. Not enough evidence to convict, but I knew that was Archie's elected poison. Then there was the arrival of Mehmet when Constantinou had got downstairs to greet him so quickly it was a fair bet he'd been sat carefully monitoring the CCTV.

I pictured Archie, probably knocked about a bit, I hoped, sitting next to Nico his hairpiece leaning toward the CCTV monitors, while they patiently waited, hoping I would be stupid enough to turn up. Then bingo, I do. Nico comes downstairs to phone Mehmet and buys

Archie a brandy in celebration. Mehmet turns up, instructions are given and Nico pays off Blondie to get me where Mehmet can discretely make me disappear.

A theory only at this point but one I could confirm from Archie, assuming he hadn't already taken a one way trip to the destination they had planned for me. Still Archie's death would confirm my suspicions anyway. Now I had a stab of fear. Clara had also been compromised. If I had been ID'd at the bar then she had too. I needed to warn her. I quickened pace.

As I neared town I was starting to run out of fields to sneak through. I was going to need to be mobile without the fear of the Merc with one tail light suddenly pulling up beside me and being very unpleasant to me. I wasn't far from Duncan's garage. I was going to have to cross some main roads, but at some point that was going to be unavoidable. I hopped a fence and began jogging along the road as fast as I could manage. Each time I heard a car approach I threw myself down in the grass verge until I was sure it wasn't Turks in Mercs.

I had been going an hour and a half when I reached the garage. My van was still parked outside, but my keys were at home. Duncan kept the spare set in the garage which silently mocked me from across the gravel forecourt, locked, shuttered and alarmed. It was going to be far easier to the break into the van than the garage.

I cast about in the detritus of a run down industrial area and soon found a rusted length of iron that the metal collectors had missed. It was a meter long length of angle iron, pointed at one end and had held up a fence at some point. I walked round to the rear of my Escort van. They always had crappy rear locks that almost any key from another Ford would fit. Mine, in common with most other rusting hulks of it's vintage had a padlock and hasp riveted to the back doors which I easily levered off with barely any effort.

With more effort and sharp jabs of pain in my chest I crawled through the rear and into the drivers seat where I popped the lock and opened the door. I got my breath back leaning against the van on my bad side and giving the other lung a chance to do most of the work. When I had composed myself I threaded the iron bar through the spokes of the steering wheel so that it stood up at about two O'clock. I took a deep breath and commenced pushing down on the end of the bar, bouncing on it with all my weight and pressure I could muster as blinding stars of pain radiated out from my ribs.

I carried on bouncing, pushing, grunting and crying out in pain like some twisted parody of sex. I lost track of the time and how many times I had bounced until I felt the crack as the van's steering lock snapped. I slumped to the floor sweat stinging my eyes and drew in lungfuls of freezing night air. I used the van to pull myself unsteadily to my feet. My legs shook and my arms felt like lead but I used the pointed end of the iron bar to jab off the cowling around the ignition barrel. With fumbling fingers I pulled three wires from the back of the lock. I twisted two together and the dashboard lit up. I waited for the coil light to go out then touched the third wire to the exposed copper of the other two. The engine turned, stuttered and burst into life.

I'd never realised how good the sound of an old diesel engine thrumming away could sound. I heaved myself into the drivers seat, tidied away the wires, closed the door and put the heater on full. The temptation to take a short nap was overwhelming, I feared if I did that I'd wake tomorrow and dreaded to think what might have happened in the intervening time. I put the van into gear and headed back into town, the streets deserted apart from the yellow sodium glow of the street lights and the sparkling diamonds of frost forming on the ash-felt.

If I were Mehmet I'd have people waiting outside where I lived. If Ali was getting his information from Archie Hayes then my flat hadn't been compromised as Archie had no idea where it was. The only other obvious source of intelligence about me was the phone they'd removed from my pocket during the kidnapping. Even if Mehmet had the technical knowledge, which I doubted he did, they wouldn't have had time to analyse the phone. Besides it was a clean phone.

I parked a street away and approached my road through a side alley. I stood in the shadows at the end and checked the street. There were no cars I didn't recognise and nothing felt out of place. I walked the length of the road first, checking in every parked vehicle for occupants and even glancing over hedges and walls. Satisfied the road was clear I hurried down the steps to my door. Thankfully they'd left me with my door keys or I'd have had a big problem.

I let myself in as swiftly as the pain in my ribs would let me, standing back and kicking each door open with a crash just in case anyone lurked behind. A quick visual check confirmed the flat empty except of a startled Brill, quickly scurrying for cover beneath a desk. I went to one of my computers and checked the logs for the wireless sensors I'd fitted. There had been no activations since I'd left and the CCTV logs confirmed this. I sat back in an office chair and lighted a cigarette with an air of relief. At least this location was secure for the moment.

My personal phone was sitting in it's cradle. I snatched it up and rang Clara. It was just past four. She could well be at the Casino still or she could be doing whatever it was she might end up doing with her client. That was if Mehmet's boy's hadn't caught up with her. The phone rang and rang out. I called again. It rang for a short while then cut off. I tried again. Straight to voicemail. It could be she'd been located by Mehmet, or more likely she didn't want to talk to me. I'd never rang her at work before, I'd have hoped she realised that my breaking that rule meant there was something serious going on. Then again I'd transgressed enough boundaries with her tonight so she could be putting my calling down to drunken, emotional behaviour and cutting me off for that reason.

I regretted never discretely putting some kind of tracking software on her phone, although that's the kind of path down which madness lays if you're in a relationship with someone. Then I realised the grey phone the Turks had did indeed have its anti-theft tracking app installed and set up. If I couldn't track Clara then I could at least track the heavies. I logged onto the site from my desktop. I hit the button to show me the phone's location and a map opened up showing a red dot moving down the main road into town. I allowed myself a smug, "gotcha" moment and settled into watch.

The car reached town and then turned around and the dot moved away again. It looked like they were searching the main road for me. Not a bad idea, but a little too late. Clearly the cuff had held the boot closed until they'd reached their destination. I considered clicking on the button to take a picture, but I wasn't sure if the flash would go off so I held off on that, not wanting to give away my best advantage tonight. Instead I clicked the button to open the microphone. It took a few seconds to buffer the audio and then through the computer speakers burst forth the muffled sounds of a car journey and a lot animated talking in what I guessed was Turkish. I could make out the two voices of the goons, slightly muffled like the phone was in stashed in a glove compartment. A third voice joined the fray. Calmer and with more authority. I guessed Mehmet. Even had I spoken Turkish the sound of his voice was too distorted to understand, probably coming through a speaker phone.

I decided to see where they'd been and pulled up the tracking log of the phone. The map filled with a red scribbles. The track started when I'd turned the phone on near the park opposite the bars and stayed there for a while before it followed me into the Vista bar via the first bar. It lost track while I was inside, the GPS unable to see any of the satellites. The red line jumped in a dead straight line to the road out of town. The phone had obviously been unable to see the sky where the Turk had initially put it. Thankfully it had moved part way through my journey in the boot. The wandering red line followed our drive out of town and down country lanes. The sharp left was there where I had rolled from the back. The Turks then had taken increasingly minor roads and tracks, even taking a wrong turn or two as the red line showed truncated spurs off of the route.

The point that the line ended in a narrow loop and paused for half an hour, that was either where they'd discovered my escape or it was the final destination. If they'd had their way, my final destination. I pulled up Google Earth and looked at that point. An old barn and some deserted farm buildings a long way from the road or any other buildings. A very likely spot for my demise. The land registry website closes at night, but I resolved to check the ownership of that land at the first opportunity.

The half hour pause was the two Turks blundering about in the dark looking for me. After that the track showed them driving out checking every side road and move out in an ever widening circle before giving up on that and focusing on the main road into town. I had no idea how long they'd keep looking for me and I had things to do. I grabbed an old combat jacket, a Surefire torch and my small set of lock-picks. I loaded the tracking web page onto my personal smart phone and tried Clara one last time.

I left her a voice mail message asking her to call me back and saying it was a matter of life and death. Then I headed back out into the night, remembering the van keys this time. It was time to see if my theory was correct. I walked back to the van and headed straight to Archie's.

I'd always pictured Archie living in some grimy tenement flat, much like mine, although I pictured him on an upper floor somewhere. When I'd done my background check on Archie I'd discovered he lived in a detached bungalow on one of the soulless estates populated by retired folk with well kept gardens and living in streets unimaginatively named for trees or flowers. These are streets that see very little foot traffic after six PM and have curtains that twitch throughout the day. I'm sure Archie gave the residents association plenty to speculate upon.

The house was still in the name of Archie's dead mother from whom I guessed he'd inherited it and hence why he wasn't still living in some dingy flat. That is unless he'd never left home. If I were Mehmet and I hadn't already reunited Archie with his mother, I'd be keeping tabs on him. That is unless he were somehow a willing participant in my kidnapping. One way or another I'd soon know.

The suburban estates of the retired are always one of the hardest places to conduct any kind of static surveillance from. The twitching curtains, the residents associations, the neighbourhood watch and most of all the not-in-my-back-yard brigade always made it a challenge. Guaranteed that a strange car parked outside a house for any length of time will provoke a proprietorial response of moral indignation that implied some kind ownership of the public road outside a house. For that reason anyone keeping an eye on Archie would stick out like a sore thumb. If it were me I'd have to do it from inside the house.

I took a gamble and drove down Archie's road, Oak avenue, although it had no oak trees and certainly wasn't an avenue. Nothing out of the ordinary, in fact no cars on the road at all, just the inevitable far eastern imports, people seemed to possessed to buy when they retire, sitting on concrete driveways. I carried onto the street that backed onto Oak avenue, this one called Ash drive. Again no Ash trees, just the bareness of well kept front gardens displaying their barren winter face to anyone walking past.

I didn't bother locking the van as the back was open to anyone that cared to look. I counted the houses down till I found the one backing onto Archie's. I let myself through the side gate and went to the back fence. I threaded my way through a bush all twigs and no leaves and stood motionless peering over the fence.

This was clearly Archie's house. It had the same air of having been once well kept, but now faded and left to ruin like Archie. The garden didn't look too bad, but that was just winter keeping the tangle of growth at bay. I'm sure in summer it was an absolute jungle. There were no lights on in the place. I kept my attention on the windows looking for any movement or the careless glow of a cigarette. Nothing. I hopped the fence landing in a crouch and fighting to control the sudden jab of pain from my ribs. I stayed in the crouch till my breathing returned to normal and I could listen for any reaction to my ingress.

Still nothing so I crept across the frozen lawn trying to minimise the crunching of the frost. I peered through the kitchen window. Nothing of note there. I stoop walked over to the back door and put an ear to the cold glass. Again not a sound. Not even the creak of heating pipes or the hum of a refrigerator.

I put my hands under my armpits to warm them up and examined the back door. Take almost any house. At the front people will spend any amount of money on large heavy doors, expensive locks, bolts and chains. The back door on the other hand is nearly always overlooked. You look at your front door every time you return to the house. It's the public face of your domicile. The back door, to most, just leads into the garden. I hadn't looked at Archie's front door, but I was sure it had more than just the six pin Yale pin tumbler lock I found in front of me. I tested the door pushing it with my foot and hand to see if there were any bolts behind. Both the top and bottom edges gave enough movement so, no. Just the latch of the Yale lock.

I slid the short end of the torque wrench into the bottom of the keyway and applied light pressure with the tip of finger, rotating the lock barrel until the biting point against the first pin. With my right hand I slid in a diamond pick and pushed up against each pin feeling for the subtle differences in resistance as the pin stack rode up the hole to the spring but one bit against the lip of the outer barrel. I pushed this pin up and the barrel rotated a minute fraction. I methodically worked through the six pins with as much deftness and subtlety as the cold allowed until with the final almost inaudible click the barrel rotated free and I pushed the torque wrench round till the door unlatched.

I opened the door a crack and listened and smelled. No sounds and only the musty damp smell I'd imagined would pervade Archie's run down bungalow. No trace of thick black Turkish cigarette smoke or the goons expensive tastes in aftershave. I pushed the door wider and crept in. The kitchen to my right I knew was empty, bathroom and toilet to my left also empty. The next door to my right was closed. I bypassed that for a second and went to the front room which was empty and still, lit only by the street lights outside. I ignored the couple of doors that were clearly cupboards. It was way beyond probable anyone would willingly spend a night crammed in a cupboard in case I happened along.

The remaining door must be Archie's bedroom. This would be a moment of truth. Either the room would be empty and Archie most probably dead or he'd be alone, a peacefully slumbering Judas. I turned the handle and pushed the door open. It creaked, but I pressed on opening it wide and stepping into a cluttered bedroom. Books and clothes strewn all over. An old wind up alarm clock ticking and tocking by the bed and below a mass of sheets and blankets the rotund form of Archie Hayes snoring quietly to himself.

I stole up to the head of the bed and crouched down. I took out the torch and despite the pain put my left hand to Archie's throat while activating the brilliant glare of one of the worlds brightest torches into Archie's face. 'Archie wake up!' I barked.

The snoring paused, he snorted and the eyes snapped open only to shut just as quickly as the glare hit them. He made to sit up but my hand on his throat checked that motion before it had begun. "?What." he croaked.

'Archie.' I barked again.

'No, please. I did what you asked.' He sobbed.

I put my face up to his ear and hissed. 'Archie, It's me, David, back from the dead.'

'No, please, I gave you what you wanted.' More choking sobs. He still wasn't getting it.

I let go of his throat and snapped off the torch and walked over and turned on the light. I stood by the door and waited while Archie got his breath back and his eyes adjusted to the new level of light.   He blinked at me myopically and struggled to sit up. Now I was a few feet back and with the room light was on I could see Archie was a state. His hair stuck out like a beaten scarecrow. The rest of him looked that way too. His left eye was a deep black and half closed and his lips were swollen and crusted with the black of old dried blood.

'Time to start talking Archie, one thing I know you're good at.'

He peered at me trying to focus and then with bloodied and bent finger felt around blindly on the night stand before locating his glasses and pulling them onto a bent and bruised nose with a noticeable wince of pain. I didn't have a lot of sympathy left for him. Glasses on he managed a one eyed focus on me and immediately sat back in shock. I was tempted to think the look of horror on his face was down to my nocturnal visit but I caught sight of myself in the mirror hanging above Archie's bed.

I wasn't far off Archie in the looks stakes tonight. One side of my face was swollen and going blue. The bruising spreading towards the makings of a good black eye. My face and torso a mass of rips and cuts from the bushes I had stumbled through and my stance lop sided from the busted ribs giving me an air of Quasimodo after a particularly brutal night out on the town. 'Look at me Archie, I'm alive, no thanks to you.'

He studied me a second. 'David, I just thought, I thought it was them back to finish me off.'

'You may start wishing that was the case. Why they haven't finished you off we'll come to in a second, but I want everything you know from the start.'

'Of course dear, er David.' He croaked, 'you couldn't just get me something for the throat, there's a bottle in the living room.'

I went and filled a glass with a good measure of brandy and passed it to his trembling hand. 'Right, from the start and make it brief I have other calls to make tonight.'

Archie took a sip and began. 'From the very, start. All right then. What you probably don't know is that a few years ago Mr Morgan had a little financial difficulty. Malpractice suit went horribly wrong for us.'

I looked at Archie pointedly.

'No, no not me, fortunately.' He continued. 'It very much ruined the firm and we were all out on our ears. You see that's when Ali Mehmet bought out Mr Morgan.'

'and you never thought to mention this before?'

'Oh, no that's the point David. No one really knows. The deal was done very discretely. In name Mr Morgan still owns Morgan, Styles and Brown but in reality it's Mehmet owns the firm. Morgan's in hock to Ali very completely. It was an arrangement suited Mehmet. The firm's not made a profit in years and still doesn't, but Mehmet doesn't seem to care. Our commercial side handles property and business deals for him and the criminal side occasionally helps out his associates that run into trouble.' Archie took another sip of his brandy. 'What you may have guessed is that I do most of the work in the firm.'

I nodded.

'In truth almost everyone else in the practice has retired and exist only as names to rubber stamp things. I,' He paused again to fortify himself with more drink. 'I, handle almost of all of Mr Ali Mehmet's business.'

'Drug business.' I added.

'I truly don't know anything about that. I don't see where the money comes from. But David, please consider what it's like for me to wake up one day and suddenly realise I've become the personal lawyer for the Mafia.'

'You never were that straight Archie.'

'True David, I may have cut a few corners here and there, but I was just playing the legal game, and it is a game. David it truly is.' He looked sadly into his glass. 'Then you realise you've become as corrupt as everyone else and you're in too deep to ever get out.'

'So is that why Mehmet hasn't disappeared you yet.'

'Partly. I realise that eventually with everything I know I'm going to become too much of a liability for Mehmet, but at the moment he has no one else. Where else do you think he's going to find a tame law firm to acquire.'

'Ok, so what about the job. What was that all about?'

'As far as I know it was legitimate. For some reason he needed to get rid of a property quickly and the insurance was the fastest way. I know he's done it before, but this time his people got caught.'

'And talked.' Archie nodded. 'two things then, one, how the hell did the case get dropped and two what did the pair say that Mehmet wants me removed for.'

'David the first I have no idea. The police just seemed to lose all the evidence and there was pressure to just drop the whole matter. The second point, you should know, you recorded the interview.'

'Archie, I never pay attention to what's being said, it's safer the less I know.'

'It's not worked out too well this time has it.' He added dryly.

'Again, no thanks to you Archie.' I snapped back.

Archie looked on the verge of sobbing again. 'David, I want you to know I didn't give you up without a fight.'

I looked at his face and bloodied hands and for once believed everything he was saying. 'One last thing for now. The club, how did that go down?'

'Back at my office, I think their plan was to give you a beating and find out how much you had heard.'

'And then kill me.'

'Maybe, but I thought not at that point. When you sent that young man in and led his men on a wild goose chase Mehmet was furious. He sent the two back to grab me. They did this to me.' He gestured to his swollen face. 'asking about you. They just wouldn't believe I had no address for you. That's when they,' His voice faltered and he looked down at the twisted fingers of his left hand. 'Left hand you see,' he sighed, 'need the right for signing papers.'

'So after they worked you over.'

'When they discovered the phone was missing they assumed you'd find out about Vista so they took a gamble on you turning up there. They made me sit upstairs and watch the CCTV monitors.'

'and I came in and acted the fool.'

'Yes you rather did.'

'Did you know they were going to kill me?'

'I hoped it wasn't the case. You can never really tell with these types, but you always hope it's just a beating.'

I still wasn't happy with Archie but the fact he'd confirmed my theory softened my attitude towards him. Besides it was clear what he knew was one of the best assets I had right then. I stole a glance at my phone and checked on the progress of the two Turks. The car was back in town and pretty much threading it's way through every street. Sooner or later they would think to check on old Archie Hayes lawyer to the mob.

'Get dressed Archie, we've got things to do before dawn.'

'David, I can't I'm not well.' He protested. I ripped back the covers revealing a threadbare set of paisley pyjamas. Very retro.

'Get dressed Archie, and do it quickly. You've clearly just become a big liability to Mehmet and you're best hope is to do what I say.' I dragged the bed sheets to the floor and headed to the kitchen looking for coffee and painkillers.

12 Friday 18th January 0441 Hours.

Evening the odds.

Archie's idea of coffee was some kind of own brand instant muck, so old it had solidified into a lump at the bottom of the jar. I boiled a kettle and poured the hot water straight into the jar and sipped at that while taking a hefty dose of some equally out of date Ibuprofen.

Archie was taking his time getting dressed, hindered by his damaged hand. I went and got the van and brought it round the front and hustled Archie into it while he was still making a valiant but ultimately futile attempt at doing up his tie one handed.

I headed straight for the Casino while getting Archie to try calling Clara on his phone, just in case it was me she was avoiding. The phone was still switched off and a knot of fear was growing in my stomach.

The Casino squatted at the centre of a leisure complex. A large expanse of concrete atop what had once been factories providing real jobs. Now chain restaurants littered the ground all providing identical prefabricated meals to customers across the land. All of these were now closed along with the cinema, bingo hall and bowling alley. The casino stayed open until at least six when the last of the die hard gamblers, usually Chinese, emerged blinking into the dawn.

The car park could have swallowed a half dozen football pitches. A few cars remained in the periphery, but the main knot clustered near the brightly lit entrance to the casino along with a train of taxis picking up the luckier customers while the unluckier ones were left with a cold walk home. I never cared for casinos. I have more than a basic grasp of maths and probability and that was more than anyone needed to know that the only winner is the house.

I checked my phone before we drove in and the car, or at least my phone was still moving about in town. I pulled into a space in the centre of the main group of cars and killed the lights. I had a good view of the entrance. We had driven a circuit of the car park first looking for any cars with people in them. Apart from one with two twenty somethings passing a joint between them and another with a flash of white buttocks bumping up and down they were all clear. I watched the entrance. Two doormen wearing earpieces. Nothing got my attention. I turned to Archie. 'Does Mehmet have any connection with this place?'

'Not as far as I know, it's a national chain.'

'What about the bouncers?'

'Maybe, he does own a couple of security firms.'

That made sense. Bouncers and organised crime have gone hand in black glove for many years. I couldn't risk going in. Even if I could be sure no one was outside waiting for me, I couldn't trust the door staff and I had no clue as to who might be in there. All assuming that Clara was still here.

'Archie, how well are you known to Mehmet's organisation?'

'um, apart from Mehmet, the accountant and the two bodyguards no one else as far as I know.' He massaged his left hand. 'and those two, they're ex Turkish wrestlers. Very nasty.' He added with a shudder.

So there was a slim chance Archie could get recognised, but much less than me and as he said, they didn't want him dead quite yet. 'Archie, you're going to have to go in and find Clara.'

'Dear boy, me?' He protested.

145

'They're less likely to recognise you and besides it'll be almost empty at this time. It wont take you long.'

'And if I find her?'

'I don't care how you do it. Get her out here now, one look at your face and she should realise how serious the situation is.' As I said it another point occurred to me. The state Archie was they might not let him in. He'd cleaned himself up a bit. I still looked like a walking corpse.

We sat in silence a few minutes while I watched carefully. The queue of taxis had dwindled. Now just one idled thirty yards from the entrance waiting for a chance fare before quitting for the night. I could see the driver alone and reading a magazine, no threat there. Time was getting on and I needed to know if Clara was safe or not.

'OK Archie you're up.'

He looked over at me, mouth open and ready to protest. My look must have shut him up and he got quietly out of the car and began to cross the car park. I could see he was deliberately going as slow as he could, trying to delay the inevitable. I scanned the entrance for any signs of trouble.

Then I saw Clara and my heart jumped in relief. The hourglass silhouette of her black pencil skirt and tight roll neck top as unmistakable as the sheen on her dark hair. Beside her walked a smartly dressed man in his late sixties. Not the fat ball of sweat I'd imagined but looking quite distinguished. The pair were laughing and smiling as they walked out to the taxi rank.

Archie seemed to recognise her and changed course to intercept. He'd need to be quick as the waiting taxi driver had put down his magazine and was about to pull forward and pick them up. Then someone caught my attention. Presence of the extraordinary or absence of ordinary in this case. A young male in a leather jacket has exited the casino behind them. What I didn't like was that his gaze was a little too fixed on Clara's client and not on her rear as any man's should have been.

I left the van and started at a brisk pace across the car park as the taxi pulled up next to the pair and the driver got out. Maybe he was going to open the door for them, but then none of the other taxi's had bothered. Then the one in the leather jacket launched forward in a kind of drop step, using the momentum to backhand punch Clara's companion in the kidneys. His back arched and he crumpled as the male followed with a knee to the head on the way down.

My mind worked quickly assessing what was going on accurately, but impotently. I had a hundred yards to cross and I could see it was all going to be over in seconds. They had taken out what they judged the biggest threat, the male and now the taxi driver, if he really was, was reaching out to grab Clara's left arm.

I saw the unfolding scene in horrific slow motion. Taxi man's right hand had barely touched Clara's left wrist when she suddenly pivoted a hundred and eighty degrees on her toes keeping her left arm at waist level, bringing herself shoulder to shoulder with taxi man. In the same fluid motion her left hand cut across her belly and her right hand circled his wrist.

It was almost like ballet. Taxi man's right arm was out at a right angle and he was bent forward still moving in his original trajectory when he'd tried to grab Clara. But now his balance was gone, he head well past his knees as he involuntarily careened into the guy in the leather jacket who still hadn't caught up with what was happening. The pair tumbled to the ground and Clara stepped over to them. Taxi man went to scramble to his feet and promptly got a stiletto in the balls. Leather jacket man was on his back and Clara crouched elegantly next to his head which she held in place with one hand while the other jabbed him expertly in the throat.

I could hear the screams now as the two would be attackers writhed and wailed on the floor. Clara pulled her companion to his feet scanning the surroundings for further threats and seeing Archie started in his direction. I got back in the van and drove it over to them just as Clara and the male reached where Archie stood agape at the scene.

'Don't talk, just get the fuck in the van.' I shouted.

The trio bundled in just as the first wailing of police sirens split the night joining the howling men like an unholy choir.

I pulled away, hopefully not too fast to attract attention. In the wing mirrors I saw the doormen running over to the two men on the floor, one still screaming the other now ominously quiet.

I just drove, not sure where to head at this point. Archie had played the gentleman and allowed Clara the front seat while he and her companion squatted in the back. I couldn't think of anything to say as the four of us rode on in silence, but I needed to break the ice. I said to Clara. 'Nice moves, I see all those martial arts classes paid off.' I could feel her looking as me while I concentrated on driving.

'It looks like you and Archie could have used a few lessons, what the hell have you been up to?' She spoke flatly, no emotion whatsoever. I'd have expected at least a little adrenaline backlash from what she had just done. Maybe she really had no emotion in her.

'Remember I said people were out to kill me.' I paused. 'It turns out I was right.' I finished smugly.

'Remember I told you to go home and leave it till the morning.' She paused for effect. 'Looks like I was right.' She added even more smugly. A heavy silence descended upon the van.

I pulled off the main road and found an empty industrial estate to park up in and work out my next move.

Archie pierced the silence introducing himself to Clara's companion. 'Archibald Hayes, lawyer for Morgan, Styles and Brown.' He announced rather formally. I didn't turn to look but I was sure he would be proffering a hand concealing some kind of secret shake.

The companion responded. 'Sir John Hamilton, Colonel, retired and honorary non executive, non voting director of various boring holdings, call me John.'

Clara turned around to John. 'And this is David.'

I felt an arm reach over the seats. I twisted and gave a weak shake wincing in pain as the move disturbed the ribs.

'Pleased to meet you David and you are Clara's?'

The question hung. I don't think either of us knew how to answer that one in a simple sentence and I wasn't sure where we stood at that point either. The silence was verging on painful. I tried for levity. 'After what I just saw I'm anything she tells me to be.'

'Yes, that was rather efficient. If that sneaky bastard hadn't come at me from behind I'd have had a go.'

'Are you hurt?' I asked.

'Hell of a bump to the head and I think the kidneys will have me pissing blood tomorrow, but on the whole I'm fine. After the Micks tried to blow me up in seventy seven everything else pales in comparison.'

'Sorry for ruining your evening.' I glanced at Clara as I said it hoping she would take it as an apology to her as well.

'Don't worry about it. I go to the casino for a bit of excitement. I shouldn't complain when I get a little more than I'd planned.' I saw Archie pass John his hip flask. I could see the two of them were going to get along. He took a nip and passed it back. 'Looks like you've made some dangerous enemies. What exactly is it you do?'

I paused again. It's difficult to explain to someone not in my world what exactly I do. 'I record people's private conversations for money.' Which was about succinctly as I could put it.

'Ah, interesting stuff, worked with some of those chaps across the water when I was with The Det. I can see how you might upset a few people. In those days it was a kneecapping if you were lucky.'

'I think they may have had something like that in mind tonight.' Added Archie helpfully.

'Ok, to business. John, I'm going to take you home. Then I'm taking Archie and Clara to a motel far away from here while I figure out how to end this mess.' Clara looked daggers at me for daring to suggest what she was going to do.

John interrupted. 'If I might make a suggestion. My country pad is only a half hour from here. Why don't you come and camp out there?'

Clara cut in. 'Oh, John we couldn't put you to the trouble.'

'Dear Clara, it would be no trouble, since my wife died I haven't used the place, it'd be fun to have some company there. I've also got a magnificent set of shot guns waiting for any of those buggers if they dare turn up. Not that you seem to need them Clara.' He looked at Archie and then me. 'But these two need all the protection they can get.'

Clara actually smiled at that. 'Well if you're sure.'

'Course I am Clara. And next time I go gambling I'm hiring you as a body guard rather than an escort, I think we'd have a scream at Epsom fighting with the Pikeys.'

While they chatted gambling, violence and mayhem I was considering my next move. Archie was certainly the best lead I had, at least until I'd analysed the recordings. What he knew about Mehmet's business dealings, even if what he said was only half true, could be the key to getting him to back down. 'Before we do anything else I need to make a stop. It may be a risky, but I think it's worth it. Archie, do you have your office keys?'

Archie fumbled around in suit pockets for a hesitant moment. 'Yes.' He eventually conceded.

'In that case we're going to stop by the office and lift all of your files on Mehmet and every business transaction, every property. In fact every damn scrap of paper relating to Ali Mehmet. I think if I can plausibly threaten to expose his whole corrupt empire he'll back down.'

Archie looked doubtful. 'Do you really think,'

I cut him off. 'You said yourself that you're too valuable to kill because he wont find another crooked law firm quickly enough. I'll be hitting him where it clearly hurts most, the wallet. As Clara said this evening Mehmet may be a mobster, but at heart organised crime is a business. Attack the balance sheet and they'll back down.'

Clara arched an eyebrow at me. 'So sometimes you do listen to me.'

I checked the tracker on my phone. The Turks had been past Archie's office and had moved on to the Vista bar. Not bad thinking, they were trying every place connected to me that they knew about. I wondered if news of the fate of the pair at the casino had reached Mehmet yet. I suspected it to be so and I hoped he was starting to get a little worried. I imagine that Constantinou was currently hurriedly erasing all CCTV at the Vista, removing all trace of my being there. I was happy with that thought.

I decided a slow pass of the front of Archie's office was in order. I had no idea how many people Mehmet could put into the field.

Clara had removed two from play. At a minimum the two Turks remained and if Mehmet did indeed own a couple of security firms he potentially had access to a lot of staff he could set watching buildings.

The plan was the slow pass then I'd park up and the four of us would head round the back the same way I'd got in to observe the meeting. With the four us, admittedly two of us invalids, we'd be able to get the boxes of files out quickly and make good our escape.

As we neared the street I got a bad feeling. I could see blue light flashing ahead, reflected from the silent walls of the buildings. As we turned in we were greeted by the full kaleidoscopic glare of red and blue flashing lights. Two fire engines blocked the road black hoses snaking along the pavement and water pooling in already freezing puddles.

Before I could stop him Archie clambered out the back. I got out to follow him and get him back. A small crowd watched the fire fighters, now sweeping up and coiling their hoses. Archie hurried up to one. 'What's happened, What's happened' The Fireman gestured to another wearing a white helmet and talking into a radio. Archie stumbled up to him. 'What's happened?'

The Fireman considered Archie. 'Is this your building?' Archie nodded quickly.

'A fire obviously, localised so luckily no structural damage but the interior is a mess.'

'Can I, may I look?' Archie pleaded.

'The buildings safe, as I said no structural damage, but it may still be a bit warm in there.' I expected him to say no, but he took pity on Archie who was in obvious distress. 'I'll get one of my boys to take you in.'

One of the other firemen walked us in. The charred smoke smell was overpowering and thin clouds of it hung in the air. The ancient front door had survived as had the stairs, but the offices were a blackened mess. As for the files, what the fire hadn't got then the water used to extinguish it had. Archie picked forlornly among the debris. Barely a printed word survived. There was nothing to be gained here. I guided Archie by the arm back to the van and we headed for John's country pad, the smell of burning as heavy and clinging as the mood in the van.

13 Friday 18th January 0611 Hours.

Graveyard shift.

They say it is darkest before dawn. There was about two hours to go before sunrise and an indistinct line of light was starting to spread in the East. It is certainly coldest before dawn. As I crouched in yet another ditch sucking on a freezing pebble to try and prevent my breath sending out clouds of vapour.

I'd dropped Archie and Clara at John's country pad. A modest six bedroomed affair dating back to the English civil war and set in more acreage than I had the time or inclination to count. Some of Archie's gloom began to dispel when Sir John produced a vintage bottle of French cognac. I availed myself of the first decent cup of coffee in what felt like several lifetimes. A medium roast made in a cafetiere. I also located another dose of pain killers.

I had wanted to get back to my proposed killing ground before it got light so I could take a look around. I was quite literally and figuratively stumbling in the dark again. Mehmet had disposed of any effective audit trail to his activities. Whether he had actually burned them in the fire at Archie's office or had removed them first made little difference at this point. While I had to take in the fact that my best source for leverage on Mehmet was gone, Archie had to accept the fact that now that he had finally become a loose end that Mehmet would want to tie up.

I wasn't sure about Sir John either. I'm naturally suspicious about people I've just met and as rule like to do some kind of background check. Circumstances had prevented that so far. It wasn't his relationship with Clara that bothered me either. It wasn't an ego boost he wanted from his paid time with Clara, it was companionship. If I had any feeling left at that time in the morning I might have found it quite touching. No it was Sir John's comment about The Dets., or 14 Intelligence company as they were otherwise known.

14 Int. were not a well publicised unit. They carried out work not unlike mine, mostly in Northern Ireland during what's almost comically called 'The Troubles'. By dropping The Dets into our initial meet and greet he'd said a great deal without saying a lot. It gave us a common frame of reference that saved a lot of my time explaining. It also accounted for his use of escorts, particularly Clara. If, as I suspected, he came from some kind of secret background there would be the same attraction between him and Clara as I had with her. He may be long retired but he'd still have contacts and I wasn't sure how that could effect me or if I could even trust him.

Sir John had lent me some gloves and a olive green woollen cap along with an Ordnance Survey map and green quilted body warmer. I was almost dressed for the hunt. He'd offered me a Beretta over and under shotgun, which I'd declined. I dislike guns anyway and while I may have been able to pose as an early morning farmer out shooting the vermin I didn't want to take the risk of explaining an unlicensed firearm.

I'd left Clara with a request to try and get as much sense out of Archie as he could remember about Mehmet's dealings. She'd followed me out to the long gravel drive of the house as I left. There was still something hanging heavy in the air between us. As I went to get in the van, I said to her, 'I'm sorry.'

She frowned. 'About what exactly?'

'Several things, but mostly about what I said to you. I pretty much called you a whore.'

'Do you honestly think there's anything you could call me, anything you could possibly say to me that hasn't been said to me before with a hundred times more conviction than you could ever use.' She was almost angry now, her hands on her hips.

I sighed. 'Probably not.' and turned to get in the van.

Clara started to turn to go and then hesitated, half turning back like she was fighting with a decision. 'It's just that's the first time you've ever said anything that hinted you gave a damn.' There might have been a tear in her eye, it might just have been the cold morning air. I had nothing I could say to that right now, maybe later when I had digested it. For now I just got in the van and drove off.

Using the OS map to work my way in I'd parked up off the road about a mile away. Yet more field hopping had got me to the spot the tracking showed my captors had stopped. My phone was currently shown as unknown location. It had lost GPS signal. It had probably been taken inside. The last trace was outside the Vista bar. They were probably trying to take a look at it. I had used the anti-theft app to wipe the phone, kill it and zap the sim card. The battery was shortly going to run flat anyway, but now all they had was an expensive sliver of plastic and metal, of minimal use even as a paperweight.

Not knowing where the Turks were I had to be extra cautious. I'd approached from the opposite side the car had driven in from going through a field marked with a rusted red sign say "M.O.D. Training area keep out." I kicked up a few ancient spent cases of blank ammunition. I hoped there were no troops out training tonight. I crossed the wood and found my ditch where I crouched sucking on the cold pebble observing and listening.

The mid winter pre-dawn is quiet. There wasn't any bird song and no leaves in the trees to rustle. The other side of the fence was the back of the old barn I'd seen from the aerial photos. I crept along the fence line until I found a section beaten down enough to just step over. I lay flat the other side again listening for any signs of life. Everything was still. I'd been going for almost half an hour and my eyes had now adjusted to the dark. I could see a freezing mist was coming down. I dropped the pebble as redundant and slowly got myself to my feet the ribs now only a dull ache thanks to the pills.

I worked around the area clockwise, first threading my way round the back of the barn and then down the side of it. It was a very large corrugated iron on a wood frame structure. It was rusted now and falling down in places. Inside I could just make out the decaying hulks of old farm equipment. Giant steel blades and hooks stuck up from the earthen floor like the fossilised bones of giant creatures.

Outside the barn I could make out the tyre tracks in the frost where the car that was supposed to have carried me had driven in a tight circle and then reversed to the mouth of the barn. Clearly the plan was to have unloaded me into the barn with the minimum fuss. I walked further in and beyond the entrance it was pitch black. I was confident I was alone out here so I used the torch.

The beam swept the cavernous interior of the barn illuminating the motes of dust hanging in the chill air. Even with one of the brightest torches available the beam barely reached the cobwebbed corners of the building, but it didn't need to. Not far from the centre lurked the rusted remains of a tractor, one wheel missing and propped up on blocks. It leaned drunkenly toward me it's missing wheel on the ground in front of me almost as if it had just rolled there. Around the over sized tyre the ground was darker as though the oil leaks from a lifetime of tractor repairs had permanently stained the floor. I almost knew what I was going to see before I drew the beam in for a closer look.

The thick rubber ridges of the tyre were also stained dark, but this wasn't oil. Chains looped round the tyre at four points with handcuffs affixed to the ends of each loop. Various farm tools lay nearby including a blood stained axe. Oddly my first thought was that these guys weren't very forensically aware. My second thought was that this was where I was supposed to have met my end. I backed out of the barn relishing the clear night air.

I told myself not to dwell on what hadn't come to pass. I began steeling my nerve to go back in and snap a few pictures with my phone when I heard the sound of an approaching car. I paused for few seconds listening trying to estimate how far away the car was, but with the twisting nature of the lanes approaching that was just wasted time. Then I saw the lights through the hedges. The car was taking it's time as the Turks must have been up as long as I had and equally must have been sick and tired of driving up here. I doubted I'd make it to a gap in the fence but there was an old tarpaulin partially covering a wall of old car tyres. I lifted the tarp and rolled under it.

I dropped a couple of feet landing on my bad side with a bone crunching thump that made me cry out. I fought back the pain and lay still hoping I hadn't been heard over the noise of the car. The car crunched on the cold ground as it drove the same circle marked in the dirt. I could hear the sound of loud Turkish music coming from the car. The music seemed so incongruous in this place it managed to send a flash of annoyance through me that at least made me forget about the pain.

The car backed up to the barn and the engine switched off, silencing the music as it went. Then a muffled banging started. They had someone in the boot. I heard some Turkish and short laugh and someone banged on the car. I wanted to see who got removed from the boot. I pulled myself up to my hands and knees. Whatever I had landed on felt soft and waxy. My hand came up damp. I smelled it. Sweet sticky with an overtone of iron. Blood. I felt around a little more and my hand met cold meat. Just like taking a joint from the fridge, soft flesh heavy with pooling liquid and a sharp edge of bone. The heavy smell of death hit me, the sweet decaying mixture of blood and shit. I wanted to get out, but that wasn't a great idea. I raised myself up lifting the edge of the tarpaulin slightly gratefully breathing in outside air through my nose.

One of the Turks had hung a camping light from the side of the tractor. The light it threw out was barely enough to illuminate a small circle encompassing the fallen tractor wheel. He walked back to the boot of the car casting long shadows in my direction. I vaguely heard more Turkish exchanged and another guttural laugh. The boot popped open and I could hear the banging and struggling of whoever was in there. One of the Turks leaned in and from the movement of his shoulder he threw a jab into the boot. The kicking stopped and the other larger Turk reached in and hauled out the figure of a man one handed and hoisted him onto his shoulder.

The figure was dumped hard onto the tractor tyre and the large Turk methodically undid the handcuffs before attaching each limb to the chains around the tyre. The smaller Turk who had been watching patiently strode over and surveyed the victim for a moment. He scratched his chin and then bent and pulled the tape from the male's mouth. He then began slapping the face with a gentleness that was out of place. The body stirred realising it wasn't all just a bad dream and began struggling violently again. I could hear him clearly from under the tarpaulin.

'*Yok lütfen! Yok lütfen!*' The voice screamed getting shriller with each repeat until it trailed off into sobbing. I thought for a moment maybe I should do something, but then again I was in a tight enough spot already. Getting out and fighting two ex-Turkish wrestlers was most definitely not my style. I ducked back into my charnel pit pulling the tarp down tight. I got my phone out and made sure it was on silent then I opened the camera app making sure it was set to video, no flash and night mode. I set it recording then shut the screen down. Just to make sure I covered the screen side with my hat.

I peered back out from my trench with the camera. There was nothing voyeuristic in my filming. This is just what I do. I'm a professional. While all I'd achieve trying to save whoever was screaming and sobbing in the barn, was a similar fate for myself, I'd be able to use this against Mehmet.

The larger of the two was stood with his back to me watching the scene with a motionless intensity. The smaller of the two, though not by much, was bent by the victim's head. He was murmuring something softly while the captive's sobs became some kind of quiet entreaty before choking to silence. The pair were clearly enjoying this. The thought sickened me and terrified me in equal amounts. This wasn't just business as I'd been led to believe. This was fun for them.

The big one made some comment and the other laughed, ruffling the captives hair as he stood, still chuckling and walked over to the axe. It was picked up and he tested it's balance swinging it between his hands letting the head pendulum between his legs. He seemed to remember the supine male now babbling incoherently to himself and strode over to stand astride the giant tractor wheel. He bent low and softly wiped the blade of the axe across his victim's cheek in a perverse caress parodying shaving with a straight razor.

The captive was silent now. Barely daring to breathe. The axe man stepped back swung the axe up quickly and buried it through the now petrified man's chest. The body spasmed and the arms and legs continued twitching. It looked as though the axe head had gone right through the chest cavity, through the hole in the centre of the tractor tyre to the ground beneath. Bright frothy blood bubbled up from the dying man's mouth and nose as he gaped like a fish on dry land.

The twitching and frothing went on for a long time. The hickory handle of the axe fixing him like a butterfly pinned to a board. The larger one walked towards the body. I could see from the bulge in his trousers that he was aroused. It took him several attempts to the pull the axe free and when it came out the ribs opened like a skeletal claw, gore dripping from the bony fingers. The axe then came down in neat efficient movements accompanied by grunts of satisfaction as limbs and head were separated.

The other Turk gathered up the body parts into a wheel barrow. It didn't need a rocket scientist to work out his next destination. I pocketed my phone and ducked back beneath the cover. It's bad enough being in a pit of decaying body parts, but to have the butchers heading your way was more than I could handle. My first thought was to leap out of the pit and start running. By the time I'd have managed to claw my way out of the blood soaked slimy hole I'd already have that axe in my back.

Instead I crept to the far end of the pit and curled myself into a ball amid the scattered limbs of the Turks victims, smearing myself with earth and blood. I lay as still as I could hoping the camouflage jacket and my coating of blood and gore would sufficiently conceal me.

The wheelbarrow had a loose wheel and it's rhythmic squeak and rumble signalled the Turks progress towards my pit. As the squeak drew closer I shut my eyes and focused on breathing. A long slow exhale. Squeak. Hold it then inhale very slowly. Squeak. I heard the barrow come to a stop and I held my breath. Then the rustle as the tarpaulin was folded back. Any second now and all hell could break loose. I tried to remain calm. Then a soft thud as a body part was tossed in. Then another and another. A pause, sounds from above and a heavier thud as the torso was tipped over the edge. Another thud and something hard hit my head. With closed eyes the shock made me see a bright flash of pain. Whatever hit me came to rest touching my face. I hoped I was staying as still as a corpse. Then the rustle as the tarpaulin was pulled back and the relief of the squeak moving back to the barn.

I stayed curled in a ball at the bottom of the pit a long time after the Turks had slammed car doors and driven away. I could find no energy or motivation to move beyond laying there and shaking. I had had enough. So much had happened in the past twenty four hours and I was just so tired. 'I don't want to play any more.' I found myself whispering to the corpses around me. The dead, my new friends, I had been destined for this pit and had ended up in it regardless. It didn't matter what I did, so why fight. I could just stay here curled up next to my dead buddies forever. 'We're all dead anyway so why fight it.' I whispered to my neighbours.

I tried to sleep. Maybe I could fall into a slumber and never wake. I inhaled deeply the sweet smell of the blood and death. Then something in my mind snapped. I could almost hear the sound of a wire pulled too tight, break with a sharp crack and twang as the strands flew apart. I could either lay here or I could fight and suddenly laying here in this pit felt stupid. I didn't have a choice, you can't just lay down and die. I decided I was going to liver forever or I was going to die trying.

I opened my eyes. The vacant gaze of the taxi driver from the casino stared back. His severed head had been what had hit mine. I grinned back at him mocking the *Risus sardonicus* of his death mask. 'The price of failure.' I told him. I stood and pulled back the cover. It was getting light. I realised I needed to get back to my flat before too many people were out and about who might take fright at my current appearance. I looked about the pit, no longer disgusted. There looked to be the remains of three bodies. I fished about for the heads and found two more. I'd take a wild guess that these had been Mikal Dinko and Grigor Malinkova. They wouldn't be talking to the police any time soon. I held Dinko by the tangled mass of bloodied hair. 'Alas poor Mikal, I bugged your interview.' I chuckled.

Something in me had changed. I was self aware enough to realise that. A kind of clarity had descended on me. I couldn't quite put my finger on it, but it was a sense of not being afraid. I realised all I had to do was keep on fighting. Live or die, it's the process not the product. Or something like that.

I fished about some more and found one of Dinko's and Malinkova's hands each and hauled myself out of the ditch with them. The pair of Turks hadn't even cleaned up. I was surprised by this. I'd have washed everything down with bleach and burned the bodies. This evening had showed two things to me. The Turks and by extension Mehmet really didn't care about getting caught. They acted with a confidence that was either pure reckless insanity or they really were beyond reproach. Even so the second point was that Mehmet appeared to be cleaning house, tying up loose ends.

I got back to the van a lot faster than I left it thanks to the growing dawn of a crisp clear winter's day. Mehmet was going to kill me, Archie, Clara and anyone else who posed him a threat and he'd get away with it. Unless I could find the reason he was so confident. I needed to get a little more under Mehmet's skin. More urgently I needed to get rid of my trusty Escort van. After the incident at the Casino there was a good chance the Police had or would soon have the registration number of the van seen driving away. The van wouldn't trace back to me, but it needed cleaning and disposing of. I couldn't very well walk into a petrol station and buy bleach and a can of petrol while looking like a member of the living dead.

I drove back to the flat. I got in and had a moment where I was unsure what to do with the hands. I opted for food bags and the stuffed them in the freezer compartment of my fridge. Then I stripped and bagged all my clothes. I would burn them later. I took a long hot shower but despite that the smell of death still clung to my nostrils.

A new set of clothes, a bottle of bleach, some rags and a can of petrol I drove out to a disused chalk pit a mile from town. It was already littered with the burned out and twisted carcasses of vehicles dumped and burned out by local joy riders. One more would attract little attention, the damaged ignition barrel and hot wiring of the starter would confirm it was just another stolen vehicle. Every surface wiped down with bleach I made a final check for anything I might have missed before liberally dousing the interior of the van in petrol and lighting it. It was starting to burn quite nicely as I walked away.

14 Friday 18th January 1430 Hours.

Pattern recognition.

Just over four hours sleep and I awoke from a strange dream in which the Turk was plunging the axe into my chest. It was odd as I watched the scene as from above, disinterested and unconcerned as the axe pierced my chest. It left me feeling strangely calm.

I'd called Duncan Mcleish as soon as I'd got in. I left him a message telling him to report the van stolen from the yard when he got to work. I also asked him for a replacement to be put at my disposal as soon as possible. Then I promptly hit the sack.

Upon waking my left side had locked up and breathing was difficult. The arm was turning nicely black in places to match my left side of my face. I tried some stretching to loosen things up and after some bone grindingly sharp pain got to the point I could hobble about the flat. Brill was mewing at me demanding his breakfast, dinner and all the meals he'd missed. With great difficulty I fed him. The injuries also presented another far more limiting problem. I now stood out. People would notice me and remember me.

Compounding that I was compromised. Mehmet knew what I looked like. The club CCTV could have provided enough pictures of me that any member of his network would recognise me up close. Clara was also compromised. I'd lost the van. I was running out of assets. On the other hand at least two of Mehmet's side had been taken out of the game permanently and Mehmet had been forced to pull up stakes on the law firm prematurely.

On balance I think Mehmet was ahead and had been calling the shots so far. It was time to switch things around, but the only methods I'd have at my disposal were now the more covert ones. It'd be nice to take the two Turk Psychos out. They knew exactly what I looked like and were going to be a constant threat to me every time I set foot on the street. I even considered ways of killing the pair but couldn't come up with a practical way that wouldn't bring down too much attention from the police.

I checked in with Clara and she reported everything was fine. She gave me a list of five more businesses that Mehmet controlled but wasn't overtly linked to, that she'd coaxed out of Archie before lunch. I added these to my database and ran a few quick checks. A haulage firm, an agricultural chemical distributor, a couple of taxi firms and Limo hire company. Archie was right as the checks I was able to do with companies house showed none of the usual links to Mehmet. I then went to the land registry and checked out the killing ground. That was a surprise. It still showed as Ministry of Defence Land. Either some enterprising farmer had long ago annexed that bit without telling anyone or the M.O.D. had just forgotten about it.

It was time to go back to the recordings and find out what it was Ali Mehmet thought I knew and try and find some clues to his get out of jail free card. I copied all the audio from the laptop I had used to my main computer. I loaded all the streams as separate tracks into some audio processing software. I fixed an espresso and then donned my headphones and got to work.

First I made sure each audio feed was synced in time. Then I cut to the interview to refresh my memory. It was still a laboured process the second time round with everything between DC Jenkins and Dinko going via the interpreter. I staved off boredom by tweaking the audio with filter settings, cleaning it up and removing background noise.

There was no logical basis for the feeling but I was sure the arson wasn't the issue. From what I knew of Mehmet's methods and resources he could easily have made the pair disappear in the months leading up to any kind of trial. No I hadn't been sent there to record that. The gold was in what else Dinko was saying.

Having a visual display of the recordings made finding the areas of speech simple. The line of the recording waved up and down in time to the sounds. At the start of the feed to one of the unused consultations rooms, I'd wired up just in case, was a very small amount of movement on the line. I copied that section to a new track and turned the audio gain way up. Some filtering and I could make the faint speech intelligible.

It was Jenkins and the silent detective talking before the interview. I hadn't been aware I'd even been recording this. They must have been in the corridor and the speaker/microphone in the adjacent consultation room had picked them up.

I heard Jenkins say. 'Sir, with respect I'd like one of my usual team in with me.'

The unnamed police man replied. 'That's not negotiable. The male is a foreign national so S.B. Want to be involved. I want to be involved, and as I'm a Detective Superintendent and you're a Detective constable I get what I want.' A Superintendent from Special Branch very odd. Was there a terrorist angle to this?

Jenkins came back quite bravely. 'Sir, I'm an advanced interviewer. I've been in major crime for eight years during which I've interviewed dozens of murderers. When was that last time you conducted a PACE interview?' I was starting to like Jenkins. He had balls.

The Special Branch officer came back, clearly annoyed. 'One call and I can have both these idiots shipped off to Belmarsh where they'll sit for years without ever seeing a court room. So unless you want some very career limiting things to happen you'll restrict your questioning to what I've already agreed.'

'Yes, sir.' Jenkins replied. The audio cut to the silence of the empty corridor as the pair walked away.

None of that made much sense. It was pretty clear to me that Dinko and Malinkova had just been a pair of hapless thugs employed by Mehmet. No reason for S.B. to be involved there. Of course Mehmet was obviously into organised crime and as organised crime was getting into globalisation there were areas of cooperation starting to emerge. I knew ninety percent of opium coming into Western Europe flowed through Turkey and originated in Afghanistan.

I listened carefully to the tail end of the interview. Dinko was listing businesses associated with Mehmet. I opened up my network diagram of Mehmet intel and ticked off each place Dinko named. Then we reached a new one. From the translator '..and this warehouse. I have once collected a package from there.'

Jenkins to the translator. 'Where exactly?' Then the translator to Dinko and back.

'He says a big white one next to airfield. Unit 14.'

Then Dinko added in heavily accented English. 'Big package.'

There was a cough in the background. Nothing else was said for a while. Had the Special Branch Superintendent just cut things off? Jenkins ended the interview then with weary resignation in his voice, so yes, probably.

I went straight to Google Earth and found the unit. One of about thirty in rows of ten on a newly built enterprise park next to the air field five miles out of town. I think it had once been a military airbase but cuts had long since relegated the place to light aircraft and skydivers. I went to the land registry again, they were getting a lot of cash out of me this week Nothing useful turned up there, the whole development was listed as owned by a holding company whose web site gave nothing up of any relevance.

I visually scanned the audio files to the point when I had shut the system down. Near the end, long after Dinko had been marched back to the cells was some movement on the channels for the unused interview room and one of the consultation rooms. I isolated those two tracks. Like the earlier one I pulled the audio gain right up and filtered for background noise. The audio was randomly alternating between the two speakers, sometimes in one, sometimes the other and occasionally very faintly in both.

I set about cutting, pasting and cross fading between the feeds. Thankfully there were only two. I started to feel Like Harry Caul in the film "*The Conversation*" which is a near to porn for us Bugmen as you can get.

The result wasn't great quality, but hey I bug people, I'm not a studio sound engineer. It sounded like it was the SB man on the phone to someone and pacing up and down the corridor as he went.

'yes, you know who this is?' He still sounded impatient. There was something inaudible. '...you are still the head prosecutor for the region you can make this happen.' The other party was saying something. '...yes, if you have to cite defence of the realm.' Then some loud buzzing as the SB man's mobile phone passed too close to the wires carrying the audio feed. 'any problems and you might suggest to...' More buzzing and no amount of filtering would take it out. '...that someone may well find a stash of kiddie porn on one of his hard drives. No it's not a bit harsh.' Then the sound of a door opening. Someone coming down the corridor. The SB man's voice faded as he moved out of range of any of my feeds.

That was it. At that point Archie had pulled the plug on the job. I still wasn't really sure what I had. The next step was to take a look at the mysterious Unit 14 warehouse. Not something I really relished with the axe murdering Turks still at large. I hadn't even started considering what Mehmet might be doing to try and find me. He certainly wouldn't be idle.

From what I had so far, it looked as though Mehmet was bringing in West Asian Heroin and somehow this was of importance to a

Detective Superintendent from Special Branch. A working theory that the stuff was somehow coming into the airport and out through this Warehouse was shaping up quite nicely. A lot still didn't make sense like burning buildings and suchlike. And why would SB give a heroin importer a get out jail free card?

It would be really useful to have a conversation with DC Jenkins, but that seemed nigh on impossible. For a start there was no reason for him to talk to me. Even if I revealed who and what I was, an act in itself repulsive to me, I doubted he'd talk. More likely he'd listen and then drop me in it.

I carried out a quick open source search on DC Jenkins. I turned up a half a dozen or so news reports of court cases, normally showing him walking out of crown court after sending someone down for a fair portion of their life. The pictures showed a thin, weather beaten man in his early fifties. Short iron grey hair and generally a tired but determined look on his face.

I got myself another coffee, lighted a cigarette and sat down to think. I'd need to make Jenkins indebted to me in some way that gave me a gentle hold over him. Then I might have the conversation I wanted. I had an idea, but first something I should have done a day ago.

I got the Turks phone I'd stolen while he followed Kash, out of its shielded bag. It was time to have quick look at that to see what it added to the picture I was building of Mehmet and his organisation. I found a cable that fitted, a mini USB-B. I fitted the battery and plugged the cable in. Then I put the phone back in the shielded bag, closing it up with just the small gap for the cable at the far end which I plugged into a computer. Through the bag I switched the phone on and waited patiently for it to boot up. It sprang to life and began searching for and failing to find a network.

The shielded bag formed a Faraday cage blocking any radio waves from entering or leaving. Should there be tracking software or any attempt to wipe the phone, the signals would be blocked leaving the phone in exactly the condition I had found it in. I used some basic command line tools to take a bit level copy of both the phone's internal storage and the attached memory card. It would take an exact copy of everything, operating system, the users files and even the empty space. The empty space would afford me the possibility of recovering deleted files. The total amounted to about 20 gigabytes of data. I went for a short nap.

My nap was shorter than expected. Duncan Mcleish rang me at five.

'Hey laddie, what're you up to ye nugget?'

'I've had some problems.'

'You must have, you burned out a perfectly good van, nice little runner that despite the rust. Oh and I've had the Police round here asking questions.'

'Is everything OK?'

'Aye, its all cool in school. They've recommended I get some CCTV to prevent future thefts. I did tell them I had a mate could probably jack that up. Speaking of mates I've got you an old Transit. Again a nice runner but getting a bit old, It's ex an British Telecom one I picked up at auction.'

'Is it still liveried up?' I asked.

'Aye just about.'

'I'll take it. If you can tart up the livery a bit so it still looks current. Oh, and forget to re-register it for a few days, it might be handy for it to still trace back to to B.T.'

'Are you not even going to ask the price?'

'Ok, how much?'

'Seven hundred quid and it's yours.'

'I'll sort you out in the next few days. Can you leave a set of keys in the gutter at the rear of the workshop, I'll pick the van up after dark.'

'OK pal.'

'And Duncan, I may need you for some overtime very soon.'

'I'll await your call. Take care pal.' He hung up.

I went back to work. The copy had finished so I switched off the phone and removed the battery. I turned my attention to the phone's data image now stored on my desktop. I first pulled off the "*contacts.db*" file. An SQLite3 database. All those contacts found their way onto my cross referenced database.

What did I really want from this phone? Twenty Gigs was a lot of data to sort through on a fishing trip. I had leads to follow already, I could come back to this later. What I wanted out of this was where the Turks lived. What would be the quickest way of getting that?

I copied out the DCIM directory where all the pictures taken by the phone's camera were stored. There were forty three images in the folder. I opened the directory in gallery view and perused the thumbnails in date order. There were some nice scenic pictures of somewhere Mediterranean. A few pictures of yet another Mercedes. What was it with these people, were they sponsored by the company? Now some photos of Vista in full swing as full as ever full of little blondes in short skirts. Then a picture of an obscenely large Sony flat screen TV, and now, hello what's this?

I think it's called a "*selfsie*" these days. A self portrait usually taken with a camera phone via a suitable mirror. All the rage with teenagers these days. The picture showed the slightly smaller guy, the one who'd buried the axe in the middle of Taxi man's chest. He was standing naked in front of a bathroom mirror letting it all hang out. I wondered who the picture was for. It was so ridiculous seeing the psychotic axe murder posing for an inexpertly taken selfsie that I laughed out loud. I laughed and then I opened the picture in a hex editor. The actual bytes of data that made up the picture revealed I scrolled through the seemingly random characters that make up the content of a JPEG picture looking for the patterns that made sense.

I found the model details of the phone, the shutter settings, the date and time and bingo!, the geographic data for where the photo was taken. By default almost all phones store this data in any picture you take, unless you're smart enough to turn it off. It was a string of numbers showing latitude and longitude.

Using the ubiquitous mapping services I plotted the location to an area the other side of town. The data probably wouldn't be that accurate. It wouldn't give me an exact street address. I opened the picture of the flat screen TV in the same way. It gave me a location very close to the first. I looked at the picture of the TV again. On the wall behind the TV was a mirror. I zoomed in on that. The mirror reflected the view through a window. I could just make out a church. I went back to the map. There were only two buildings in my search radius with that view of the church and one of those was set of retirement flats, hardly the place the Turkish enforcers would hang out. The other was a run down building converted into flats. That looked to be the spot, I reckoned second or third floor by the angle on the church. I should go and take a look to confirm it for sure.

15 Friday 18th January 2000 Hours.

Interference.

Nicely dark and usefully cold. The weather providing ample excuse to have a scarf wrapped round half my face, leather gloves and woollen hat pulled down low. I sat on a park bench with a good view all round me and waited for Kash to arrive. I carried a small black rucksack with a pair of frozen hands and a pair of encrypted radios in it. Under my dark green coat I wore a black vest fitted with multiple pockets. In these were a range of my extensive lock pick collection and a few other tools that might come in handy.

I'd never liked the expression "The gloves are off." I always thought it the wrong way round. In my world when things turn serious and more drastic covert action is required, the gloves come on. Mine were firmly on at this point.

On the way I'd carefully scouted out where I thought the Turk was living. I couldn't at this point assume both lived in the same place, but there was a chance it was so. I'd walked via the church yard looking up at the windows of the flats. There were about four possible flats the picture could have come from. I circled the building alert for the pair suddenly arriving or leaving.

Out the front was the Mercedes death car. Easily identified by the boot lid dented from my efforts with the jack. I knew I had the right building so now the task was to isolate the correct flat. I carded the communal door and checked the heap of mail piled on top of an old iron radiator.

This building was a microcosm of the town itself. Built to house a large and prosperous family it had probably stayed with the same lineage for several generations before an inheritor decided to the sell off the family assets denying future generations it's worth. Bought by a property speculator in the eighties it was now in the hands of an absentee landlord living in London and never visiting the long term unemployed, heroin addicts, single mothers and low income workers that made up his tenants. It was just like my place.

There was no mail to indicate the flat number of the Turk. Most of it was addressed to people who must have long ago moved on to the next flat and the next absentee landlord.

I didn't go any further into the building. No sense in taking risks I didn't have to, so I went and waited for Kash at our prearranged spot.

I made out the silhouette of Kash bounding across the park, his hood up. Just a vague outline of a teenager, but by the walk I knew it was him. He stopped in front of me peering out from under his hood. 'Hi Chatar!' he greeted.

'Kash.'

'I have some great news.' He spoke too quickly when he was excited.

'So tell me.'

'I've had a conditional offer from Kent to study Electronic engineering.' He paused. 'It's dependant on my grades.'

'Good news, Kash. When all this mess is over we'll focus on those exams.' I personally hate exams. It's not what you know, its what you can do that counts. But still, Kash needed to get where he could access the knowledge he was hungry for. If that meant jumping through the state's hoops of formal education then jump he would.

'Tell me what the job is tonight?'

'I haven't time to explain everything but things have got a lot more serious. Those guys who followed you yesterday. They tried to kidnap and kill me last night.'

Kash let out a whistle to show how impressed he was.

'I'm going to try and neutralise the threat those two pose us. All you have to do is be a look out.'

'OK boss. Lookout for what.'

'I'll explain on the way, but what you need to know now is that should anything go wrong at all you're to get the hell out and make your way back home taking all the usual precautions.'

Kash nodded.

'There's an encrypted file on Dropbox. The key is your full Sikh name backwards. If anything goes wrong you are to follow the instructions in the file to the letter. Have you got that.'

'Yes.'

'Good, then lets get going.'

I had Kash stationed in the shadows at the end of an alley way up the street. He should have had a clear view of the entrance to the building. I'd brought Kash up to speed during the walk over. Glossing over some of my more embarrassing moments, but giving him enough to appreciate the gravity of the situation I was bringing him into. I'd then worked my way round to the back of the building,

I had one of the radios stashed in an inside pocket with a small earpiece fitted. Kash had the other. I tested the link when I got round the back and Kash reported back with a clear signal. I walked up towards the church. The streets were deserted and cold lent everything a crisp clear aspect. I found one of the few remaining working payphones in the town and pushed through the heavy door into it's kiosk. I had Mehmet's mobile number from the captured phone and I slotted in a handful of well cleaned coins from a small money bag. Then I dialled the number.

It rang for some time. Mehmet wouldn't recognise the number, it would either appear on his caller ID as a local number or unknown. I feared for a moment it would go through to voice mail but he eventually picked up. With everything that had been going I didn't think he'd fail to let curiosity get the better of him.

'Hello.' He spoke in unaccented English. My first time hearing his voice.

'You should know who this is.' I told him, making no attempt to disguise my voice.

'I think you have the wrong number.' He said flatly.

'I thought I'd call to thank you for the V.I.P treatment at Vista last night.' That should make things clear enough for him. Unless he'd had more than one unwitting victim taken out the back of the bar.

'Why are you calling me.' A trace of an accent appearing. Annoyance, fear or something else? I couldn't tell, but he'd had enough self control to not ask me how I got his number.

'I was thinking after last night's drama it would be in all our interests to come to an arrangement.'

'I don't see how that would benefit me. I'll see that you are receiving the V.I.P treatment as you put it, very soon.' Yes, definitely annoyance there making the accent shine through.

'Ali, you're not looking at this clearly are you. Your dogs might catch up with me. But I can see that taking a very long time and costing you a lot of money and effort and you can avoid all of that. Look at it this way, in the time you are looking for me there's a lot of things I've seen that could get made very public.' I paused. I'd keyed on him being a visual person. When he spoke he "Saw" things rather than "heard" or "Thought" or "felt". I was using this pattern of language back at him. Creating empathy and subtly manipulating him, I hoped. 'So, what I propose is that you and I meet, face to

176

face. I can give you all the recordings and an assurance of my continued goodwill and silence. You can give me the sum we agreed upon. Surely, you can see that working out for the best?'

'I see we may have something to discuss after all.' He wasn't agreeing to anything. I could almost feel his mind turning things over. No negotiation, no threats. He was clearly only interested in an opportunity to meet me. Time to dangle the carrot.

'In that case Ali, meet me outside Unit 14 in twenty minutes and come alone, if I see anyone else there I'll leave.' I hung up without waiting for a response. Of course Mehmet wasn't going to come alone, of course he wasn't going to actually pay me and of course I wasn't going to be there either. But, the big "BUT" this wasn't an opportunity Mehmet could afford to pass up. On the off chance I was stupid enough to actually be at the shipping unit he'd have to send his two thugs and they wouldn't have a lot of time to try and get there and get set up ahead of me. Using Unit 14 also raised the stakes quite nicely in Mehmet's mind. Now he knew about that I felt sure he'd move heaven and earth to find me.

I pushed the PTT on my radio. 'Stand by, stand by.' I said to alert Kash. I heard two clicks of his PTT in response as I jogged back to my view of the rear of the Turks building. I found some suitable shadows to stand in and watched. A light went out on the top floor. I pictured a hurried call from Mehmet to the two large psychopaths, no doubt spending a relaxing evening watching TV programs about home improvement and tips for sharpening their axe blades.

Ninety seconds later Kash's voice erupted into my left ear. 'Two targets leaving the building. Positive ID on both.' I depressed my PTT twice to acknowledge that and waited. Twenty seconds later. 'Both subjects in vehicle and heading away from my location.'

'All received, keep watch for them returning' I replied to Kash and made my way quickly to the front of the building. This time of night it would take them less than fifteen minutes to get to Unit 14. If I'd had time and resources I'd have liked to have someone bedded in covertly watching the unit to give me the nod when they arrived and more importantly when they left. No sense in whining about what I didn't have, so I calculated on the side of caution. Ten minutes drive each way with a minimum of ten waiting for me. That gave me half an hour to do my work. I set the stopwatch going on my watch.

I once again carded the communal door. These older door entry systems always were fitted so poorly most would give with a sharp slap and all of them yield to a thin rectangle of mica. I quickly made my way up the stairs, dodging bicycles, prams and bags of rubbish. First floor had sounds of a baby crying and the smell of burnt chip fat. Second floor the hall light was broken, smell of cannabis crawling out from under the door. I produced a packet of crisps from a pocket, ripped open the packet and scattered the crisps at the bottom step before heading towards the top floor. Light working. No rubbish just a solid front door. I walked the landing to where a wooden framed window did nothing to keep out the cold. I looked out and could make out the alley where Kash was watching from the shadows. I couldn't see him. Good lad.

I keyed my radio. 'In position at the flat door.' I reported.

Kash came back to me. 'I see you in the window. Everything clear in the street.'

I double clicked the PTT and moved to the door. There were pros and cons about my location. Being on the top floor meant there would be no passing traffic so I could work on the door without fear of interruption. However, if the pair of Turks returned I'd have no way to leave the building without passing them. Clearly a prospect not conducive to my good health.

The door was a good solid one. Clearly better quality than the others I'd passed on the way up. It had two locks. A pin tumbler midway and a curtained mortise below it. Not too surprising, but I'd hoped for just a pin tumbler.

I pulled out the curtain mortise picks from a vest pocket. I used the wire pick to the feel the inside of the lock and had a peek with a small penlight torch. I counted five levers. So far so good a British Standard lock, not too complicated to pick, but time consuming as I tend to get less practice on these locks than I do on pin tumblers.

Concentrating on the lock I inserted the wire into the handle and then fitted the handle in the lock. I turned it gently to engage the curtain slightly. I started carefully lifting each lever while feeling for resistance as I turned the handle. I got three of the levers into the correct position before over lifting the fourth. I dropped tension on the handle and let all of the levers drop and started again.

I was completely focused on the lock. All my concentration was used in visualising what was happening inside the mechanism. This is why you need someone watching your back. You can become so engaged in teasing the lock open that half an army can march up behind you. I started lifting the levers again, trying to remember the positions from last time.

The radio crackled with three urgent key clicks of Kash's PTT. I pulled the pick out and went to the window. Three clicks was for a problem. A sudden wave of panic washed over me and adrenaline flooded my already tensed nervous system. I glanced down into the street. No sign of the Mercedes deathmobile. I relaxed slightly. I looked further down the road to Kash's position. I could see some figures moving at the end of the alley. I keyed the radio up. 'What the hell's going on Kash?'

The response was Kash holding down his PTT. He didn't speak but I could pick up voices in the background. He left his radio open mic and I turned up the volume on mine.

A male voice, local doing a fake south London accent. 'What you doing here bruv, why you coming to our ends?'

'I'm waiting for a friend.' Kash replied.

'You aint waiting nowhere blood.' Came a fainter voice.

'I'll only be here a few minutes.' Kash put forward plaintively. They were interviewing Kash. Establishing his suitability as a victim and he was passing that test with flying colours. I wondered what to do. I could rush back out there and hope the presence of a witness would disrupt the territorial violence that was about to occur.

'You not waiting in our ends without paying no rent kid.' Came the first voice.

'What you here for blood? You selling weed on our postcode?' The second voice becoming more accusatory. 'Cos' that's just disrespecting us.' The voice building in volume and rising in pitch. Working himself up and simultaneously pre-justifying the violence to himself. This was bad news.

'Look, what do you want?' Asked Kash firmly establishing himself as the victim.

Collateral compromise, we call this in surveillance terms. Third party interference that while not as bad as being detected by your subject it can nonetheless destroy a good surveillance job. I made to head down the stairs when another voice joined the fray.

'Ah, you little fuckers! Piss off.' An older voice, male. Local accent. I headed back to the window. The front door to the house adjacent to the alleyway was open spilling light onto the street and illuminating three hunched hoodies and a man in his sixties holding pick-axe handle the white hickory glinting in the light.

The first hoodie's voice. 'What old man? You not gonna do anything to us.' Spat almost contemptuously.

I watched as the man advanced into the group shouting 'I'm sick to bloody death of you shits hanging round here dealing your dope. I didn't do twenty two years in the army to let you fuckers rule my streets.' The voice breaking in places in sheer frustration. I watched as the man jabbed the bat out quickly rather than swing it. The jab gave the hoody nearest no warning and no time to avoid. I heard the crack, muted through the radio link.

The hoody staggered back clutching his nose. He turned and stumbled back down the road. He was clearly the alpha of the group as the other two slowly turned and trailed him up the street mouthing back abuse towards the man as they retreated.

The man spoke to Kash now. 'You OK sonny? I heard all of that, little fuckers. Come inside, I'll make us a tea while you wait for your friend.'

'Thank you sir, may I sit by the window to watch for my friend arriving.?' Kash replied. Then he cut the open mic and gave me two clicks of the PTT to confirm all was copacetic.

I looked at my watch, six minutes wasted. I went back to the lock. I had to start over. I got back to three levers feeling about right and still the fourth was giving me a problem. I skipped it and set the fifth with no trouble. I reset the lock again and set levers one to three and number five. The earlier surge of adrenaline was leaving me and as I crouched my legs began to shake. I stood and breathed out slowly counting to ten. I did this several times while clearing my mind and asking my body to relax.

Crouching to the lock. I closed my eyes and sent my minds-eye inside the mechanism. I visualised each lever rising up till the level of the slot for the bolt was at the same place for each. I tentatively turned the handle of the pick felling for the bolt catching slightly on the lip of the groove. I exhaled slowly and raised the last lever into place. My left hand on the handle of the tool felt the last resistance as the bolt started to slide through the slot. I turned with more force and felt a deep satisfaction as I heard the solid clunk as the bolt turned unlocking the catch from the mortise.

Ten minutes down and one lock to go. I put away the mortise picks and examined the Pin Tumbler. It looked like an ASSA five pin. The door and frame were well fitted and I wasn't going to be able to card this one. I slotted a sprung loaded circular tension tool into the keyway and held it in my left hand. I used a diamond pick in my right. I had just begun to apply a little torque to the lock barrel when I heard a door open on the floor below. I quietly shuffled backwards beyond the view of the stairs.

I crouched just past the top of the stairs listening to a muted conversation below while watching the seconds tick by on my wrist watch. There was dragging of feet as the pair shuffled around the first floor landing. I heard a distinctive crunch as one of them stepped on the crisps I had scattered. Christ! The good byes were taking a long time.

It felt like an eternity but I eventually heard one of the voices say 'Later bruv.' and shuffle down the stairs while the first floor door slammed with surprising violence before the shrill tones of a domestic erupted in the flat.

Kash radioed in 'One adult male leaving the front door.' I gave him the double click answer and got back to the pin tumbler lock. No more interruptions and on more familiar ground I quickly had the breaks in the pins at the sheer line and twisted the tension wrench. I let the door open a crack.

I'd seen the lights go out from the rear of the property, but to assume that means no one is home is dangerous in this business. I put my ear to the crack and listened. Just the hum of a refrigerator. The smell of a strange aftershave and a stillness in the air. I swung the door a little wider and slid in sideways. I got my penlight out. I'd modified it by putting a plastic cap on the end with a hole just larger than a pin prick. Using that to survey the room, I stepped slowly placing my toes gingerly down and testing the floor gradually increasing pressure before unwinding the rest of my foot.

To my right was a kitchenette. Fridge-freezer, sink, cooker, microwave and cupboards. It was open to the living room with a bar to running the width of the cooking area. I snuck behind it and carefully probed the room with the torch. The huge flat screen TV was mounted like a mirror on the world and was hanging off of the left hand wall. In front of me was the back wall of the building, it had windows running its entire span. Light and airy I believe the estate agents call it.

Leather sofa in a tasteful dark brown, also practical for any accidental spillages of blood. A glass topped coffee table littered with minuscule coffee cups, Turkish cigarette packets and Turkish magazines with glossy covers of dark eyed beauties gazing out vacantly. There was a door in the middle of the right hand wall straddled by a Vettriano print and a vintage black and white of the New York skyline. I guessed the flat came fully furnished, I figured the Turks more for C. M. Coolidge in artistic taste.

I made my way to the door slowly. All this was taking precious time, but I was getting one shot at this job, I doubted I'd find another way to guarantee the Turks were out for long enough and if they suspected I'd been near this place I definitely wouldn't get another attempt at it. I turned the handle to the door then used that to provide upward pressure on the whole door, relieving the hinges of some of their burden and lessening the chances of a creak.

A short corridor devoid of anything except a wall socket and three doors. One left and two right. I went left first. The door was half open. I slid in and checked the room out, it was a bedroom with the same light and airy views as the living room. It had large double bed, fortunately empty. It also had the all pervading strange aftershave smell that instantly bought back memories a large Turkish wrestler leaning over me while he stuffed me in a boot. I put the thought aside and went to the first right hand door. Empty save the clutter of a shared bathroom.

Last door. Same precautions led me into another bedroom. This one was empty and smaller and lacking the light and airiness of what was clearly the Alpha Turk's room. It was also untidy. It put me in mind of writing a book called the seven habits of successful psychopaths. I allowed myself a grin as I stood up to full height and switched on a light. I called to Kash. 'Flat cleared, it's empty. I'm starting work now.'

Kash called back. 'OK. Be quick.' I looked at my watch. Twenty minutes of my self allotted thirty had gone. I walked back into the living room turning on lights as I went.

In the living room I put down my rucksack and stripped off my leather gloves. Beneath these I wore a pair of purple nitrile gloves. Affixed upon each digit of each hands were a set of prints taken from the severed hands. I'd used the same method as I did to fool the fingerprint machine, although it was easier this time when I actually had my hands on the hands in question.

The only problem I encountered was that fingerprint residue is made up of oils secreted from the skin. My little plastic prints were not of course going to leave any deposit. I figured the best solution to that was to apply a little hand cream to my finger tips. I stood in the living room and did this. I used a common brand name hand cream. I was working under the assumption that actually analysing the chemical constituents of a print was was beyond the imagination and certainly beyond the budget of the police. Even if they did they would have to conclude the two victims were just fastidious about getting dry skin.

I set about laying a trail of prints all over the flat with great gusto. I even went into the hard to reach places. I wasn't concerned with trying to create an elaborate crime scene for the 'tecs to follow. They would soon have better things to do.

After I'd printed up doors, windows, wall, the fridge and the TV. I did a load on the headboard of the big Turks bed. I scratched what I hoped would look like nail marks with a small pin. I hoped the police would spend some time figuring that one out.

Back in the living room I put on another pair of nitrile gloves on top of the first. I took out one of the hands from the back pack. It'd been defrosting for some time and while it was still a solid lump but a little of the blood had pooled in the corner of the food bag. I pricked a hole in the bag with the pin and dripped blood into one of the corners and under the sofa. I dripped a few drops around the bedroom and also into the plug hole of the bath. I did the same with the other hand. Satisfied with my artistic endeavours I pondered what to do with the hands. I didn't want them to be found by the Turks, but equally they had to be somewhere credible. I couldn't just put one down the back of the sofa and expect the police to believe it had been misplaced like a TV remote control.

I opted for the freezer for one. My first thought had been the freezer so why wouldn't an axe murdering psycho come to the same conclusion. I laid the paw behind some crispy pancakes and a tub of out of date ice cream. Before I could think of placing the second hand, hand, one not so careful previous owner, somewhere, I noticed the land-line.

Too good an opportunity to miss. I lifted the receiver and dialled 17070. An automated female voice told me the number of the circuit. Gold dust to a veteran bugman like me.

As I cast about holding the remaining mitt the radio sprang to life. 'Stand by. Stand By.' I heard Kash call out.

I froze. The stand by was a possible call to action. I awaited the update.

'Subject Vehicle approaching, repeat subject vehicle approaching.'

No time to lose at all. I dropped the hand back into my back pack and pulled it on. I quickly went round and turned off all the lights. Then left the flat pulling the door shut behind me and hearing it

185

latch. There was no time to re-latch the mortise lock. That would involve re-picking the lock all over again. Certainly no time for that. I would just have to rely on them either not remembering they locked it or on the pair blaming each other for forgetting.

I made it down to the first floor landing and radioed Kash. 'Update please.' My voice carrying more than a little urgency.

'Hold on. They're parking directly outside the building.' His tone even and calm, but then he wasn't the rat in the trap.

'Have I got time to get clear?' Me controlling my voice and breathing to remain calm, to be my normal cool headed self.

'Negative, they'll see you. They're starting to get out of the car.'

Shit and double shit. I went back up the stairs to the top floor. I went over to the window and looked down upon the roof of the Merc and the two heads of the Turks pulling their bulk from the leather upholstered seats. I noticed the larger one was going quite bald on top, I'm not sure why that seemed important to me, but then you don't really imagine psychopaths worrying about the signs of ageing.

First thing I did was try not to panic. The second was to consider going out the window and aiming for the roof of the car. My stunt man had the day off so I ditched that plan. The third thing was to loosen the light-bulb in the top floor landing light so it went out. Maybe I could crouch under the window in the relative shadow and they wouldn't notice me. It was while gently undoing light-bulb I heard the front door open and low tenor of the Turks conversation.

Glancing up at ceiling during my work I noticed my potential salvation. A loft hatch. Secured by a padlock and hasp. I stepped up on the banister so I could reach it. It was a cheap brass padlock. Probably three pins. I considered just ripping the hasp off, but there was a risk the Turks would hear.

I could hear them making their way up the stairs to toward the first floor. I was glad for the first time that they were so large as they plodded their way up the stairs slowly. I had a pick and tension tool out and exhaled slowly to calm myself. I got the tension tool in and using my left thumb to give the gentlest caress to it about a third of the way from the end. I used a rake pick and see-sawed the snake like edge up and down as I dragged it along the brass pins.

The single sharp click was a the sweetest sound I'd heard in a long time. I put the picks between my teeth, popped the hatch and chucked the padlock up into the void. Then I mantle shelved silently into the loft just as they hit the darkened first floor landing. Squatting with my legs astride the opening I saw the tops of their heads as the pair walked along the hallway. I slid the hatch into place a quietly as I could while the pair crunched over my debris of scattered salt and vinegar crisps.

I stayed as motionless as I could while the pair cursed as the top floor light failed to come on. They trudged up the stairs still moaning and grumbling to each other which despite not knowing Turkish I could follow with ease. There was a grunt as one of them tried the mortise lock and found it not as he expected. The discussion I was waiting for never happened. I heard the door open and the pair trudge inside. The door closed and then I heard the clunk of the mortise re-engaging.

O.K. So they weren't planning on coming out any time soon or they'd have not bothered to lock the mortise. I switched on my penlight to locate the padlock. I pocketed that and looked around as the radio burst into life again.

'Hey man, you all right?' Kash almost whispered down the radio channel.

I didn't even risk a whisper. I double clicked my status. I scanned the loft space. Dust, more dust and fibreglass insulation sheets. I itched just looking at them, never mind the minute glass dust getting under my clothes. A few old boxes and tea chests scattered here and there on boards suspended between the ceiling beams and a water tank in the corner.

I made my way over to the tank balancing on the beams, careful not to drop through the plaster board ceilings to the flat below. I wasn't sure quite how the Turks would take me as an uninvited guest descending from above, but I'm sure it wouldn't involve them making me a strong Turkish coffee.

I pulled off my backpack and took out the food bag with my remaining spare hand. I opened it and dropped the hand into the water tank. When that defrosted the DNA would be everywhere. Have that you fuckers.

I duck walked back to the hatch and gingerly lifted it. Peering an inverted meercat like head downward I surveyed the hallway, now lit only by the orange sodium haze of street lamps. All was quiet. I lowered myself to the banister and re-padlocked the hatch. With a slowness that was forced against my natural instincts I descended the first flight of stairs avoiding my patch of half trampled crisps with the deftness of ballet dancer and began heading for the ground floor. I radioed Kash. 'Stand By, exfil in thirty seconds.'

I heard a double click response and slightly more quickly went down the stairs to the ground floor. With huge relief, pride and a generous dose of smugness I left the front door and out into the chill night air. I turned right. Kash was to egress left. I hit the radio button. 'All clear, pull out.'

Kash responded. 'Wait, wait, He's just got the biscuits out.'

I followed my pre-arranged ex-filtration route.

16 Saturday 19th January 0830 Hours.

Meeting of minds.

Morning found me at the computer again. I set up two Hushmail accounts that I accessed using Tor. I then went back to my data slurp from the police network a couple of days ago.

I'd woken to a cold flat and a seized up left side as my battered ribs protested about the gymnastics the night before. In addition to that the weakened left lung was obviously building up fluid that was resulting in a annoying cough. I'd need to sort that out before I engaged in some of the later moves I was planning.

I'd got up and gone through a painful series of stretching exercises culminating in forcing some deep breathing that filled and expanded my lungs to capacity, the broken ribs crunching and cracking as I forced my left lung into it's full range of movement. I finished off with some dead hangs and reverse pull ups on my chin up bar. My only real hobby is climbing and while I don't get out much I try to stay in shape as some of the skills transfer to my work, like pulling yourself into a loft hatch ahead of a pair of large psychopaths.

Coffee and painkillers administered I reflected on last nights little job. I had left the building going right and following a twisting turning route through town while Kash had done the same after leaving his new friend and going left. We'd met some time later back in the park.

I was very pleased with Kash's performance, more so than the little follow we had done days earlier. In this line of work it's the simple tasks that really test a person's suitability. Give someone a complex task and they may struggle, but it will occupy their full attention and they will stick with it to the bitter end. However, give someone a very simple, boring task and many will become distracted or invent reasons to move off from position and modify a carefully thought out plan.

Over the years I'd worked with many such people in the surveillance side of the private detective business. You can tell the types as soon as they turn up on a job. They're often loaded up with gimmicky gadgets. They also tend to dress like they're trying to look like someone working undercover. I'm sure if they could have found a T-shirt or baseball cap with " Surveillance Operative" written on it, they would have worn it. The team would be plotted up on a subjects house in static positions and after an hour or two you'd spot these fools wandering about muttering about a better idea they'd had. Just one reason why I prefer to work alone if possible.

Kash was none of this. He'd stayed in position and when forced to move by collateral compromise he'd found a better one and stuck with it. He'd expressed concern over his little altercation with the Hoodies. I'd tried to explain that people who lurk, figuratively and literally in the shadows are often visible to others in similar clandestine worlds. He asked me what he should have done differently and I tried to explain that sometimes you need to get a little aggressive in guarding your shadow. Kash had expressed confusion at this, I guess because it ran counter to everything I'd taught him. I think it was a lesson I was just beginning to learn myself.

My morning's work on the computer was stuttering to a halt. I lighted a cigarette and phoned Clara.

She picked up on the third ring. 'Hi, David.' A little cool, but about what I was expecting.

'How's things in the country?'

'OK, but I'd rather be in town. How much longer do we need to hide out here?'

'A few more days, a week at the most. If I haven't found a way to sort this out by then I think I'll retire to the country myself and keep bees or something.'

'Would you?' Clara asked.

'Keep bees?'

'No, retire, not necessarily to the country.'

This was out of the blue. My comment had been offhand and now she was developing the theme and I wasn't sure I was comfortable with where she was going. 'I hadn't really thought about it.' Was all I could morosely add.

'I mean, if we both got out of our abnormal lives, would things be different between us?' Hesitant. I don't think she was thinking this through either.

'Of course they'd be different. What would we do for money?' Ever the realist.

'I don't know David. I hadn't thought that far ahead myself, but maybe we could have a, a something more like a relationship. Instead of a...' She paused struggling for the right description. I doubt she'd ever find it. I wasn't sure I could.

'Instead of a casual arrangement.' I finished her sentence for her.

'If that's what you want to call it.'

'I thought it works out fine.'

'So did I David, so did I.' I didn't like her use of the past tense. There was an implication there that made me uncomfortable, about as uncomfortable as her suggestions in the possible future tense. Why spoil something that was working just fine? Sex and companionship when required. Deep down I suddenly realised two things: First was that it was me who had spoiled things by crossing unwritten lines and secondly I suddenly realised with those three words 'sex and companionship' that I had become just another client. Only difference was I didn't pay.

What could we do anyway. Throw away both our means of income. Try and step out of the shadows of deception and human frailty into a suburban utopia and pretend that the world was really a nice place. Ignore the signs of deceit and deviance amongst our neighbours and friends while throwing ideal home dinner parties and spend our weekends choosing wall paper for the guest room?

I didn't see that working for a moment.

'Look, Clara, lets get this mess all sorted then we can return to normality and figure this out.'

'Return to abnormality you mean David.' I had never seen a trace of dissatisfaction at her choice of life before. That disturbed me more.

'I'll be grateful just to survive the next few days.' I realised after I'd said it I was turning the conversation back to me. Me, me and me.

Clara changed subject and tone. 'Archie's had his hand sorted out by an Army doctor friend of John.' No "Sir John" this time. 'He's got several fingers in splints and his left hand now looks like a giant white paw.'

'Has he remembered anything else useful?' I asked.

'Nope. Between the painkillers and the vintage brandy I'm not getting a hell of a lot from him.'

'And Sir John?'

'What about Sir John.'

'Can we trust him?'

'You mean can you trust him.' She corrected me. 'David, you don't trust anybody. You never will and I honestly don't know what made you like that, but in your terms you can trust him as much as you will need to for your purposes. We're safe enough here and your secrets are safe enough.'

Clara was right. She knew me too well. It still stung but what she said was mostly the truth, but not entirely. I wanted most of all to know she was safe. I just didn't phrase it that way. I got to thinking about the smell of her long dark hair, the curves of her body and the liquid black eyes. I had the feeling I needed to say something else important to her, but I couldn't think what. 'OK Clara I'll check in with you tomorrow.'

'Yep, talk later David.' A cold black dismissal. She hung up.

I sat there dumbly holding the phone for a few moments before I came out of my trance and turned back to the computer. Now for phase two of last night's shenanigans. I needed to have chat with DC Jenkins and it needed to be on my terms. Therefore I needed to intrigue him enough to get him to meet me alone and at a location and time I chose.

I pulled his office extension from the force's directory I had obtained earlier. "Detective Constable Harold Jenkins, Major Crime." I converted it into a direct dial number based on what I had learned of their phone system. From the earlier research I'd also learned the format of the organisations email address. Using one of the Hushmail accounts I sent Jenkins a one line email containing the number of one of my few remaining disposable phones.

It looked like I was going to need a trip to stock up on throw away mobiles. That would require finding a shop or maybe even two or three shops selling cheap pre-paid mobiles. They had to be shops with no CCTV and I would pay in cash, buying no more than one or two phones in each shop. Then repeat the same process in different shops to get the SIM cards. Then all over again in yet more shops to top up the SIM cards using cash. All in all the process of acquiring a half dozen throw always takes a whole day and a couple of hundred quid.

That's the price of anonymity these days.

I took the mobile with me but left it switched off and headed out to a phone box that wasn't covered by Big Brother. I found one after about half an hour. The going was slow as I had to be cautious and keep a look out for any of Mehmet's men that were out hunting for me.

I dialled Jenkins' number. A local male voice answered. 'DC Jenkins' phone, this is DC Reynolds.'

'Ah, hello could you get me DC Jenkins''

'He's in an interview at the moment, he should be back in about half an hour. Can I take your number and he'll call you back.'

'It's Tom Conran senior CPS prosecutor. Um, I'm not sure what extension I'll be on in half an hour. I'll call back.' I ended the call. At least he was on duty today.

I went and sat in a park for forty minutes and then called back. This time I got Jenkins. I recognised the hard London accent that sounded like it didn't take any shit. That quality could count for or against my plan depending on how well I played it.

'DC Jenkins.' He answered sounding both bored and resigned.

'Hello Harold, or do you prefer Harry?' I asked.

'Who is this, and yes it's Harry.' Slightly edgy, wary of being mucked about. I'd better play this straighter.

'Harry, I may be in a position to help you.'

'Oh, how's that then son, hurry up 'cos I'm a busy man.'

'You didn't like that SB man interfering in your interview did you?'

Silence. I could feel his mind going over *"How the hell does he know that"*. I'd baited the hook. 'Not sure I know what you're on about sunshine.'

'I've a feeling you're as mystified as I am about the Dinko and Malinkova case. I might be able to help you resolve some of your doubts about that and lead you to where they are.'

'Don't yank my chain. That case is closed and I've got more than enough ongoing ones to worry about.'

'From the way you spoke to the SB man before the last interview I'd guess you're not the sort of man to let that drop.' Right now Harry Jenkins would be figuring me for some sort of nut case or a psychic. 'Look, Harry I don't expect you trust me just like that. Do one thing for me. Try and get hold of the translator you used for the interview. I'll bet you that you can't. If that allows you conclude some thing's not quite right then check your inbox. There's a mobile phone number there. Leave me a message with your personal number and I'll call you and tell you some more.' I hung up. It was a slight gamble that he'd just ignore me. In which case I'd need to think of something else, but if I was even half right in my assessment of Harry Jenkins, he'd make the checks and call back. There was also an equal probability that he'd be disturbed by what I knew, or rather how I knew it. Jenkins may choose to alert either the SB guy or his superiors or possibly both.

If that was the case I was making it as impossible to track me as I could. The email address should be about as untraceable as you can get using the combination of Hushmail and Tor. The mobile phone I was leaving switched off. I'd only switch it on every so often when I was out and about at random locations. Any effort to track me by that would be nigh on impossible as well.

I went back home and remembered to eat. Brill came in meowing and I fed him too. Then I went out for another walk. I switched on the phone sitting on a bench in a church yard. There was a message waiting for me. It was a simple text with a mobile number. No way of telling if it was really Harry Jenkins' number. I called it.

''ello.' Harry's gruff voice.

'So was I right?'

'Yeah, you were, but that doesn't prove anything.'

'I agree. But there does exist a lot of evidence that can prove things. We need to meet, just you and I, so we can see we're both on the level.'

'That wasn't some bullshit masonic reference was it, 'cos if you're part of that nonsense you can take a running jump right now sonny.'

'Harry just a turn of phrase, but it's starting to sound like I've found the right copper to deal with.' For some reason that reaction warmed me to Jenkins. 'There will have to be a bit of cloak and dagger stuff however as I need to protect my anonymity when we meet.'

'Go on.' Suspicion in his voice.

'Take a drive to town, come alone. Bring this phone with you. Park up in the multi-story and walk out front. I'll let you know what happens from there.'

'This had better be worth it 'cos if not I'll give you a damn good kicking sunshine.' He cut the call.

I switched off the phone and headed back home. I picked up my personal mobile and a phone jammer. A small black metal unit bought online from China for a few pounds. The unit took out all the mobile phone bands and the GPS as well. It also chucked out a hefty dose of electromagnetic radiation. A device to be used sparingly.

I found a bus stop about a hundred yards up the road from the multistory with a decent sized queue to hide in. It was still cold so no one gave a second glance to my baseball cap and scarf wrapped round my blackened and bruised face.

Two buses and ten minutes later I saw Harry Jenkins emerge and stand hesitantly by the entrance to the car park. I switched on the phone and sent him a text. *"Walk through the alleyway into town and wait outside the grocers."*

A few seconds later I saw Jenkins reach into the pocket of grey suit jacket he wore. He read the message shaking his head at the absurdity of my precautions. He headed over the road and up the alley. I waited five minutes to see if anyone came out after him. No one did.

I took an alternate route and got into a coffee shop overlooking the grocers. I ordered an espresso and sat back from the windows and watched. Jenkins was pacing outside the grocers. I watched carefully to see if he was in contact with anyone either by phone or a covert radio. I saw no evidence of that and no one nearby seemed to be interested in him.

I gave him ten minutes of that then switched the phone back on. There was a message from Jenkins. *"Hurry up you bloody fool. It's cold out here."* I chuckled at that and then replied.

"Walk to the cinema, via the old market place." I sent that and finished my coffee.

Harry received the message and reluctantly started to trudge in the direction I'd given him. I noticed he walked with a very slight limp. It looked like one of his hips was giving him problems.

I followed him at long distance letting him get well ahead and often out of sight. I could do that because I knew in advance where he was headed and also because I needed to be outside the box of any team that might be following him looking for me. He reached the cinema and I was as confident he was alone as I could be. While he paced outside I went in and bought a ticket for a film starting in half an hour. As it was the first showing of the day the theatre was empty so I went into the darkened hall with it's odd non-smell that all cinemas have and made myself comfortable at the back.

I kicked away some empty pop corn containers the cleaners had missed and composed a last message to Jenkins. *"Buy a ticket for the 1130 showing of the Disney film. Come and sit in seat K13"* That would put him in the row in front of me. I sat and waited. This was about as good a location as I could find. It was nicely dim. With the gloom, the hat and the scarf he shouldn't get too good a look at me. Sitting down wearing a winter coat he wouldn't be able assess my height and build. The theatre had three exits, two at the rear and one at the side which would lead out into the crowded foyer. It also had two fire escapes leading directly outside. Should this not go according to plan I had several escape routes in place.

I heard one of the doors creak at the rear of the auditorium. I switched on the jammer. A wedge of light arced across the floor briefly before the heavy door swung shut leaving the hall in gloom once more. Old Harry was good. He had come in the exit at the rear, not using the entrance as anyone would naturally do. He clearly had street sense. I didn't look up as he threaded his way over between the rows of plush red seats, but I could hear him coming down my row. Was he planning on making a grab for me or was this just a show of exercising some control over the situation?

The creak of a seat being unfolded next but one to my left relieved my anxiety. Harry lowered himself slowly into the seat. Definitely a hip problem.

'Hello Harry.' I said. 'What's up with your hip?'

'I didn't do a fucking dance all over town just to talk about my health. I'll go to the doctors if I want to do that.' Gruff and irritable. I hadn't detected a trace of that when listening to the interview recording. While questioning suspects Harry must adopt some kind of calm, unruffled persona. Everything I was learning about Harry Jenkins was putting him higher and higher in my estimation. I pondered why at his age why he was still a Detective Constable. I was sure this was not the best time to ask.

'Sorry about the precautions, but I'm in a very vulnerable position.'

Harry grunted an acceptance to that. I stole a glance at him. He looked pretty much as he did in the pictures I'd seen. A thin wiry man in his fifties. Lean but developing a beer gut. His hair was prematurely and uniformly grey and cropped short, almost military short. His face was deeply lined and pitted and the bags under bloodshot eyes told of late sleepless nights. The grey suit was rumpled and creased and his tie half loosened.

'I won't waste time beating around the bush. I'm assuming you'd like to nail Ali Mehmet and his two thugs.'

'What I'd like to do to that slimy shit and his two pit bulls would send me to the big house for full life term, but yes, in lieu of that I'll settle for putting them away.' Spoken with a weary resignation. This was man familiar with the production line of justice.

'I'd like to help you do that. For reasons I can't go into Mehmet wants me dead. The two Turks have had one go already.'

'Then I'm surprised you're still around. I don't know how he does it but witnesses and rivals all just seem to disappear.'

'I'll let you in on his little vanishing trick, but first I'm taking a big risk talking to you. My methods are best described as unorthodox.'

'You mean illegal.' Harry cut in.

'Sometimes. For that reason and my mania for personal privacy I like to stay as far away from Police and official records as possible. I'm going to have to trust you that my involvement, even my existence doesn't get passed up to your superiors.'

Harry pondered that for a moment. 'Then just be very careful what you say to me. I'm happy to keep this under the table, but I won't have you putting me in a position where you or anyone else can put the squeeze on me.' I was hoping to do just that, but in a subtle, gentler way. With luck he'd never even notice. 'I may bend the rules, but I've never broken them so I'm not going to start now, even for a prize like Mehmet.'

"Fair enough Harry. Then it's Chatham House rules.'

'Chatham fucking what. Speak English.'

'Everything we discuss we can use, but we keep it all unattributable. I'd like to know your thoughts on how the arson case got dropped?'

'I thought you were going to tell me something useful?' Harry grumbled at me.

'I'll do better than that. You'll be able to have both the Pitbulls in custody by tonight and a shot at Mehmet. However, there's something about all this that doesn't make sense. I feel I'm missing something, missing something important.' The enduring mystery to Mehmet's get out of jail free card was bothering me. I had a suspicion it was very important.

'It worries me too. But it' not unheard of for the crown prosecution service to drop cases. Also evidence went missing as did witnesses and now even the translator's gone AWOL.'

'Tell me about the Special Branch man.' His presence in the interview bothered me and it had clearly annoyed Harry. I was thinking this topic might open him up a bit.

'Never seen him before, never seen him since and I don't care if I never see him again. But that's how those boys operate. Half of 'em think they're some kind of Secret agent. He showed up before we'd even finished booking Mehmet in.'

'What's his name?' I asked.

'Detective Superintendent Dan Jacobs. Though he's very young for that rank.'

'And where does he work out of?'

'Buggered if I know. Why are you so interested in him?'

'I have a feeling there's a link between him and Mehmet. You know he was talking to the Crown Prosecutor while you weren't around.'

'That doesn't mean anything, of course he'd bloody be talking to the prosecutor.'

'Not like this.' I pulled my phone out and held it out in front of him. I tapped the screen and the phone started playing the recording from outside the interview room after Jenkins and Dinko had left. I'd edited it to just the intelligible speech for brevity and I'd cleaned the audio up as much as I could.

Jenkins leaned forward straining to hear and decipher the faint speech.

"yes, you know who this is?" ...you are the head prosecutor for the region you can make this happen ...yes, if you have to cite defence of the realm..... any problems and you might suggest to...' ...that someone may well find a stash of kiddie porn on one of his hard drives. No it's not a bit harsh."

Harry grunted as the recording stopped. 'I don't want to know how the fuck you got that. You certainly are unorthodox and so is bloody

Detective Superintendent Jacobs.' He sat back in his seat and exhaled. 'This is getting mucky.'

'It's a lot muckier than that. I'm not really in a position to look into Jacobs, you are.'

'I'm not sure how I'll do it, those SB lot are very secretive.'

'In the meantime Harry it's time for the main feature.' I brought up the video player on my phone and set it going and handed it across to Harry. He took the phone in his hands with careful deliberation as if he was afraid it explode. In a way it was going to be just as devastating.

I sat back and watched Harry's face as my snuff video from the barn played out. The lines in his skin brought out in sharp relief by the glare of the tiny screen. His face went from suspicion to interest to concentration as he realised what he was watching. If I expected to see shock I was disappointed. Harry's expression set in focused grim mask. There was no shocking Harry and even if there was I don't believe he'd let anyone see it.

The film finished and Harry breathed out. 'Jesus fucking Christ.' He carefully handed the phone back to me and unconsciously wiped his hands on his trousers.

We both sat in silence for minute then Harry said, 'of course it's no bloody good as evidence. Unless...'

'Unless I agree to take the stand you mean.'

'Yeah, and I take it you won't be doing that any time soon.' He spoke sadly.

'I might not have to.'

'There's more?' Harry asked.

'Much, much more. In a pit, near that barn are most of Dinko and Malinkova.'

'Most of?'

'Well almost all of them. And a few others.'

'Fucking hell. You've gone up in my estimation.'

'Well you've gone up in mine.' I offered.

'Steady on old son, lets not get engaged just yet. I still need something I can use. We old style police usually like to have a little of what we call "evidence". We're a little quaint like that.'

'Well then Harry. A little more cloak and dagger stuff.' I handed Harry the throw away phone I'd been using to communicate with him. 'Keep hold of that. All communication between us will go through that. I'm assuming the police monitor all their phones and computers with great zeal. So that phone will be reasonably secure.'

Harry turned the phone over in his hands like he wasn't sure whether to accept it. I could understand his hesitation. He'd probably run informants before and this was a turn around. It would feel a little like I was running him, which was partly correct. He pocketed the phone. The deal was done Harry was mine, well as much mine as any trained bloodhound could be.

'Now I'm about to give you a big hand, well two actually.' I resisted laughing at my own razor wit. 'I'll text you the location of the killing ground. I suggest you take a healthy winter ramble in the location and accidentally discover that place this afternoon.' I handed him over the phone I'd stolen from the Turk. 'You'll find that laying around the barn. It seems those sick fucks were recording their crimes. On the phone you'll find a copy of the video you've just watched. I've modified the metadata on the file to fit the phone.'

'The meta what?' Harry barked.

'Never mind, but It'll keep your forensic boys happy and will look good in court.' Harry nodded. 'In the two Turk's flat you'll find enough fingerprints and DNA from Dinko and Malinkova to keep any jury happy that they were at the flat. You'll also find some trophies that pair have kept.'

'Trophies?' Harry was intrigued.

'Body parts. The bits of Dinko and Malinkova that aren't in the pit. To be exact a pair of hands. One from each. One is hopefully still in the freezer the other is in the water tank.'

'I'm starting to think unorthodox is little weak for what you do.' Harry muttered. 'The only problem is I can't just go waltzing into the flat even if I knew where it was. There's still that little inconvenience of the law. So far I've got nothing I can take to a magistrate for a warrant. Unless..'

'unless I become a witness.' I added.

'and yeah I get it and to be honest I don't blame you.'

'Getting in won't be a problem.' I said not able to keep the smugness from my voice. Sometimes I'm just so sharp I cut myself. 'Remember Section seventeen of PACE.' More bounty from the hours of tedious research I'd done prior to my recce at the Police Station.

'of course the police have a power of entry for saving life or limb or preventing serious damage to property.' Harry parroted it out. He must have learned it by rote. 'But I don't see how that helps me.'

'Later this evening there will be a call to a disturbance from that address. The call will give the police enough cause for concern that they'll be happy to force entry to the flat. Just make sure you're on duty and happen to be passing. With the killing ground, the video and the forensic evidence you'll find at the flat you should have enough to take the pair off the streets.'

'Done up like a bloody kipper.' Harry chuckled. The first time he'd shown anything remotely like a smile. 'I just wish there was something to connect all this to Mehmet.' He added.

'So do I. There's a chance you might get them to talk, but these two aren't low level hired help like Dinko and Malinkova. Leave it with me and my unorthodox methods and I'll get you something on Mehmet.'

'Well I honestly thought I'd be wasting my time meeting you. I was wrong about that.' Harry pulled himself to his feet with a grunt as his bad hip stuck. He turned and held out a hand to me.

'So do I escape the kicking then?' I asked him leaning forward and took his proffered hand in my gloved fist. As I shook I pressed my thumb down on his first knuckle.

Harry chuckled. 'For now sonny, for now.' He turned and started shuffling along the seats, he paused and called back over his shoulder. 'I know you're not going to give me your real name, but what do I call you?'

I thought for a second. 'Call me the Bugman.'

Harry nodded and made his way out.

17 Saturday 19th January 1930 Hours.

Kippered.

I'd stayed and sat through the film. Seventy minutes of Disney's latest piece of cultural theft and distortion, punctuated by the occasional crying child and the conversation of the bored adults accompanying them. I was fairly confident Harry hadn't brought anyone along with him and wouldn't have anyone waiting outside for me, but I still felt it sensible to wait and leave amid the crowd when the film finished.

I was pleased with the way the meeting with Harry had gone. As far as our interests coincided I was starting, not to trust him, because that would just be foolish, but to have a certain confidence in the way he would act.

I stayed in and off the streets until it was dark and time for my next act. I packed a small satchel with tonight's tools, wrapped my scarf up high and pulled on my gloves and hat. It had warmed up a little due to heavy cloud cover that felt like it lurked just above the street lamps, reflecting the yellow glow back down to the damp streets.

Once away from the house I turned on my last disposable phone reflecting that somehow Mehmet was going to have to pay for the expenses incurred. I sent a text to Harry asking how he was doing. I got a quick reply.

"Finally back at the station. Invigorating day out in the country. Met up with our two friends."

I took that to mean he'd completed the first part of our plan and *accidentally* discovered the crime scene. So far so good.

I sat in the church yard looking at the windows to the Turks flat through a small pair of binoculars. The lights were on and the

colourful flickering coming off the walls told me the giant TV was on.
I couldn't see any movement. I went to the phone box round the
corner I'd used to phone Mehmet yesterday. I dialled the landline of
the flat with the number I'd obtained. After a few rings it was
picked up with a gruff voice. 'Buyrun!'

I put on a local accent. 'Hi, is Gavin there.'

'No. No Gavin here. Wrong number.' And the phone was slammed
down.

The car was out front so it looked as though the Turks were in. I
went back to my ecclesiastical vantage point and spent another ten
minutes observing through the lenses. I really wanted to positively
ID both Turks so the Police could pick them both up at once. I
realised I was delaying unnecessarily. Even if Jenkins didn't get
both, the remaining one would be forced into hiding and would be
removed from the game.

I had the new van I'd yet to pay Duncan for parked a couple of
streets away. I walked back to it and pulled on a hi vis vest and a
white hard hat. I'd already followed the phone lines back from the
flat, across a telegraph pole and down into a green cabinet up the
road. I drove to that now and parked up next to it. I retrieved a tool
box from the back and put it down next to what the telephone
company call a PCP, a primary connection point.

I used my cabinet key. This was one of the older ones that opened
with just square shaped tool like a socket spanner. Inside was a
tangle of hundreds of pairs of wires coiling around the metal
shelves, some affixed by cable ties and some not. Some labelled and
some not. This PCP was a mess. Some you opened and they were
neatly laid out with each pair of wires methodically numbered. This
wasn't. I searched through the punch down block were the pairs
terminated. This could take a while to find the correct pair.

I wasn't worried too much about where I was. I was a guy in a hard hat and a hi-vis. These alone are usually enough to make you almost invisible and gain you access to the most surprising of locations. In addition I had a fake ID card I'd made some time ago, it looked almost as aged as the Telephone van parked beside which would even check back to the company if its plate were run through. It was late enough that most legitimate phone engineers would be off the road. I was just a poor worker fixing an urgent fault at the weekend.

I took an engineer's handset from my tool box. I connected the handset to the first potential wire pair and dialled 17070. I got the circuit number read back out to me. I kept on with this for about half an hour until I got the right line.

I checked the street was empty and got my mobile out. Saved on it was an audio recording of shouting and fighting in Turkish. I had scoured YouTube for a clip from a suitable Turkish film. I set that playing and held it near the microphone of the handset then dialled three nines.

The operator answered on the first ring. 'Which service do you require?'

I did my best effort at a vaguely Eastern European accent. 'Police please, hurry.'

'Putting you through now.' I heard the click as the line was connected through to the police control room.

'Please help!' I pleaded in an accent somewhere East of the iron curtain. 'They try kill me.'

The operator tried to calm me down and get some sense out of me. I kept quiet and let her hear a good section of the *background* noise. I came back on the line. 'They kill me, they kill friend. Hand in fridge. Please come fast.' I deliberately forgot to give them the address, it would be on the screen in front of them anyway.

I unplugged and closed the cabinet and got back in the van. Five minutes later I heard the banshee wail of approaching sirens. Two patrol cars sped past me without a second glance. I moved the van nearer the church and went back into its grounds.

I set myself up with the binoculars and sat down to watch the show. I didn't need to do this, but I wanted to. I'm a watcher not a participant, I'm paid to observe other people play out their most private dramas. This little escapade was my first time orchestrating the mayhem. I loved it. Sitting in the shadows watching the seeds of chaos, I had carefully sown, flower into confusion. It was a heady drug.

I saw movement. A flash as the TV went off. Even from this distance I could just make out the hammering on the door. I regretted not bringing out a parabolic mic so I could hear the scene play out. One large figure came to the windows and was looking out. I saw the shadow of the other hovering by the door.

More sirens as another marked car arrived. One officer walked round to the rear looking up at the windows and talking into his radio. I got up into a crouch prepared to move if the policeman worked out, as I had, that the best vantage point were where I was currently lurking.

I picked up a muted thump which I was guessing was the flat door being put in. I saw shadows move and then one of the Turks pressed up against the windows two policemen behind him clearly pinning him against the window while they cuffed him. He stared angrily out the window towards me. He couldn't see me or know I was out there, nevertheless it sent a chill down my spine. He was pulled away from the window.

I left my spot and ambled past the house. A cluster of police vehicles lights still flashing gave the street a surreal feeling as blue and red shadows strobed over walls. I couldn't resist walking past. The front door to the building was open and a uniformed officer stood there writing in his notebook. I carried on as a blue Skoda was parking up. Harry Jenkins got out arms full of evidence bags and boxes of rubber gloves. As we passed on the pavement he gave me subtle nod. Beneath my scarf I grinned.

The two Turkish psychopaths well and truly kippered as Harry had put it.

This was hubris writ large. This feeling of power, of being able to reach out and manipulate events from the shadows was intoxicating. I started thinking I might do a bit more of this. No more vicarious observation. I could be the puppet master pulling the strings.

I went back and parked the van a couple of streets away from my house. A celebration was in order, I could walk the streets without fear that the pair of ex-wrestlers would suddenly turn up and cart me off to my doom. I headed for quiet local hostelry, 'The Copper Beeches' for a pint or two.

I was just heading towards a quiet corner with my pint when I heard a text message come in on the "*Harry*" phone.

"*Two friends staying with us for a while. Thanks for the hand(s).*"

So phase two complete. By now Mehmet should be feeling the pinch and hopefully running a little scared. I was slowly slipping control of the situation from his grip and into mine. I sipped my beer and idly surveyed the customers in the bar. The Harry phone buzzed again.

"*Quelle suprise, Jacobs has just turned up.*"

This was unwelcome. How had he got there so quickly? I'd only just left the Turks flat within the last twenty minutes. I doubted the pair had even reached the police station yet. The more I encountered Jacobs the more I was convinced that he was a key piece in this puzzle. There was also the very disturbing thought that maybe

Jacobs could pull his trick again and get these two released. That idea was going to sit in my head and ruin my evening off.

I used my personal phone to do a bit of web searching and compiled a list of local newspapers and radio stations. I threw in a few national ones for good measure. I went to the bar and changed a ten pound note into coins. There was a pay phone in the corridor leading to the games room. I went to it and started dialling.

An hour and forty minutes later my voice hoarse from talking and my change depleted, I called it quits. Some had been closed, some hadn't been interested, but I managed to leak selective details to a half a dozen media outlets. If they could be bothered to follow my tip off, things should soon start appearing on the news. What news organisation wouldn't want to follow up a tale of multiple murder and a gruesome death pit.

I was on my third pint and starting to get about as close to relaxed as I'm able. I was periodically flicking through a few news web sites when I got a hit. A breaking news story on a national daily's site. One I hadn't even called. Some ambitious reporter had probably sold the story on.

The headline read: *"Pit of Death! The police today made a gruesome discovery of a pit containing several dead bodies. None of the victims have yet been named but a police spokesman confirmed that two males are currently helping police with their enquiries."*

That should slow Jacobs down if he was protecting Mehmet. I doubted even Special Branch would be able to interfere now the story was out and going global.

18 Sunday 20th January 0834 Hours.

Trust.

I had woken early partly because there was a lot to do preparing for my next phase against Ali Mehmet and also because I wanted to revel in the results of my actions. I don't posses a TV so I had content myself with watching the news via the web. The story was everywhere. It must have been a slow news day because my story led. I ended up wasting an hour to pure indulgence. One TV news station had even chartered a Helicopter to overfly the death pit. I clearly wasn't the only one overjoyed at the coverage. I noticed the Home Secretary had taken the opportunity to quietly announce more surveillance and interception laws. The furore from the death pit relegated that piece of liberty sapping news to an also ran.

I doubt many people ever get to watch the breaking and news and sit there satisfied in the knowledge that they did it and no one else knows. I began to understand the exhilaration some serial killers get from their work. Here I was sat concealed in the shadows on the edge of civilisation covertly and quietly directing the affairs of men. I had become the trickster God, Loki, Prometheus, Coyote or Tengu. Take your pick. And nobody saw me walking amongst them. No one even guessed I existed. No one except Harry Jenkins.

Harry sent me a message at just gone nine. It read simply, *"Let's meet."* I pondered what that could mean. Was this now the point at which he drags me in, maybe to try and coerce me into being a witness? Or was there some problem with our little plan. I sent him a reply. *"Why?"* and got an almost immediate response. *"Need to talk about Jacobs."* This didn't put my mind at any greater ease. I didn't want to have to waste the time in setting up a secure meet again, however if his message was true then Harry could have information I needed.

212

I grabbed up my jammer and the small pair of binoculars and walked through town. On the way I sent Harry a message. *"Same starting point as before."* I made sure I got there well ahead of him again and this time went up to the roof of the multi-story. I stood directly under one of the CCTV cameras monitoring the car park, out of it's field of view so none of the operators would become suspicious at my lurking.

A little after ten I saw Harry's Skoda turn in. Looking down from above he seemed to be the only one in the vehicle. A minute later I recognised Harry's limping gait stop outside the entrance. I sent him a further text. *"Coffee shop in Duke street."* I was going easy on him this time giving him much less of a walk. I stayed at my eagle's perch watching and getting more confident.

If I had been tasked with catching me I'd have put a team into the car park ahead of Harry along with some foot mobile operatives in the surrounding streets. A ten man team would have just about covered it. Harry trudged out of sight and I remained vigilant. A couple of minutes after that I sent Harry the last message. *"Get yourself a coffee and wait for me."* and prepared to move. As I did so I noticed a silver Ford Focus pull up opposite the multi-story, directly beside the alleyway Harry had used a few minutes before. Something didn't feel right about this car.

Staying one step ahead of almost anything unpleasant relies a lot on *gut* feeling. When something doesn't look, smell, sound or feel right it's worth a second look. A false positive is a lot less problematic than missing the signs of incoming trouble.

Using the binoculars I took a closer look. The car had extra antennas fitted. A glass mounted mobile phone one and the characteristic loaded whip of a TETRA radio on the roof. That pretty much confirmed the car was police, or at any rate government owned. A short haired man in a grey wind cheater got out the passenger side and headed down the alley without a second glance.

213

The annoyance of this development was slightly offset by the satisfaction that my elaborate precautions had paid off. The car pulled away and I started in haste down the stairs and managed to reach the end of the alley just as the foot operative got to the other end. I hurried to catch him up. I was analysing the situation as I went. They hadn't been in visual contact with Harry, they'd arrived too long after him. However they did seem to know where he'd gone. That could be explained if there was already a team in place, but I didn't see anything to confirm that. There were two other explanations, either Harry was in contact with them or they were tracking him some other way.

I followed Grey Anorak through the High street keeping him in sight. He didn't seem to be in communication with anyone. He turned into Duke street and went into the coffee shop. I gave him five minutes and walked past the front, glancing carefully in. He was sat with a large cappuccino way back in the shop clearly keeping an eye on Harry. I moved on wary that there was at least one other guy working in this team.

There was no easy way to resolve this situation. I felt slightly sad as I wanted to be able to trust Harry. Well, trust him as far as was operationally necessary. I sent him another text. *"Guy in a grey anorak over your left shoulder. Know him?"* I hit send and waited. Harry would know he'd been busted and I guessed he would be man enough to admit it, not only that but it would force the whole team to stand down now that they had been compromised.

I got the reply quickly. *"No. Should I?"* Was Harry playing it dumb. He'd seen my work now and he knew how good I was. I decided to play along giving him a little benefit of the doubt and some more rope to hang himself.

"He's Police and he's following you, but you should know that already." I sent, typing furiously.

A little longer to reply this time, maybe Harry was weighing up his options. *"No one knew I was coming here."* If I were to assume Harry was being honest with me it would mean something else was going on here, something bigger and a lot more worrying. That hypothesis clearly didn't fit Occam's razor. The simplest explanation was that Harry was setting me up. The nagging doubt I had was that no one sends a two man team to catch someone like me. Harry certainly wasn't that stupid. You could only rely on a team that small if you had some kind technical advantage.

I had to quickly think up some kind of way to test that theory and thereby either clear or Damn Harry. I couldn't explain why I was making this effort instead of just walking away. Harry could be a useful ally, maybe it was a simple as that. I formulated a plan in my mind. Not perfect as it used the same location as yesterday. Never a good idea to repeat yourself, but it was the nearest crowded place with multiple exits.

I headed off, first going back into the high street and making a quick stop in one of the shops that sell everything for a pound. I spent two pounds and bought a pack of fridge magnets and some glue. I then walked to the cinema and bought a ticket to a random film.

Once through the gate I went into the toilets where, ensconced in a stall, I used my penknife to prise the thin magnet from the colourful front. I sent Harry a text asking him to head to the cinema for the second time in two days and then I went into the theatre. Same as yesterday the hall was empty which was what I had hoped for. I worked fast stashing the jammer under the back of seat F10 and then walking towards the glowing green sign for a fire escape door in the right hand wall.

I coated one side of the thin strip of magnet with glue and held it for a moment while the adhesive started to set and become tacky. In the top right corner of the door frame was the contact switch for the alarm system. Opening the door would set the alarm off. I didn't want that to happen. I slipped my magnet carefully between the contact switch on the frame and the magnetic strip on the door, making sure the glued side was facing the switch. I gave it a minute to take then cracked the door open with the push bar. No alarms and no staff rushing in to check. So far so good.

Back in the foyer I went to the teenager working the box office and explained my friend was running a bit late and asked to buy a ticket for seat G10 and could I leave at the office for him. The kid obliged and kindly put the ticket in an envelope which he labelled with his name. I then got back outside where I found a card shop with a nice view of the front of the cinema. I sent Harry his final text instructions and then pretended to browse birthday cards while watching the street outside.

Crunch time was coming up. Harry arrived, his shambling gait crossing the street in front of me and going into the cinema. The grey anorak arrived a few moments later. For a two man team they were giving Harry a lot of distance. That told me they either were in cahoots with Harry or they had some kind of technical tracking going on. Either way in a few minutes I'd know.

By now Harry should be collecting his ticket from the box office. Grey anorak hurried inside, he wouldn't want to let Harry get too far away in a building. I kept watch for a little while longer and soon spotted the second part of the team. Short haircut again, but this time a blue jacket. He kept watch on the doors from the street outside. If Harry were following my instructions he would be retrieving the jammer from the back of the seat where I had hidden it. He would switch it on and leave by the fire escape all before grey anorak could queue up, buy a ticket and follow him in.

I moved on from the birthday cards to the anniversary ones just as blue anorak took a phone call. Still talking into the phone he rushed into the cinema. My ever suspicious mind told me this could still all be an act and Harry was setting me up, but another part was hopeful that Harry wasn't involved.

I ended up buying a *"congratulations on your new house"* card to avoid looking suspicious. Fifteen minutes later the anorak wearing surveillance pair emerged blinking into the winter sun. They didn't look happy as they paced in front of the cinema in hot debate. No doubt blaming each other, or more likely the tech guys for losing their quarry. When they weren't looking I slipped away.

Harry was waiting for me in another cafe down a side street on the other side of town. Well away from any CCTV cameras just to be on the safe side. I did a circuit of the street checking the area front and back. Things looked clean so I went in.

Harry was seated at the back where he had a good view of the door. I went straight over to him.

'More bloody cloak and dagger.' He grumbled at me. On the table in front of him were three mobile phones, the one I'd given him and I guessed a personal phone and a work phone. All were stripped down, batteries and SIM cards removed. He was showing me he was clean. He saw me glance at the table. 'Search me if you want.'

'Either it's already too late or I can trust you.' I told him.

'So who were they.' Harry asked.

'Take a guess. The car was fitted with an Airwaves aerial, so I would assume your lot.'

'They weren't local or I'd have recognised them.'

'Who knew you were coming?'

'No one. I'm not even on duty today officially.'

'Harry, potentially that means they are keeping tabs on you all the time.'

'Of course I bloody realise that.' Harry was angry. 'We can assume I wasn't followed yesterday morning or we'd know about it by now. So that means something I did yesterday has upset someone.'

'We can assume the phone I gave you is secure or they'd have known what the plan was at the cinema.' I said re-assembling the phone. 'Therefore I'd say they're tracking you by one of the other phones.'

'Fan-bloody-tastic I've only had my new phone a month.' Harry shock his head in disbelief.

'Chuck it away and claim on the insurance.' I told him.

'Leave off, that wouldn't be honest.' He chided me and then pulled himself to his feet and limped over to the next table. He snatched up a discarded newspaper, glanced at the cover before flinging it onto the table top in front of me.

I looked down at it and the headline *"Death pit!"* glared back up at me. Harry lowered himself back down with a grunt. 'Your doing?'

I nodded.

'Wouldn't normally condone something like that, leaking details to the gutter press, but in this case well done.' He grumpily conceded.

'How so?'

'Let me take you through it.' Harry said tapping a forefinger down on the newspaper. 'Before I'd even got to the station with that pair of rottweilers, Jacobs was waiting and he wasn't a happy man. I can tell you he didn't buy that story of my accidentally discovering the barn and the pit.'

'Yeah, that was a bit weak, you don't really fit the profile of a rambler.'

'Be that as it may. Jacobs may not believe it, but he can't prove anything. Anyway, where was I? Jacobs starts wanting to know what evidence I've got and where I got it from. Then he goes into the whole business at the flat demanding to know who called it in.' He paused and looked at me. 'I got the distinct impression he knows you're involved.' He paused. 'Well, he suspects someone's involved.'

'But he can't prove anything?' I asked.

'No. The only one knows about your part in all this is me and you can rest assured I won't be bubbling you up, for one thing it would drop me deeper in the shit than I could swim out of.'

'You're wrong about one thing there Harry.'

'What's that?' I could see his mind turning trying to figure out what he'd missed.

'You're not the only one who knows my involvement are you? Mehmet knows full well I've seen the death pit. He tried to send me on the one way trip there and he must have guessed I'm behind the rest of it.'

'OK, so what you're suggesting is that when I lifted the two Turks, discovered the killing site. Mehmet shits himself and calls Jacobs to fix the problem. i.e. to locate you.' Harry drummed on the table deep in thought. 'But why call Jacobs, what is he to Mehmet?'

'The question, Harry, is what is Jacobs?'

Harry's face brightened. 'Yes, what is Jacobs, there's something doesn't smell right about him and it's not just his aftershave. He doesn't really talk like a cozzer and he's too young to be a detective Super. There's just too many things don't add up.' Harry scratched his head. 'He just breezes in and out like he owns the place.'

'So if he's not Police, then what is he?' I asked.

'Search me, SOCA or maybe even Box. They're about the only people who can come swanning in and out of a nick like that.'

'I think you're getting warm Harry. Box have got the access to do something like track your phone. But if that's the case we're in deeper shit than we realised.' We both paused and sat in silence for a while. 'So what does that make Jacobs to Mehmet, his handler? Is Mehmet an informer for him or something else?'

'Sunshine, that's the bloody key to all this. I'm limited with what I can do. This might be time for some more of your unorthodox methods.'

'Where's Jacobs now, if he is Box then that makes my job much harder.' I wasn't relishing the prospect of going toe to toe with Mehmet and the security services.

'Funny thing that, as soon your leak hit the headlines he vanished like a cockroach when the light comes on, scurrying for cover. That all backs up our idea about him doesn't it?' Harry shook his head sadly. 'still no bloody evidence against either him or Mehmet though.'

I left Harry advising him to watch his back. He grumbled something about being a bloody grown up and able to look after himself. I needed to plan my next move very carefully. I was starting to become more aware of what I was up against and none of it was very comforting.

19 Sunday 20th January 1340 Hours.

Background Checks.

Sunday afternoon on a bright clear winters day. Perfect for a spin in the country. I'd got a protesting and hung over Duncan McLeish out of bed to borrow a car and was headed out to Sir John's country pad, but I wasn't enjoying the scenery. Instead I was focused on the latest developments and what the hell I was going to find when I got there.

After meeting Harry I'd taken a more cautious and paranoid circuit home. Once there I started some basic web searches on the name Dan Jacobs. As I expected it didn't turn up anything that could possibly be a link to our mysterious Detective Superintendent. I was going to give up when I remembered I'd intended to do a quick background check on Sir John Hamilton.

Being a "sir" made the job fairly straightforward. It's not so easy to hide when you've been knighted. There were news reports covering the death of his wife a year ago and there was the New Year Honours list of a decade ago where he got his promotion. Lt. Col John Hamilton (ret.).

I dug a bit deeper and looked historically. He'd mentioned being blown up in Northern Ireland in nineteen seventy seven. I dug around a bit and found reports of an explosion in a Laundrette and a Captain Hamilton was mentioned as being injured. So far he was checking out. I did some more research and while it didn't specifically mention that laundrette it appeared the 14th Intelligence company had been running a laundrette as a front for intelligence gathering.

So that was likely Sir John's background. He'd obviously gone on to greater things as I doubted they gave away knighthoods just for being first in the canteen queue. I moved on to companies house and found his entry listing all his many and varied directorships. I was about to close down and start preparing equipment for my next move when I realised something was nagging me.

I rechecked the list of Sir John's directorships and something was staring at me, but I couldn't figure out what. I opened up my connection diagram on Ali Mehmet and started scrolling through the list of entities. I found the point of convergence that had been nagging away at my subconscious. *"Fortis holdings"*, the company that owned the business park containing Unit 14. And old Sir John was a director.

There's no such thing as coincidence. Even if there is it pays to behave as though there isn't. This one little link could mean so many things. Sir John's entry into this little drama wouldn't be co-incidence. That would in turn mean someone had linked Clara to me. My mind was spinning off into infinities of conspiracies. Why we all weren't already chopped into pieces somewhere was a mystery.

The fastest way to resolve all this was probably not the most sensible, but I was pushing the accelerator of the little car as hard against the floor as I could while I sped along the dual carriageway to confront Sir John.

I parked up just off the country lane in front of the gate to a field. Sir John's sprawling acreage was a short hop across the field. I climbed the gate and made my way along the hedgerow. A gap in the hedge permitted me into a part of the garden full of stunted fruit trees. I circled the house looking for anything that made me uneasy. Satisfied I knocked on the front door.

Clara opened the door. 'I wasn't expecting you back here so soon.'

I cut her off. 'Is that a problem?' I asked, unsure why that had slipped past my lips.

'Of course not. What's up? Why so serious?' Her brow furrowing.

'I need to have a chat with Sir John.'

'You're not getting all paranoid on me are you?' Clara asked a edge of concern in her voice.

'It's not paranoia if people are out to kill you.' I said flatly.

Clara sighed and led me down the hall and into the front room. A couple of good quality sofas with floral patterns and the almost anachronistic touch of antimacassars suggested this room had been furnished by the late Mrs Hamilton.

Sir John stood from where he had been taking tea in one of the armchairs. He was wearing green cords, a brown checked shirt and a cream coloured woollen cardigan with over sized buttons. The veritable image of a kindly old uncle. Only the hard lines etched into a face clean shaved every morning with military precision betrayed the carefully studied character I assumed he was playing.

'Would you like some tea David?' He asked politely.

I declined with a wave of my hand. 'I need to have a chat.'

'A chat.' He repeated back slowly taking time to ponder each word. 'That sounds ominous. Please have a seat.'

I sat in the chair he'd indicated and he lowered himself opposite me picking up the bone china cup as he sat and sipping as his Earl Grey. 'What would you like to *chat* about?' Sir John enquired.

'I'd like to talk about Fortis Holdings.'

Sir John looked at me blankly. 'And this is because?'

'You're listed as a director.' I proffered, hoping he's just spill the beans and save me the time of going through various charades of ignorance.

'David, I'm a director of so many companies. I honestly can't remember the names of all of them. In fact I suspect I'm director of companies I haven't even heard of.'

'Explain please Sir John.' I wasn't believing his ignorance for a second, but I'd let him carry on spinning his yarn till I had something I could tie up his deceit with.

'As I intimated to you the other night, during my army career I found myself in the Dets in Northern Ireland doing the sneaky beaky work trying to catch terrorists.'

'Yep, the 14 Int. I got that reference.'

'After our intelligence gathering operation was compromised and I got blown up, I came back to London and was put to work in certain other government departments. Mostly admin. Boring stuff, but secret stuff, but it saw me through to my pension and got me a knighthood.'

'So cut to the chase Sir John, what does any of that have to do with Fortis Holdings?' He was rambling and what he was telling me seemed merely a diversion from what I wanted to know.

'From time to time these government departments need to engage in, shall we say, semi legitimate activities.'

'Semi legitimate. That's a good one.' I congratulated Sir John on his double speak.

He ignored me and carried on. 'In order to do that and insulate Her Majesty's government, shell companies, holding groups and the like are often set up. A lot of so called private military and security contractors are in reality fronts for the other government departments.'

'So what is Fortis Holdings?' This was interesting, but it still wasn't getting me anywhere.

'Old boys like me, trusted old boys with good names and good credit are used to set these companies up. We give it an air of legitimacy. We get to still be of use to our country and we get a nice little bonus and expenses.'

'So what the hell is Fortis Holdings.' I was getting annoyed now.

'I honestly don't know. A lot of the stuff gets set up with my name on it and I haven't the foggiest what's really going on, it's the old need to know.' Sir John surveyed his empty cup as if trying to divine from the tea leaves in the bottom. 'Can you tell me what the significance is?'

'Fortis owns a development of industrial units, one of which seems important in the business of Ali Mehmet.'

'Could be a coincidence, but,'

'but you don't believe in coincidence any more than I do.' I finished his sentence for him.

'Quite.' Sir John added.

There was a pregnant pause which I broke first. 'On the subject of coincidence.' I began, but as if on cue I heard the sound of tyres crunching over the gravel drive. We both rose at the same time and both found ourselves peeking through the net curtains.

'I'm not expecting visitors.' Pronounced Sir John solemnly.

The car was a black Range Rover. One of the high end models with tinted windows. It didn't give me a good feeling. I backed away from the window. 'Any idea who that is?'

'Not a clue.' Answered Sir John.

'Not very clued up today are we.' I added not being able to help myself.

Sir John turned to me looking slightly irritated. 'Get the others and go and wait in the Kitchen, I'll find out what, whoever it is, wants. Best stay out of sight. I think the less people know you're here the better for all of us.'

I didn't like the idea. I hadn't finished our *chat* and I certainly wasn't inclined to be very trusting of Sir John with all the unanswered coincidence hanging over him, however there wasn't really much alternative. I left the living room and found Archie loitering in the hall peering at the movement of an ancient Grandfather clock. I tapped him on the shoulder. 'No time for that Archie, follow me.' Archie looked at me blankly but followed in his staunch gait towards the Kitchen.

We met Clara coming out holding two tea cups. Archie and I blocked the hallway quite effectively. I said nothing but motioned Clara back into the kitchen. We dropped down a step and despite not being very tall I had to stoop under the lintel into the oak beamed kitchen.

This must have been the engine room of the house and probably the most comfortable part of it. The kitchen was larger than my flat and dominated by a giant Aga cooker at one end heating the space to an almost tropical temperature. In the middle was a large table and by the litter of glasses and mugs I guessed this was where Archie and Clara were spending most of their exile.

Clara went to protest my undue caution so I hushed her with a finger to my lips as I pulled the door closed behind us. I stopped short of completely closing the door and bent towards the gap with my left ear. I remained hunched over listening while I scanned the kitchen for a way out should I need it. There was a door in the wall to my right.

'Where does that door lead to?' I whispered to Clara.

She bent to my ear and whispered. 'It's the pantry.' No use as an exit but Clara's breathy whisper sent a shiver down my spine as I smelled her leaning in close.

'Any other ways out of here.' I asked.

'Only the kitchen window.'

'Do me a favour and open it as quietly as you can.' Clara nodded and went to the opposite corner of the room. I heard the doorbell go with a short angry buzz and Sir John's measured pace up the hallway.

The front door unlatched and I felt the slight change in air pressure push against the kitchen door I was holding as it swung open. I could make out people talking, but not what was said. Then the stamp of feet on the door mat and low pitched thump as the front door latched shut. Two sets of steps, Sir John's measured stride and another lighter pace.

'Come this way, this'll be a more comfortable place to talk.' From Sir John.

'Thank you Sir John. I hope I'm not intruding.' Another male voice. No discernible accent. I guessed early thirties or very late twenties. I recognised the voice. I'd heard it before. I couldn't match it to a face, but it had a familiarity to it.

'No, no you're not intruding. It's just I rarely get visitors.' Sir John's voice trailing off as he turned into the front room. Then all the sound was attenuated as the door to that room was quietly and carefully closed.

Then my mind made the connection. It was the link with conversation in the hallway and it being cut off. It was the Special Branch officer. Dan Jacobs or whatever the hell his real name was.

My pulse beat quicker. Not fear, not quite. This was something more like excitement. The fact Sir John hadn't dropped us in it already was a good sign. Still I wanted desperately to be a fly on the wall of their conversation. This is what I do and I do it well. The Bugman is the fly on the wall.

I closed the kitchen door and walked over to the table. I had no equipment with me, I hadn't planned on bugging anyone. I would have to improvise. I took stock of what I had on me; a penknife, a phone, some change and in my wallet a small mirror and a micro set of lock picks. Nothing especially useful. I glanced around the kitchen. All standard stuff, tea towels hanging under the sink, pots and pans nothing I wouldn't expect.

On the kitchen table was Clara's phone, the headphones still plugged in from where she must have recently been listening to music. I turned to Clara. 'Mind if I borrow these.' I said picking up the ear buds.

'I suppose so.' She frowned at me. Much more of this frowning and she'd get lines on her face. I took it as a yes and unplugged them from her phone. I looked at the jack plug on the end. Four rings. These were the kind of headphones with a mic built in so you could use them as a phone head set.

I unfolded the blade of my pen knife. The microphone was housed in the little plastic bulb along with the volume buttons. I used the blade to prise the plastic case open.

Clara gasped. 'What the hell are you doing?'

'I'm borrowing your headphones.' I answered without looking up, now engrossed in my work.

'Wrecking them you mean.' Her voice rising.

'Keep your voice down.' I calmly told her. 'I'm re-purposing them to a higher calling.' Out the corner of my eye I saw her fold her arms angrily across her chest and bite her lip. She wasn't a happy girl. Archie stayed sensibly quiet.

I freed the tiny electret condenser mic from the housing. It was attached by two gossamer thin wires. I used as gentle a touch as I could as I freed the mic and stripped away as much of housing as I could. I then cut both earphones off. I heard Clara sharply exhale. I dropped the wires onto the kitchen table and began scouting around the kitchen looking through drawers. Clara just stood and glared.

I found what I wanted under the sink. The tea towels were hanging from a small hook attached to a rubber suction cup which was affixed to the side of the porcelain sink. I pulled one free and chucked the tea towel onto the work top. I took my prize to the table. I used the penknife to slice of the thick square of rubber that held the hook. I discarded these and went back to one of the drawers from which I removed a meat skewer.

I opened the door to the firebox of the Aga and laid the skewer in it. I went and retrieved the tea towel I'd thrown earlier. When the end of the skewer was a nice deep red I used the tea towel to pick it up. I went over to the table and bored a hole through the middle of the rubber suction cup. I then quickly fitted the tiny mic into the hole using the hot end of the skewer to ensure a tight seal of melted plastic.

Another rummage in the drawers and a reel of electrical tape added the finishing touches. I plugged the other end into my phone and set the audio recorder app running. I counted quietly to five in front of the mic. I played the recording back. I was good to go.

I pocketed my phone and microphone and hauled myself through the kitchen window. I dropped down into the garden and keeping bent down below the level of the windows I threaded my way around the outside of the house.

Once at the front I used my pocket mirror to peer carefully around the corner checking the car in case anyone had remained in it or near it. The tinted windows prevented me being certain, but the car looked empty. I got flat down on the semi frozen ground and inched my way below the windows. I was hoping the winter remains of rose bushes would conceal me in case I had missed someone hiding in the car.

Below the living room windows I rolled onto my back and took out the mic. I licked the suction cup and slowly reached up until I'd reached the bottom of the pane. I slowly stuck the cup to the glass and then withdrew my hands. I plugged the cable into my phone and started it recording before concealing the phone beneath some stones and dried up old leaves.

I inched my way back round the corner every movement dragging my ever suffering ribs along the flower bed. Once safely round the corner I lay there with my mirror watching for the S.B man to appear. I'd quite like a look at my adversary.

It was starting to get dark and it had already got cold. I looked at my watch. I had only been laying here for twenty minutes. In my mind I ran through the possible perpetuations and combinations to explain what was happening. Harry Jenkins and I had come to the conclusion that Jacobs was most likely from one of the security services. Sir John had admitted that he had a connection to the security services. I wondered what he wasn't saying. If he were willing to admit to some kind of link, was he hiding something even more significant. None of this was tying in with Mehmet. It was his relationship to the spooks that bothered me most. There was a piece of the puzzle missing, probably several.

I heard the front door to the house open. I quickly slipped my mirror out and angled it around. A male in his late twenties stepped out, turned and shook hands with Sir John who was following a few paces behind. Hello Dan Jacobs, a small thin man with short dark hair neatly parted at the side. He had fragile features below thick black eyebrows and almost incongruous pale blue eyes. He wore a light grey suit, Green Barbour jacket with a black scarf hanging loose around his neck.

Hands shaken Jacobs walked over to his car, pressing on the key fob on the way. He walked with a proprietorial confidence that gave him an air of self entitlement. He didn't look back as he slid into the Range Rover. The car started and slowly rolled across the gravel and away down the drive. I heard the front door shut and gave it another two minutes before I scrambled round on hands and knees this time and retrieved my phone. I had seen a small summer house at the back of the garden during my approach to the house earlier. I headed there now to listen to my recording.

Not the best recording I'd ever made, but compensated by being done in a environment with almost no background noise. Jacobs and Sir John must have been talking a good few minutes by the time I got the bug placed it began with Jacobs. *"pleasantries aside Sir John, I'm under the impression you're retired."*

"That's correct I suppose, but as I'm sure you'll eventually discover, you never really retire from the service."

Jacobs ignored that and went on. *"Yet you still call in the old boy network for favours."*

"I don't follow young man."

"Two days ago you called Bertie Danforth to ask for a background check." Jacobs pressed on.

"Ah, Bertie. Good fellow. I often call him."

"Specifically you asked for anything we had on a certain freelance technical surveillance operator. What's your interest in him?"

"Oh, that, I'd forgotten all about that. I think someone mentioned something in the club, I was curious."

"So you've not met this person? He is a person of interest in a very sensitive job I've got running."

"Is he, oh that's a coincidence, and no I've never been introduced." Replied Sir John.

"Well Sir John, lets leave this as an unofficial visit that never happened and take this as a warning to steer clear of active operations." Jacobs must feel he's got some kind of pull talking to man almost three times his age like that.

I didn't want to waste time listening to the whole thirty seven minutes of the conversation so I began skipping through until I was interrupted by the door to the summer house suddenly opening. Sir John stood in the doorway. 'I think you'll find it easier and more comfortable to just ask me.' Then he turned about and headed back towards the house through the gathering gloom. I followed him.

This time we went to another room off of the main hall. The room was a deep brown leather and mahogany study. This one was clearly all Sir John's design. He took a large wing backed armchair and motioned for me to sit in a similar one set at a forty five degree angle. From a decanter he poured two measures of amber liquid into crystal tumblers. I brought mine up to my nose. It had the unmistakable peaty aroma of Laphroig.

'Well then.' Sir John broke the silence as he sipped his whiskey. I looked at him and said nothing. 'I think the time has come to clear up a few,' He gazed into the tumbler, 'misconceptions. Go ahead and ask anything you want. If it's something I can answer, I will. If it's not then I'll tell you.'

I had a lot of questions but no idea which were the important ones. 'Who is this Jacobs?' I tried for a starters.

'Jacobs? Is that what he's calling himself. He is Security Services. A rising star. One of the new breed. Made quite a name for himself in certain circles.'

'Why was he here?'

'My fault. I'm a little out of touch with service loyalties it seems. I have to confess after meeting you I made a couple of calls on the old school tie network to see who you were.'

'and you found out?' I cut in curiosity about what the state knew about me overriding everything else.

'Not a lot. There is a file on you. A couple of jobs you've done have indirectly been for us, all via cut out companies.'

'The sort of companies set up with you as a director.' I interjected.

'Quite. And the government likes to keep track of people like you.'

'They seem to want the monopoly on surveillance.'

'Yes, it would seem so. There are rumours in the house that the Home Secretary is planning to make your profession licensed. I imagine that will put a damper on your business.'

That last comment struck a nerve. Being tracked, catalogued and filed by the government would pretty much end my career. 'So how much does anyone know about me?'

'Not a great deal. We know your work but almost nothing about you personally.' If Sir John was telling the truth that was a small source of comfort. 'Refill?' asked Sir John holding up the bottle. I nodded my assent. 'We did know that you were linked to Clara though.'

That got my attention. 'Go on.'

'Much like yours, her business occasionally overlaps with the business of state security. Some of her richer clients are often persons of interest to the Service. Like you she has unknowingly worked for us.'

'So us meeting wasn't a coincidence?'

'My meeting Clara wasn't. I regularly hire her and she passes over bits and pieces she picks up while hob nobbing with rich Arabs.'

'That's still one coincidence too many and we haven't even got to Jacobs yet.'

'Fair point David. My attempt to tap up the old boys for information on you got back to Jacobs, as you call him, very quickly. Being retired and out of the loop I'm not privy to the office politics, but what I suspect is going on is the replacement of the old guard by the new breed, people like Jacobs.'

'None of that does anything to explain Jacobs connection to a Turkish drug boss who wants me dead.'

Sir John looked over his glass at me. I detected a slight glint in his eye. 'You're too focused on your own problems David. Don't lose sight of the bigger picture. Jacobs wouldn't have the slightest interest in drugs.' He took a long sip of the whisky. 'But the drug business does teach a very useful skill set.'

'You're talking in riddles.' I told him.

'I'm being as honest as I can, also consider that I may be as much in the dark as you about this.' Sir John rose from the arm chair. 'Now, I think it's high time you went out and actually did what I assume you're planning for Mehmet.' He held the door open for me.

As I walked out into the chill hallway I couldn't help but feel I was being subtly played. There were things going on the background I probably would never understand.

I found Clara and Archie sitting in the kitchen finishing the remains of a rabbit stew, from the shotgun leant casually against the sideboard I would have put money on Clara having killed the meat herself. I dropped the now truncated headphones onto the table.

'Thanks.' I said to Clara. I paused then couldn't resist a dig. 'So, how much did you tell Sir John about me?'

Clara's nostrils flared and she tossed her head back making the dark sheen of hair fall back off of her shoulders. There was even a little colour rising in her cheeks and she took a breath to say something and then suddenly paused as though she thought better of it. She smiled a sly reptilian smile. 'I've suddenly worked out why you're attracted to me.' She glanced down at her slender legs and shrugged. 'It's not my body. I've known what effect it has on men since I was thirteen. I'm used to that now. But oddly enough I don't think that's why your attracted me.' She looked away. 'It's my job.'

'Your job?' I asked dumbly. Everyone was talking in riddles today.

'My job. Maybe it's too oblique for you, but because I'm off at night with other men it means you've never really had to trust me have you?'

'Trust you, what do you mean?'

She let out a deep sigh. 'I can never be unfaithful to you can I? By definition you never have to trust me to be faithful.' She locked her eyes on me. 'That's what I've come to know about you. You are incapable of trust.' She held my gaze, but I was looking through her eyes, at what I couldn't tell.

After several deeply uncomfortable seconds ticked away Archie made a brave attempt to break the silence and change the subject. 'The farm.' Archie slurred out. 'Mehmet often joked about his farm.'

'What Archie?' I snapped. Clara had managed to wound me and now Archie was picking at the scab.

'It's just odd is all. Mehmet never owned a farm.' He hiccoughed.

I didn't dignify that with answer. I turned and left the house walking over the newly frosted field back to the car.

20 Sunday 20th January 1930 Hours.

Midnight in the garden of good and evil.

Time to really get things started. If I were going to get Mehmet off my back and unravel what had been going on I was going to have to do it using my methods. Now Mehmet had an idea of what I looked like I was limited to the set of techniques I could utilise.

Sadly Mehmet didn't have an office. The closest thing to that had been Archie's building that I was assuming Mehmet had burned down. Therefore the only place to really run him to ground was at his house. My plan was simple. Do a number on his house. Wire it for every bug I had in my arsenal and sit back and wait for the solution to come through my headphones.

Early evening found me standing in my hallway sweating from the thermal base layer, fleece top and trousers and set of combats over that. I wore a black woollen watch cap and leather gloves. Beside me was a large camouflage rucksack, some Hessian sacking and a roll of chicken wire.

I heard the solid thump of a diesel engine pull up outside. I cracked the door and confirmed it was Duncan McLeish in the ex-BT transit. He jumped out and slid open the sliding side door. I lugged the kit out quickly. Lest the neighbours see and jumped in. Duncan slammed the door behind me and got back in the driver's seat. He pulled quickly away.

'Evening old pal.' He greeted me cheerfully.

'Duncan.' I replied.

'Ok pal, take me through it one more time.'

'Simple Duncan, don't worry about it. We do one pass along the road to check everything looks OK. Then we go away and twiddle our thumbs for a bit.'

'Aye, I can do that right enough.'

'The second pass is crucial. Did you study the map I emailed you?'

'I did that.'

'So at the point I marked you slow the van to a crawl. I open the door.'

'And I do a quick three sixty to check everything's cool.'

'Correct and then I toss the gear into the ditch beside the road before rolling into it myself.' I said while applying cam cream to my face.

'And I accelerate away, not so much I spin tyres. Then I brake a little hard at the next junction to shut the sliding door.'

'That's it Duncan. Then you come to the RV point forty eight hours later.' I confirmed with him.

'I still think you've gone a bit soft in the head pal. No one wants to be doing a wee rural OP this time of year.'

'Have you taken out all the internal lights in this bus?' I asked.

'All done pal.'

'Ok Duncan, lets do it.'

We passed through the late Sunday evening streets all cold and empty, past houses where the ghostly blue flicker of TV screens back lit the curtains. We passed through town barely seeing a soul and the roads got more empty as we passed into the suburbs the houses we passed getting slightly larger with each mile out of town.

I'd spent some time studying satellite photos, ordnance survey maps and Google street view as well as the plans of the house I'd bought from the Land Registry. Mehmet's house was most definitely out of my price range, a moot point as I doubted I could afford a garden shed at today's prices. The building itself was two storeys high and had five bedrooms and three bathrooms. It had an attached garage and some out buildings that looked like a disused stables. A driveway ran some thirty meters from a gate at the road to a small hard standing outside the house.

The house was surrounded by several acres of grass which terminated in hedgerows. On two sides the grounds backed onto the golf course. On one side a farmer's field. I'd chosen the farmers field for the OP, it was the only choice really. The relief of the ground put that boundary a good few meters higher than the sides adjoining the golf course. Most of the way along the edge I'd have a clear view of the front door, garage and hard-standing. In addition the sun would be at my back most of the time it was above the horizon, lessening the chance of the low winter sun reflecting off of my optics and giving me away.

'OK Dave,' Duncan called from the front. 'We're coming into the target area now.'

I raised myself up so I was leaning against the back of the front bench seat. I peered carefully into the gloom outside as hedges whizzed past on both sides. There were no street lights out here a small fact that would make my job easier. We passed Mehmet's gate and I took a good look right. Lights were on in the house and a car on the driveway. Someone was home.

A few seconds later we passed my chosen de-camp site. It was just a grass verge with a small ditch and a hedge. Nothing untoward here. No cars in the vicinity. It all looked good. We drove away from the area and Duncan wasted twenty minutes idly driving round country lanes. We completed several large loops and headed back.

We came up the road the same way as before. This time slower. As we passed Mehmet's everything still looked the same. Duncan slowed still further and I carefully slid the door back doing my best to minimise the noise. I took hold of the first bit of kit and noticed Duncan do his all round mirror check.

'Ok pal, all clear.' He called back to me.

I grabbed the chicken wire and tossed that out into the ditch as Duncan used the gears to slow us to a crawl. The Hessian and rucksack went next as we slowed still further.

'Good luck pal.' Called Duncan as I jumped out, feet together hitting the grass verge and rolling out. The wind was almost knocked out of me, I was ready for that, but the ribs still jarred as I rolled. I lay still and flat in the frozen tufts of grass as Duncan's tail lights disappeared up the road as he gently accelerated away. There was a brief flare of red as he touched the brakes at the junction a few hundred meters up the road.

It was suddenly very quiet. I rolled into the ditch beside me and remained motionless, listening for any sounds that I had been observed. Nothing moved in the frosty landscape. I gave it another couple of minutes, not even a car passed. I then worked my way up the ditch collecting the gear I had thrown from the van and stashing it well into the thick grass growing out from the icy centre.

Listening out for any sounds of approaching vehicles, I left the kit where it was and crossed the road quickly stepping over the wire fence surrounding the field. I kept low to the fence until I came to the start of the hedgerow which screened me from Mehmet's property some fifty meters the other side. I checked out the whole length of the hedgerow till I judged I had found the best spot then I went back and retrieved my kit.

I went in low, burrowing in at the foot of a fat well grown section. I pulled the chicken wire in above me and pushed into the middle of the hedge, expanding out with the wire and using a pair of secateurs to create a small cave. I scraped away dirt from the ground, depositing what I dug up into a handy rabbit hole. I lined the little cave with the Hessian sacking sheets. Then I pulled in my rucksack before crawling outside to clear up any signs I'd been there and check the hide was invisible from that side. Satisfied I crawled back in.

I got my sleeping bag out from the top of the rucksack and wiggled my way into that. Getting into position and building the hide had worked up quite a sweat. Now sitting motionless in sub zero temperatures I was going to get quite cold.

Next I set up the optics. I pulled out my Canon digital SLR, then my heaviest bit of kit, the night vision lens. These things cost a few thousand, if you can get a supplier to sell one to someone who isn't police or military. Way above my budget. However an old image intensifier tube can be bought on the surplus market for under a hundred quid. Mine came from the periscope of a submarine, but was essentially the same bit of kit as a military Starlight Scope. While heavier, larger and emitting an audible buzz these triple cascade tubes could still outperform the smaller and lighter modern generation three tubes.

To make my lens all I'd had to do was fit a suitable primary lens and an adaptor to fit the front of my DSLR. I'd mounted the whole lot in an aluminium tube with a battery pack and an on-off switch then I sprayed the whole lot matte black. All for under £200 quid.

I set the camera and scope on a small sand bag, it was far too heavy for a tripod. The end of the scope well back from the edge of foliage. I began my watching.

Getting into a house to plant bugs has some similarities to burgling a house as far as not getting caught inside goes. However my task is much harder. Not only do I have to get in and out undetected, but there has to be no suspicion anyone has been in that shouldn't have been. By comparison a burglars job is easy.

In order to do it successfully I've found it necessary to follow certain steps. At the start is the reconnaissance. You need to spend as much time as you can to learn the layout, habits and patterns of the house. In this case I was doing that via a rural observation post. I'd already done the research and obtained plans and maps. Now I had to sit and watch and learn who came and went, what times they came and went, which parts of the house were used when and what security was in play. Once I had that information I could carry out the CTR or close target recce. Then I would go in close and take a good look at the access and egress points, locks, cameras and alarm systems. Only then would I be able to formulate the plan for getting in and out, if it were at all feasible.

I fervently hoped it was feasible. I didn't really have any other cards to play at this point, unless Harry Jenkins came up with something, which I doubted. In fact I had started to get the unwelcome feeling that both Jenkins and Sir John were relying on me to get the goods on Mehmet and his mysterious relationship with Jacobs. It was an odd situation I found myself in with both a policeman and a retired security service officer banking on me to help them. While all I just wanted was rid of Mehmet and the threat he posed me.

Stitch up.

I locked the flat door behind me and tossed my rucksack to the floor. I hadn't slept in over two days apart from the almost trance like doze you get during a long period of surveillance. It's almost like sleeping with your eyes open, but alert to any movement from your subject. I felt surprisingly energetic but grimy. I'd been wearing the same clothes for forty eight hours and my face was streaked with the dried and fading cam cream. I stripped off in the hallway and headed for the shower before remembering the faintly unpleasant task that would be better done before I showered.

I opened the rucksack and removed the sleeping bag from the top. Beneath it was a black sack which I carefully removed. In it was a wide necked bottle full of two days of my piss and two freezer bags of my shit. There was no way I could leave those in-situ. Apart from the smell potentially giving me away to humans it would be like a beacon to animals.

The odious task completed I was more than ready for a shower where I spent a long time trying to get clean. Out of the shower the flat was so cold I shook rather than shivered. During the OP I had been comfortably snug in four layers of clothing and a sleeping bag. Within the little cave in the hedgerow the temperature had stayed quite mild and apart from the odd chill gust of wind, it had been a pleasant stay.

I was now quite familiar with the ground around Mehmet's property. The routine and rhythms of it's daily cycle now logged and recorded. The paper-boy, actually a fifty something male on a bike who deposited a broadsheet in a mail box at the gate. The postman who pulled up in a van and came to the door with packages too large for the box, the times Mehmet got up and about and the time the lights went out. I'd mapped and photographed the positions of camera's and alarm boxes and I'd observed Mehmet's routine when leaving and arriving.

I'd even grown accustomed to the movements and routines of the foxes and badger that visited the grounds. One fox, I'd gone to the trouble of naming James, even came up and gave the hide a sniff, checking out the strange intruder to his patch.

The second night I set out on my CTR. I had waited till gone three before I worked my way onto the golf course then up to the back fence. It had been a cloudy, moonless night full of enveloping darkness and convenient shadows. The front of the house was covered by two cameras. One large unit housed in a box with two powerful infra-red lamps pointed up the drive to the gate. The other a smaller camera surrounded by a ring of infra-red LEDs covered the front door.

True to form I found no cameras at the rear. I used the night scope to check for any beams of infra-red light spilling out, a sure give away for a camera, but the rear was clear. I slowly inched my way around the back of the building. There was no back door, but a set of double patio doors opened on to a paved area with a garden furniture and a barbecue. All the doors and windows were fitted to a high standard and all were alarmed.

This was a fairly secure house. Not military grade, not over the top, but better than average. I crawled round the garage. It was set into the side of the house and a tiled roof came off it at an angle to join the main roof of the house. I reached the corner and used my mirror to peer round the edge. I got a view of the front door. Too far away to get any detail so I scanned the alarm box and cameras, but again my 600mm lens with a two times converter had got me in closer during daylight. I made my way back out of the grounds.

Now wrapped up well in a sweatshirt and a fleece and with a strong hot cup of coffee I sat at the computer updating my detailed plan of the property. I still needed some more information before I could come up with a plan to get in and out, but those would have to wait till daylight. It was half eleven now and I was about to turn in when I remembered to check my various phones for messages.

A couple of bland non committal *"Hi how are you?"* messages from Clara. I was slowly but surely losing her, if it could even be said I'd ever had her. The problem was I didn't even know why and what made it worse was that problem was way down the list of things I was contending with. I moved on to the Harry phone. Two missed calls and a message saying *"Call me."* Maybe Harry had made a breakthrough. I called him straight away not bothering to go for a walk with the phone.

'Where the hell you been?' Barked Harry.

'Working.'

'Made any progress?'

'Getting towards it. These unconventional methods take time and planning to go properly.' I told him.

'Well old son, take my advice and ditch the whole thing. Pull up sticks and take a nice long holiday.'

Harry's sudden change of heart was disturbing to say the least. 'What the hell are you on about Harry?'

'Sunshine, we've bitten off a great deal more than we can chew here.'

'Harry, we suspected we were up against more than a local hood.'

'Ok, Let me tell you what's been going on in my sad little life. Yesterday morning I stroll into work all ready to continue the interviews with the your pair of axe murderers.

Well everyone is giving me the cold shoulder, OK, not an unusual happening when you are the model of charm and sunlight that is Harry Jenkins. So I get to my desk and all the files for the case are gone. Guess what Harry does next, he bellows around the office for the moron who's borrowed them. Instead of a reply from the sick, lame and terminally stupid that make up my team, I get called into to the D.I.'s office. Can you guess what happens there?'

'No Harry.'

'I thought not. No, I get arrested. Two clowns from Professional standards, a DS and a DI that looked about twelve fucking years old are waiting for me. They nick me then walk me out to the car and take me to another nick thirty miles away 'cos they can't use this nick in case anyone knows me. Fucks sake, I work all over the county every bugger knows me.' Harry was almost doing a good job at keeping his anger in check. 'Anyway, the allegation is that I stole a wedge of folding from the two amigos. Apparently they found some of it in my car. So they have turned that over and turned my house over while I spend almost twenty four hours in a cell.'

'I found the cells quite restful.'

'Sonny, this ain't the time to get smart. The net result is, I've been bailed while they investigate. Investigate what I don't know. There wasn't any cash and even if there was I wouldn't have taken it. So I've also been suspended from duty. No police powers for the first time in twenty years, well almost the first time. So if I were you I'd pack a case and go somewhere sunny, or failing that just get the fuck away from here.'

'Finished?'

'No. I'm just getting fucking started.'

'Good man, we're too close to give up now.'

'How exactly are we too close. We still haven't a fucking clue what's really going on, have we.'

'I get your point Harry, but the only way we we're going to find anything now is through my less than legal methods. One point Harry. This phone we're talking on, how did they miss it and are you sure they missed it?'

'That's the only bit of luck I've had in a few days. I left it round the ex's by mistake. So they have definitely missed it. There is one other issue though.'

I took a deep breath. 'Go on Harry.'

'The Turkish axe men. Looks like they'll make bail now. Basically the case against them is in danger of going into one giant fucking implosion. All the evidence I have touched is now tainted, so the forensics, everything from the death site and most of the interviews. Those two are probably back on the street already.'

My heart sank. Well it did if that expression means feeling like your stomach just dropped and came out your arse. 'I wish you were joking Harry, but I doubt you've ever told one in your life. But as a small consolation that gives us the motive for someone fitting you up.'

'It don't help me though. Just who are we up against?'

'I'm not entirely sure yet, but the fog is starting to clear. Harry stay by the phone, I need to accelerate things a little and I may need your help.'

'Well it's not as if I have anything to do now, is it.'

This whole affair was starting to feel like it one step forwards and two back. I pondered the sanity of taking one of Sir John's shotguns and waiting at the side of Mehmet's garage for him to come out in the morning and then letting him have both barrels in the chest. I

247

meditated on the image of his middle section spraying out in a liquefied mass of organs, bones and flesh while his confident smile disintegrated into a look of shock and horror. It's not my style but the thought did make me feel slightly better.

My personal phone rang, it was Clara. I didn't really feel like a heart to heart chat at this point and almost didn't pick it up. Still I'd get to hear her voice, so I picked up.

'Hi Clara how's it going?' Trying and failing to be upbeat.

'We've got a problem.' Definitely not upbeat, in fact deadly serious. If my heart could sink any more it would but it was already in the basement and the lift was broken.

'Just what I need, what is it?'

'It's Archie, he's gone.'

'What do you mean gone? In his permanent state of drunkenness he can't get far. The man runs off brandy fumes.'

'He's taken Sir John's MG.' I pictured both it and Archie either in a ditch or wrapped around a lamppost already.

'What the hell's got into him?' I couldn't imagine anything getting through the fog of alcohol to provoke that kind of rashness from Archie.

'We were watching the news and a small article at the end caught his attention. A short obituary of Mr Morgan from Morgan, Styles and Brown. It seems he died last night of a heart attack at home. Next thing we knew Archie was gone and all we saw were the tail lights of the MG weaving dangerously out of the driveway.'

'Shit, shit and shit. Fuck it Clara, I've just found out the two psychopaths are probably on the loose. This looks very much like a trap. Has he got a phone on him?'

'Not that I know of. His old Nokia is still here.'

'Damn it, I don't even know where Morgan lives, which is I guess where Archie is going. This is going to be like a needle in a haystack.' I really didn't have time for this. 'Look I'll call Duncan and get a clean car set up, then I'll try and find him.'

'Carry on what you're doing.' Clara's voice suddenly very stern. 'Sir John and I will take his Land-rover and go and look for Archie. Mehmet's men shouldn't know what Sir John looks like and I'll try and keep my head down.'

I was going to cut her off and tell her it was my problem and to stay put, but something changed my mind. 'OK, Clara, be careful. I'll do some research and see if I can find an address for the late Mr Morgan and I'll ring you back.'

'I'm always careful honey and thank you.' Her voice back closer to the seductive purr I'd come to know.

'For what?' Confused yet again.

'For not trying to stop me helping, for trusting me for once.' She purred and then hung up.

I sat stunned for second, not only did I not know what I was doing wrong, I equally didn't realise when I was doing the right thing with Clara. I shook out of my reverie and got to work on the computer.

22 Wednesday 23nd January 0430 Hours.

Teamwork.

Cold, dark and damp. Pre-dawn on a winter's morning. I don't think anyone would have been here had they much choice about it, but I'd pulled in a lot a favours and stretched a few loyalties to put a team together.

I hadn't got much sleep. It had taken me only a few minutes to come up with Morgan's address, which I duly passed on to Clara. Then I'd spent the rest of the night getting the kit ready for the morning's work. Before going out on an Op there are a thousand and one things to remember. I charged batteries, packed tool boxes and rucksacks and checked the technical gear. Having been in this game for so long, most of it is automatic now. I took my time deliberately in attempt to distract myself from worrying about Clara and the search for Archie-bloody-Hayes.

I'd had an update from Clara about midnight. No sign of Archie or the MG. I put thoughts about where he might be out of my head. He was a grown up and made his own choices. I remembered the watch I'd had Kash wear during the meet with the Turks. I dug it out and downloaded the video which I used to pull some stills of the two Turks. I emailed them to Clara with a warning to be on the look out for the pair then I got on with preparing for morning.

I'd selected the remote rural car park to a nature reserve some miles away from Mehmet's pad as our rendezvous point. Duncan, Kash and I rode in the ex Telephone van. The wheels cracked and crunched through frozen puddles as we drove a three sixty around the empty gravel. We parked in a far corner facing the entrance and waited for the others to arrive.

Harry arrived first driving a nondescript Vauxhall provided by Duncan the night before. He shuffled out of the car wrapped in a huge duffel coat and scarf. If I'd doubted Harry could appear any more grumpy than his normal surly self, a freezing winter's morning proved me wrong.

Next up was "Our Kev", or Kev the Scouse. He was actually from Birkenhead. Kev glided in on a bicycle coming to a stop by the two vehicles with a screech of brakes. He waved towards me. 'Ey, it's the solid state ninja.' He exclaimed towards me. That was everybody. I hoped it would be enough. As it was I'd had to break my rule about compartmentalising my personal associations and bring most of the people I knew together at once.

I stepped out of the side door of the van and handed round maps to everyone. No one seemed in the mood for talking.

'Tea, anyone?' Kev announced holding out the steaming flask.

I shook my head. 'No thanks Kev, I don't drink tea.'

Kevin looked at me like I was a creature from Mars. 'You don't..' He started to wonder, but Harry interrupted by taking the flask and thanking Kevin with a grimace that only passed for a smile because I was getting to know Harry's taciturn expressions.

I handed out radios and we quickly checked them amid squeals of feedback. Then I briefed everyone.

Kevin set off first, his primary task to cycle past the house and check for anything out of place. Easier to do at the speed a bicycle travelled than in a car. He'd then position himself at the road junction after Mehmet's house and pretend to mend a puncture. Harry would be sitting in the car at a junction in the opposite direction. Between them we'd have boxed Mehmet's house in as far of vehicular access went.

Next Duncan, Kash and I mounted up. I pulled on a set of telephone company overalls as we threaded through the country lanes to where I had identified the green cabinet for Mehmet's land line was

251

located next to a row of new builds about half a mile away from his house. I guessed his internet connection speed wasn't that great, but it was a plus point for me being able to tamper with it well out of sight.

Duncan pulled up right in front of the box bringing two wheels up onto the grass verge. I'd be out of sight to anyone except the local residents looking out of their side windows. I jumped out toolbox in hand and quickly opened the front of the cabinet. It took a few moments with the engineer's handset to find the correct circuit, but once I did it took only a second to disconnect it. I'd come back after and reconnect it with the addition of some recording equipment, but for now, I wanted Mehmet's house cut off from the outside world, just in case he had a burglar alarm that dialled out.

I stripped off the overalls as Duncan bumped down of the verge and we headed back to the main road past the house. It was now 0507. I had ground to cover before it got light. Kash handed me my kit as I suited up in a black load vest filled with the tools I'd need. I pulled a camouflage jacket over the top of that.

As we sped down the road I radioed Kevin and Harry to check we were clear fore and aft before I repeated the covert de-bus of the other night. It felt like rolling out into a field of glass as I flattened frozen stalks of grass. This time having cover at either end of the road I didn't have to worry too much about passing traffic and quickly made my way into the field and past my previous OP site. I headed to the rear of Mehmet's house, crawling the last fence line till I had a clear view of the back of the house.

Duncan's voice broke through the radio. 'In position.' He should now be sitting in a lay-by uphill half a kilometre, with eyes on the front of the house. Kash should be in the car with Harry. Now to exercise caution. No sense in rushing. I used a small night-scope to examine the back windows. Curtains were drawn and no sign of any movement. I started a very slow crawl towards the side of the garage. I wasn't sure whether a quick dash would have been better, but from what I knew of Mehmet's routine he should be asleep right now, so slowly and quietly won.

I reached the corner of the garage but stopped short. The grass and weeds were slightly longer here, I hunkered down, more against the cold than to hide. These kind of jobs always consist of ninety nine percent waiting, usually bored and cold and then one percent pure panic. This morning was no exception. I had to lay here and freeze at my point of maximum exposure and wait for an alignment of *"ifs"*. If Mehmet didn't vary the routine I observed the other day, if my hastily constructed electronics worked, if no one else turned up at the house. If all these and many more variables all lined up I should have a shot at getting into Mehmet's house undetected.

A freezing mist had formed in the lower lying areas and the cloud cover was thick. There was a hint of snow in the air. I looked at my watch. It was barely quarter to six. I shivered. I distracted myself by running through what I had to do in my head. I visualised it in detail, playing out the possible permutations and combinations if things went wrong. Every half an hour the team checked in on the radio their voices breaking into my thoughts via the ear piece. I acknowledged each of them with a double click of the PTT, too close to the house to risk talking.

Around eight I heard the first stirrings of movement in house, or rather I felt the vibrations of water running through pipes. It seemed Mehmet was up and using the bathroom. If he kept to the same routine I'd observed I shouldn't have more than an hour left feeling the frozen ground leech the warmth out from beneath me.

I tried to relax into the cold and stop the shivering, it made little difference. No matter if I froze to death here, I had to make this work. I was painfully aware this was my last play. I had no other tricks up my sleeve and I was committing all of my resources, the last of my resources, at trying to find our Mehmet's secrets.

I felt my phone vibrate in my pocket. Almost everyone with the number was somewhere around here with one of my radios. It could only be Clara. My bones creaked as I rolled partially to one side and fumbled with numb fingers to pull out the phone. I got the message up on the screen.

"Resuming search for Archie. X"

Damn her, why couldn't she wait a couple of hours. I really didn't like the fact the two Turkish psychopaths could be at large. However if things went as I hoped I might get a fix on those two, which would allow Clara and Sir John some freedom to hunt for Archie. I started to type a reply, a frustrating process with frozen fingers through gloves. I pulled off the gloves with my teeth and hastily in-putted a message.

"Hold off one hour or so will text when all clear."

I poked the phone back into it's pocket. The cold air on my bare fingers burned and kept burning even after I replaced the gloves. I lay with my hands folded into my armpits for warmth and waited.

A little before nine Harry called over the radio. 'Stand by, stand by.' I lay very still. 'Charlie two passing my location.' Charlie two was the Turks Mercedes. A few seconds later Duncan's voice announced calmly. 'Charlie two past my location. Bravos two and three inside.' The two Turks were heading this way. Both good and bad. They hadn't been at liberty when I had carried out the observations on this place. If they were to come in and sweep the grounds or anything like that I'd be quickly discovered.

I kept my head down, listening and picturing what was going on from the commentary. Duncan's voice came through my ear piece again. 'Charlie Two now static outside Alpha one. No movement.' I hoped this would mean they were going to wait at the gate for Mehmet. Now, so long as he took his own car and didn't walk out and travel in their death-mobile, we would be in business.

I heard movement in the garage I was laying against. If Mehmet did the same thing today he'd be getting into the car, opening the garage door with a remote control fob, starting the car and driving out. I fished in one of the pouches on my vest and pulled out a small black plastic box. It had a big red switch and an aerial. With a little luck and a of lot ingenuity Ali Mehmet's labour saving gadget was going to save me a lot of work.

With a rumble and a whirr that startled me, the garage door began rolling upwards and I heard the car start behind it. Duncan updated the net. 'Charlie Two still static. Charlie One now visible in the garage.' I switched on my little black box.

During my CTR, when I'd crawled round here I'd noted down the make and model of Mehmet's security system. It was quite a high end one complete with all mod cons. I'd downloaded the brochure. It proudly boasted how everything was integrated, no more carrying several fobs for your garage door, automatic gates ect., now everything could be controlled from one click. One click to open the door and one to close it and arm the alarm system.

A little more digging on the Internet and I'd located a copy of the service manual for the system. A glance at the circuit diagram of the fob and I worked out the frequency it transmitted on. A few hours with the soldering iron and I'd constructed a simple jammer which I mounted in the black box.

The trick relied on Mehmet not looking back to check on the door. I hadn't noticed him doing that the other morning. The modern human is a creature of habit, if that garage door had closed without problems a hundred times before, why wouldn't it again? I tensed up ready for action, still keeping myself flat on the ground next to the garage.

Duncan called in. 'Charlie One, mobile toward gate. Bravo one driving, and I've got Bravo two decamped from Charlie two at the gate.' What the hell was the Turk playing at? I heard the pitch of Charlie One, Mehmet's car raise as it must have accelerated forwards. With more creaking of cold and tired joints I pushed up into the start of a press up. The radio crackled again. 'Bravo two opening the gate and Charlie one now half way down the drive.' I caterpillared forward, keeping low and reaching the corner of the garage in one bound. I barely glanced up. The car was well down the drive, the big Turk holding the gate to the road open and looking towards his boss driving towards him. The car starting in the sub zero air had caused a fair amount of smoke, which was a bonus. I rolled into the mouth of the garage grateful that my device had worked and prevented the door rolling back down, and more importantly the arming of the burglar alarm system.

I kept rolling until I was well into the relative darkness of the garage. I snapped my head up and began searching for the manual door control. Duncan radioed an update. 'Charlie one now static on Red.' Good Mehmet was out on the main road now. I spotted the door control by the internal door leading into the house and crawled over and hit it. The door began whirring and grinding as the motor pushed it back to ground level leaving me in a sudden darkness.

I sat on the ground getting my breath back and waiting. Duncan chimed in again. 'Charlies one and two on red toward green.' Both cars were heading away. I hoped they'd be gone for a long while and give me time to really start getting under Mehmet's skin.

Kevin's Birkenhead tones now came on. 'Both Charlies left onto green, toward blue.' Good. They were heading into town. Kash's higher voice now broke in. 'We are static on Green.' As soon as the convoy passed them Harry would pull in behind and follow at a safe distance. Hopefully I'd now know wherever they went. In addition I had Duncan covering the front of the house with a long lens to warn of anyone approaching and Kevin at the end of the road. I allowed myself to relax a fraction and pulled out my mobile and quickly sent Clara a message that she was clear to look for Archie Hayes. The message sent I switched the phone off and activated two commercially bought jammers I had placed in my load vest. These should take out all the mobile phone bands and any wireless camera, wifi or GPS devices to a radius of thirty feet. All that radiation was probably mutating my DNA while I worked, but should the Burglar alarm be active and have a GSM backup, this would stop it calling out. I'd already taken care of the land line.

The door leading into the house was a low grade internal door with half of it a pane of single glazing. I looked through it at the alarm control panel on the wall. It looked to be un-armed. Time would soon tell. I pulled a pair of paper overshoes from a pocket and put them on. Then I removed my cold weather gloves, replacing them with two pairs of latex gloves. I tested the door. It was unlocked, Mehmet was overconfident in the merits of his automatic garage door.

I stepped in watching the alarm panel closely for any sign I'd triggered it. So far so good. Duncan called up. 'All clear out front.' Duncan would be watching the building and also relaying any updates from Kash and Harry who would be out of range for the radios now.

I had a fair idea of the internal layout of the house. I quickly and quietly went room to room in case there was anyone still home. The building was empty in more ways than one. It reminded me a lot of Clara's flat in that there were no personal effects, no photos, no souvenirs, no odd mismatched pieces of furniture kept for sentimental reasons. It was neat, very clean and tidy and expensively decorated but it had more the air of an hotel room than a home. Knowing my time might be limited I toured the house prioritising what I had to do. The phone line was covered, I could tap that at the green cabinet. I found a spare bedroom set up as an office. It was nothing fancy, just a desk with a high end laptop and a phone. I poked around looking for papers or ledgers. There was nothing of that kind, so I assumed everything was stored electronically.

The computer was switched off, which was another bonus. I used the camera on my phone to record to the positions of everything before I started moving things. I took out a memory stick and a couple of CD's from my pockets and fired up the computer. I interrupted the boot sequence, entered the BIOS menu and set the first boot device as a removable drive. I inserted the memory stick and rebooted.

Now instead of booting into what most likely was Windows 7, it would boot from my thumb drive into a heavily customised Linux based operating system. The system came to life quickly, the customised OS was a very slimmed down version. Once the machine was up and running I poked around in the operating system files and registry entries on Mehmet's hard drive. Having identified the correct version and service pack of Mehmet's operating system I copied across a few files and DLL's, replacing the original ones in his machine.

Now whenever Mehmet booted his computer it would load up my modified files as part of his operating system, right inside the Kernel to be technical about it. I hadn't added much functionality, but his machine would now open a reverse shell via an SSH tunnel right to my computer. What I had done in simple terms was place a back door in his operating system. One to which I alone had the key. So long as the laptop was connected to the Internet I'd be able to do pretty much anything I wanted. It would have been nice to take a full forensic level copy of his hard drive, but that could take several hours and the less time I spent here the better.

I removed my thumb drive, rebooted and set the BIOS back to how I had found it. Duncan broke through on the radio. 'Both Charlies and all Bravos complete at Alpha 3.' So they had all gone to Vista, well with the law offices burned down it was probably the closest thing to a workplace that they had. Now the plan was, if it were safe and feasible, Kash was going to stick a GPS tracker under the vehicles so I could track them remotely. I was slightly worried about this part of it because the two Turks had seen Kash before. I put that out of my mind and carried on with the task at hand.

On the floor behind the desk was the telephone jack. I got down on my hands and knees and quickly unscrewed the front cover and then wired in a small circuit board with a microphone on it. It was a quite basic parallel tap, powered from the fifty volt telephone supply line and transmitting audio back up the twisted pair in ultrasound. I left the office and found another telephone jack in the kitchen. I did the same here.

Duncan called up again. His calm and quiet Scottish voice over the radio always welcome on these type of jobs. 'All clear outside Alpha one, mobile unit has placed the trackers.' So still clear outside and hopefully Duncan would be also watching the laptop in the van and keeping an eye on the two vehicles. It would have been handy to bug both the cars, but I couldn't come up with the right combination of circumstances where I'd have enough time and unobserved access to them to do what was necessary.

I wasn't sure what to bug next. I took the cover off an electrical socket in the kitchen and wired in a radio bug as a back up to the one on the phone. I added another of these in the living room and then placed a final one in the office. I was covered in all the important areas. Knowing I was fairly safe from interruption I took a more careful look round the house.

Everything was well ordered and neat. Even the toiletries in the bathroom were arranged in a neat row. The fridge was quite sparse, but clean and sorted into sections. Someone like that had to keep records and I figured they would be on the computer. I couldn't wait to get started on that. I went once round the house comparing each room to the photograph I had taken, making sure everything was exactly as it had been before I arrived.

259

I then found the unit for the CCTV system, it was a stand alone hard drive unit. I erased the last three days of recording just in case it had picked something up on a camera I was unaware of. There was chance this might be noticed, but that would be a lot less catastrophic than Mehmet seeing footage of me skulking around his house.

Back in the garage I carefully closed the internal door and radioed Duncan. 'Exfil in thirty seconds, am I clear?'

'Aye, looking good.'

I hit the button for the garage door and waited for it roll completely up. Then I hit the button to close it and rolled out underneath the descending shutter. I shuffled around the corner and made my way over the back fence and took a leisurely stroll across fields to where Duncan was waiting to pick me up.

23 Wednesday 23nd January 1240 Hours.

Intercepts.

Duncan and I went back to the green cabinet. I connected an extra circuit in series with the subscriber loop. Everything coming down that line, both Mehmet's phone calls, and the feeds from my bugs would be transmitted a short distance. We left the van a couple of streets away. Kevin took the first shift sitting in the back and monitoring the feeds. The rest of us piled in the car with Harry.

Switching my mobile back on I had a message from Clara saying she was resuming the search for Archie. I'd deliberately forgotten about him so I could focus on breaking into Mehmet's house. For a second I considered joining the search, but sober reflection told me I could be of more use doing what I was doing. Almost as an afterthought I decided to text Clara the URL for the vehicle trackers, at least with her smart phone she could safely avoid Mehmet and his cronies while she and Sir John searched.

We dropped Kash in town near to his favourite burger house and then Harry near where he'd parked his personal car. Duncan left me a few streets away from my flat and was then going to relieve Kevin on monitoring duty.

I was priming the espresso machine when I got a text from Clara.

"Found John's MG, intact." So old Archie hadn't crashed it. Whether he was intact was still in question.

I pulled up the tracking page on my main computer. I'd made the trackers myself using GM862's a combined GSM phone and GPS unit with a built in python interpreter. They were easy to write code for and having made the devices myself, if they were discovered there would be no audit trail that tracked back to me. I had about two days before the battery would run out and I'd need to swap them out. The screen showed the Mehmet crew still static at the Vista bar.

Another text came in from Clara.

"Car was near a pub we are trying all the local pubs." A fair bet if you're looking for Archie.

I then logged into the proxy server I was bouncing the reverse shell from Mehmet's laptop through. Nothing yet. The only drawback, and it was a fundamental one, was that the computer had to be on and connected to the web for me to do anything. That could happen at any time or not at all if he either didn't use that computer or used another one somewhere else. I started to ponder if I should have hit the Vista bar rather than his house. I didn't really have the resources left for another B&E job like I'd pulled this morning, getting into Vista and up to the office would be a challenge.

I put that out of my mind for now and lost myself for a couple of hours writing a quick script in Python that periodically checked the proxy server for an active shell and then sent me an email when it found one. If Mehmet came online I'd have to work quickly.

It was almost five when Clara called. I picked up quickly.

'We've found Archie.'

'Is he,' I started.

'OK? He will be.'

'Did they, did Mehmet.' I tried again.

'If you'll let me finish,' She cut in impatiently, 'you might find out.' I sensibly kept quiet. 'We started on the pubs, and sure enough we'd found out he'd been in most of them. It looks like he somehow got back to town without crashing the MG and got diverted into the first pub he found. He seems to have conducted a one man wake of epic proportions. After finding eight pubs he'd been in I decided to take a short cut.' She paused, giving me an opportunity to appreciate her flash of inspiration.

'A short cut?'

'Yes dear, after visiting that many licensed premises I deduced the most obvious place to find him was either in A&E or a cell.'

'Which was it?'

'A&E, with alcohol poisoning. He's now feeling very sorry for himself.'

'What now?' I asked.

'They're keeping him in overnight, I'd say he's in as safe a place as any. I can't see Mehmet getting to him on a very public ward. I'll go and check on him in the morning.'

'I'll do that, it's a long drive from Sir John's.'

'It's OK, I'm going to back to my place.'

'You're what? You know that's not safe.'

'I'm fed up with hiding in the country, besides you sent me the link so I can track the opposition. I think I'm equipped to take care of myself.' I could hear more than a trace of annoyance in her voice now.

'It's just for a couple of days and then...' She cut the call. I rang back, it went straight to voice mail. I grabbed my jacket and headed round to her flat.

It should take Clara about fifteen minutes to get to her flat from the hospital. I got there in five and did a circuit of the building. Nothing was out of place so I went and loitered in a doorway on the opposite side of the road. A taxi pulled up shortly after and Clara stepped out. I hurried across the road and caught up to her as she went through the front door.

'You're not going to change my mind.' She announced with a toss of her hair as she let go of the heavy glass door. I managed to catch it just before it closed and latched. I followed her through and into the stairway almost having to run to keep up with her brisk, long legged stride as she went up the stairs.

We reached the door to her flat, she paused with the key in the door. She sighed. 'What is it you want?'

'I'm not sure.'

She opened the door and then looked at me. 'You better come in, we can't argue in front of the neighbours.'

I followed her in. She dropped her shoulder bag onto the kitchen work surface. 'Well done in finding Archie.' I said quietly.

'Is that all you came here to say?'

I'm smart enough to know something else was required here, just not quite smart enough to know what. 'I've not been myself recently.'

'Oh, you have been yourself, you just can't see it.'

I couldn't figure that one out either. 'I've been quite scared.'

'Nope, it's because you haven't been in control of the situation and you don't like that.' I wasn't sure which situation she was referring to, the Mehmet one or our situation.

'I'll give you that.'

'Look, David, I didn't want to have this conversation now, like this. Especially while all this other stuff is going on, but what are going to do with us? I know ours isn't what you would call a normal relationship, but.'

'But what Clara, maybe I play things too close to the chest, but you're perceptive, you must see how much I care?' I hadn't planned on saying so much, my mouth normally doesn't run away with itself to that extent.

I hit the target, Clara went quiet. She brushed some loose hair from her eyes and looked at me. 'How are we going to fix this then?' She took a step closer to me, fixing me in an intense stare. I wouldn't be able to lie my way out of this.

'When this job is over, it'll have been my last. I don't have a clue what the hell I'll do, but I'm getting sick of the lowlifes I have to work for.' I was definitely talking too much, but Clara had previous for making men do that.

'You'd do that for me?' Clara asked, her voice softening.

I wasn't even sure if I was telling the truth or not. I was getting pretty tired of the game and I couldn't imagine being with any other woman than Clara. 'You'd have to retire as well, I mean, if this were going to work out.'

Clara smiled and her dark eyes lit up and maybe I was going soft in the head, but I swear there was a tear in her eye. I didn't think she could do that. 'Of course, yes whatever you want honey.' She beamed like I had just proposed to her. I think what I had said was far more than that. She took the remaining step forward and kissed me, pulling me in close. My mouth was really running away with itself now, but in a very different way as I was enveloped in her thick dark hair.

The kiss lasted an infinity until she reluctantly broke it her hands gentle on my face pulling my lips from hers. 'Do you really mean it?' she breathed.

'Yes.' I breathed equally as huskily. At that moment I meant it more sincerely than I'd ever meant anything. She pulled me in close again, my face in her hair smelling her.

She whispered in my right ear, her lips teasing the ear lobe. 'When this job is finished, lets go away and plan our retirement.' She gently bit the lobe. I murmured some kind of a "yes", but not in any language I was familiar with.

Before I knew what was happening she had guided me through to the bedroom. I was still sightless, lost in a world of cascading hair and her urgently searching lips and tongue. She gently pulled me down to the bed and time stood still as we made love tangled up in half removed and twisted clothes. This was different to any of the previous times we had had sex. There was no artifice, no pretence and no subtle seduction. Just pure passion between us like I'd never known.

As we lay together, still entangled in discarded clothing feeling the heat of her sweat drenched body pressing against mine and still kissing, though slower and more gently now, I realised that she had never given herself to me like this before. Prior to tonight she'd always been holding something back, and probably so had I. We undressed properly and went to sleep holding each other. I felt like a teenager again and fell asleep with a smile on my face.

I was woken by a beep somewhere on the floor nearby. It took me a moment to realise it's importance. I rolled over and felt round on the floor for my trousers and retrieved the phone. It was the email I'd been waiting for. Mehmet was online. I slipped out of bed trying not to wake Clara, then stopped went back and kissed her gently on the forehead. She smiled in her sleep. I was getting too old be going and falling in love.

I dressed and looked at my watch it was two in the morning. I jogged through the freezing fog back to my flat. I got straight on the computer without even setting the coffee machine going. There it was, the black text window of a console open on my desktop.

I checked the tracking system. Mehmet was back home and had arrived there about half an hour ago. So, he'd come back from Vista and logged on. Now to work quickly as I couldn't know how long he'd leave the computer on for.

I started by taking a peek around his hard disk looking for interesting files. There was a directory of spreadsheet files and another of word processor documents. I TFTP'd them up to a server. Then I looked for and then snatched his mail archive and address book. He was still online, so I kept going. I took a copy of the windows registry, then I went searching for his web history. He used a browser that stored user names and passwords so I had those as well.

Mehmet logged off about half past three, but I was more than happy with my night's data haul. I made coffee and set to work going through it.

It was tough work. Most of the stuff was in Turkish. I made full use of online translators, but the going was slow and rendered imperfect results. Still I was getting a feeling for much of what had been going on. I had been right about one thing, Mehmet kept meticulous records, but I was coming round to the idea that records were part of his job.

Just before six I gave Harry a call. He was about to finish his shift in the van and hand over to Kevin. There had been no phone calls, Mehmet had returned about half one, turned the TV onto a Turkish rock music station and by the sounds of clicking had been working on his computer. I knew all of this apart from his music tastes. I thanked Harry and got back to work.

At quarter past seven my phone started ringing. I looked up expecting it to be Kevin reporting something from the van, I was puzzled when I saw it was Singh, Kash's father calling.

'David, is Gianprakash with you?'

'Um, no. He should be home.' I was puzzled.

'Ah, I thought he might be helping you with something, that's all.'

'He was yesterday, I dropped him town yesterday afternoon.'

'OK, I'm just getting a bit worried he hasn't come home yet.' I was starting to get that sinking feeling again.

'Mr Singh, does he have a girlfriend or someone that he visits.' I was clutching at straws here, I was fairly sure he didn't.

'David, you'd probably know more about that than me, youngsters today.' I pictured him shaking his head sadly while saying this.

'Mr. Singh let me make some checks and I'll get back to you.'

I hung up and rang Kash's mobile. It rang and rang out. At least it was still on. I had one more ace up my sleeve. I'd got Kash to give me the login for his phone tracking software a while ago, just as a precaution while he was running errands for me. I hunted around for the notebook I'd written it in. I found that and logged in. It seemed to take forever for the map to load. When it did I was stunned.

The red dot of the phone was showing square in the middle of the death farm, I shuddered at the thought of the place, my brain working overtime to figure out the meaning of this. What ever it was it didn't look good. This sinking feeling in the pit of my stomach was getting to be all too familiar. Clearly Mehmet had got hold of Kash, what he had done with him I'd surely find out. I put aside the growing self recrimination for getting the lad involved in this and started figuring out what to do.

24 Thursday 24nd January 0740 Hours.

Doing deals.

How the hell was I going to tell Kash's family? Maybe I could think of something and not have to. I took a deep breath. Take this one step at a time. I grabbed my jacket and went out to find a discrete phone box. I called Harry on the way and filled him in. He resisted any *"I told you so"* comments which I thought was quite charitable under the circumstances. I knew what happened next he'd be listening to.

I phoned Mehmet's landline. It was picked up quickly.

'Yes.'

'Mehmet, you know who this is?'

'I was expecting your call.' He was calm and relaxed, he held all the cards so why wouldn't he be. 'I was very disappointed you let me down the other night. We had an arrangement.'

'Cut the crap Mehmet, let the boy go.' I was no mood for criminals and their theatrics.

'Come and meet me and we'll discuss that.' I knew how far his idea of discussion went. It wasn't a very attractive prospect.

'OK, Mehmet, where and when?'

'You already know where, come whenever you like, but if you don't get there by eight this evening I'll dispose of the boy.'

'How do I know he's OK?'

'You don't.' Mehmet hung up.

Well I guessed the phone had been left there to show me where to go, or to entice me there. Either way Mehmet was starting to get wise to my methods. Had he guessed what else I was doing? I rushed back to my flat. I was hoping my call would prompt Mehmet into action, and action I could overhear and track.

I called Harry. 'What have you got.'

'I've got your call loud and clear. After that he made a mobile call, I couldn't hear much and besides it was all in Turkish.'

'Was it a long call?' I asked.

'Nope, very short. Look, I think you should really consider calling in the police on this.'

'Think about it Harry, we can't trust them, certainly not while Jacobs is around.'

'I hate to say it but you're probably right.'

'Ok, Harry call me the moment you hear anything else. Oh, and stay alert, I'm not sure how aware of my methods Mehmet is, but there's a chance he getting wise, I'll call Duncan and Kevin and get them out to you, that way they can keep an eye on the van.'

I made the calls and asked Kevin and Duncan to set up covertly and watch the van. Then lighted a cigarette and considered my options. I felt I had an inside track on Mehmet now, but Jacobs was still the wild card. Almost anything I could do to Mehmet, Jacobs could counter. Well almost anything.

I copied the relevant files from my Mehmet data trove to a laptop and stuck it in a bag. I was going to have to go out and about, what I was about to do I didn't want linking back to me in any way, shape or form.

I got an update from Harry, he had overheard Mehmet making a mobile call in English. He could only hear Mehmet's side of the conversation, but the gist of it was that the loose ends would be tied up soon. I guessed he was probably talking to Jacobs and the loose end was most likely me.

I took a walk around town and found a coffee shop with free WiFi, ordered a double espresso and sat down to work in a dark corner of the place. It's tricky working in a public place when you're up to no good. I had a corner seat and kept the screen in front of me. The whole job would have been far easier and faster at the flat, but I didn't want any of this going through an internet connection that could track back to me.

I then made some very tricky phone calls to London. My preparation as complete as time allowed I had one unpleasant visit to make.

As I stalked into Singh's shop he wordlessly beckoned me though the back and up the stairs into the accommodation above. I'd never been up here before. He offered me a seat and went to fetch me some tea. Sitting on the sofa opposite were two of the largest Sikhs I'd ever seen, they sat silently intimidating me with their impressive facial hair.

Mr. Singh came back in and handed me a cup of tea. He sat down and gestured to the two silent Sikhs. 'These are my brothers.' He said by way of explanation. 'Tell me David, What do you know?'

'Kash has been taken by some very bad people.'

Singh stroked his beard. 'I suspected that. What are we to do?'

'I'm going to get him back this evening.' I said scrutinising the his two brothers trying to see where their Kirpans where concealed. I explained my plan to Singh and his brothers, who sat impassively listening to me. Singh wanted me to take the two brothers with me as back up. They didn't really fit into my plan and it took some convincing to get Singh to let me play this out my own way. Eventually we compromised and I gave them a role in the plot.

Eventually I left the shop alone with just a couple of loose threads to tidy up. I wasn't entirely happy with the situation. Once again I wasn't in full control of the situation and my plan involved too much winging it for my liking.

25 Thursday 24nd January 1440 Hours.

After leaving Mr Singh I'd called both Harry and Clara to meet me at the café for a council of war. I left Duncan and Kevin at the van monitoring Mehmet's house. You can't have too much information.

We sat down with our coffees, back in my favourite discrete corner. 'Ok people, what is Mehmet's business?' I asked.

Harry sat silent. Clara ventured, 'Drugs?'

'Good guess, but no. Well not primarily.' There was a slight look of confusion on Clara, but I could see Harry's mind working. 'I've been through Mehmet's secret account spreadsheets and with the picture I've been building up his business portfolio I've got a pretty good idea of what his job is.'

'Go on.' Harry prompted leaning forward.

'Think about what we already knew. He runs, bars, kebab shops, car washes, hairdressers and tattoo parlours. The one thing they all have in common is that they are cash businesses.'

Harry very nearly smiled. 'He's laundering.'

'Exactly, he's legitimising the Turkish mobs cash in this country. From his online banking he is sending a lot of money to banks in Cyprus.'

Clara now leaned forward conspiratorially, I savoured the view it offered down her blouse while she spoke. 'So let me get this straight. He sets up these businesses, with Archie's help. But the profits they make are really the profits from organised crime. Which he then pays into legitimate accounts in Cyprus.'

'Well semi legit, but that's the gist of it. Why else would one town have twenty tattoo places, there's enough that this place should be looking like a Polynesian Island with all the body art. Why else in a recession are hand car washes opening left and right around the place? Every time you pass one there are ten people standing around doing nothing.' I sat back grinning to myself at my powers of deduction.

Harry cut to the chase. 'So Sherlock, where the hell does the spooky Jacobs fit into this?'

'I've an idea, my next meeting should throw a little light on that question. But consider this, what are the Turkish Mafia really good at?'

After a moments thought Clara cut in. 'Moving things, people, drugs, goods across borders.'

'Spot on, I guess for reasons of geography and history they've got really good at moving things across borders unnoticed. I'm sure that's where Jacobs fits in.' I briefed the pair on my plan for the evening. Harry volunteered to drop me the meeting. Clara was visibly not happy with not coming along. I explained that I needed someone who knew everything in reserve in case it all went horribly wrong. I didn't tell her that I half suspected she'd rip Mehmet's throat out if I let her get anywhere near him.

I gave Harry the details for later and left to go and pick up a car from Duncan's yard. I ordered two more coffees and sat back down with Clara. She was still frowning, I guessed because of my cutting her out of the endgame. I passed across a USB stick. 'You need to keep hold of this. Should anything go wrong It's got everything on it I've uncovered about Mehmet and the Turks operation.'

She picked it up and examined it at arm's length. 'What do I do with it?'

'Read through it all, I'm sure you'll come up with something. If you don't hear from me by tomorrow, then open it up Everything should be there.' I didn't tell her about the message I'd also left in the file, just in case. No sense in worrying her.

'So it's nearly over?' She asked.

'This time tomorrow, with a little luck, yes.'

'And this time tomorrow?'

'And this time tomorrow We'll be retired and heading away somewhere sunny to plan the rest of our lives.' I hadn't realised she had been holding her breath. She let it out all at once.

'You really mean that David?'

'I promise.' She brightened at that. Not sure what possessed me but I suddenly leaned across and kissed her. Clara was as shocked as I was. That was the first public display of affection I'd ever let slip out. It seemed right and after tonight I was sure I'd be trying that again. 'I have to go see your friend Sir John now. But get packing and I'll see you in the morning.' I kissed her again, on the forehead this time, and left.

Next I met Sir John in the park at the edge of the strip. He wore a vaguely military looking duffel coat and a brown fur trilby. I fell in beside him and we walked through the park.

I started straight into him. 'You've known exactly what's been going on all along haven't you?'

He looked sideways at me as we walked. 'Of course.'

'I've been played haven't I?'

'Yes, you have, but you've done very well, I'm quite impressed.' Sir John conceded.

'I need a favour. I need Jacobs kept out of the way this evening.'

Sir John paused in his walking and turned to me. 'You credit me with more influence than I have, but let me tell you about Jacobs.' He paused to find the words and then resumed walking as he spoke. 'The country needs men like Jacobs, men capable of working on their own initiative, on their own, without back up or support. He is a very capable operator, he can play a Police Superintendent, an army officer or an investment banker. He's quite ruthless and very driven.'

'Some kind of secret agent.'

'More a facilitator. He sets things up, plans and runs things which allow the er, secret agents if you wish to call them that, to do what they have to.'

'So Jacobs works for you?'

'No. He's so far off the books he doesn't work for anyone. He knows what he has to do and goes and does it. We don't pay him, as I said he is a very special asset.'

'I can't see any difference between him and Mehmet.'

'Ah, David, that's globalisation for you.'

'Globalisation?'

'The past twenty years we've seen terrorism become a super-national entity, much like business has gone global, so have our enemies. Likewise organised crime is now transnational. Borders don't mean anything to these people. Unfortunately states haven't evolved the same way, we're still bound by international law and border controls. In order to fight these people we've had to evolve like they have. It was logical for us to use the services of large organised criminals to help us achieve covert ends. But we had to keep ourselves insulated.'

'Hence Jacobs. My guess is Mehmet has been privately investing the money he was laundering to feather his own nest and got his fingers burned in more ways than one. Hence the spate of insurance jobs.' I added.

'Exactly, and Jacobs steps in offers him a way to recoup his losses while helping us. He's a very shrewd operator.'

'And that was bringing things in through the airfield and unit 14.'

'David, I can't possibly comment on that.' So it was true, hardly rocket science to figure it out.

'And you've known this the whole time?'

'Well, Jacobs has been exceeding his brief. We needed some way to clip his wings, without any official involvement or course.' Sir John paused again and looked at me. 'That's where you came in. When Mehmet got arrested this looked like the perfect opportunity to get control over the situation and rein Jacobs in a little. When they hired you I saw the means by which we could bring Mehmet down and slow Jacobs down.'

'How exactly?'

'We know quite a lot about you. People who are any good at what you do are of interest to us. We can't have you going and working for the other side can we?' I wondered who the hell the other side was meant to be. Sir John continued. 'I've been keeping a close eye on you all along. I began using Clara just in case I needed to get closer to you. So when it was necessary to give you a little nudge in the right direction I did.' I felt slightly sick. I'd been played all along, while I thought I was in the shadows pulling the strings I had actually been the puppet.

'I'm not sure I like what I'm hearing.'

'I'm sure not David, but needs must when the Devil drives and all that.' He resumed walking. 'Now, you're going to go and deal with Mehmet and get your young friend back. I'll do what I can to keep Jacobs out of the picture while you finish things, but I can't promise anything.' I wouldn't have believed him even if he had. I turned to go. 'You know David, come and see me when this is over. I can use a man of your talents.'

I was getting the feeling that Sir John was a lot higher up the food chain than he let on and also a lot less retired than he made out. I stopped and looked back at him. 'I'm not really a joiner, Sir John. I don't think I'd fit in with your kind of organisation.'

Sir John looked at me sadly. 'A pity.'

I started to walk away but turned back. 'Besides, after this I'm out. Clara and I are retiring.'

'Really?' He said with a slight raise of an eyebrow.

26 Thursday 24nd January 1840 Hours.

Exchanges.

Blundering about in the dark again. It seemed that I'd spent a lot of the past ten days blundering about not really sure what was going on. I thought I had a pretty good idea now as Harry dropped me close to the execution barn. I hoped I hadn't got wise too late in the game.

There was no light here at all and I stumbled my way up the country lane colliding with the grass banks and sloshing through partially frozen puddles until my eyes adjusted to the dark. It was deathly quiet and the only noise was my haphazard progress.

Gradually my night vision kicked in. The hedges and trees began looming at me out of the gloom. I found the entrance to the yard and as I walked across the gravel a sudden glare opened up in front blinding me. I stood still shielding my eyes with my arm while my sight readjusted to a pair of Mercedes headlights at full beam pointing at me.

I noticed something at my feet and bent to pick it up. It was Kash's phone. I walked over to the car. I wasn't surprised to see the two Turk psychos. The larger one got out of the car and walked over to me grinning. I showed him the phone. 'Drop something? You people really must learn to be more careful with your phones.' I said with a lot more confidence than I felt. The big Turk produced a gun and with one hand and took the phone off me. He motioned me into the back of the car and then slid in next to me. There wasn't a lot of room next to his bulk. I ignored the tent in his trousers with a suppressed shudder. There really is a point where you can take enjoying your work too far.

It was just the Turkish Tweedle-Dum and Tweedle-Dee in the car. We pulled out of the yard and onto the road. I hoped I was right about our destination as we wound our way back through the increasingly familiar country lanes. Tweedle-Dum kept the pistol pointing at my ribs, it seemed a redundant act. I don't have much capacity for violence and even if I did I doubted I'd have been able to make much of an impression on him.

We pulled into the industrial estate next to the airfield and stopped outside Unit 14. Mehmet's car was already there. The driver got out and opened my door. My large companion in the back prodded me out at gun point.

I stepped out into the glare of the wide open shutters of Unit 14. Bright fluorescents illuminated the hard-standing. I glanced in the unit. It was mostly empty save a few boxes and packing crates. One was open and I saw Kash sat tied up in it. It looked like we were going to be extraordinarily rendered.

Mehmet strode out to meet me. He was dressed in what appeared to be his habitual striped shirt. A blazer and a heavy wool overcoat augmented it for the weather. He stopped a few paces short and looked me up and down.

'So, we meet at last.' Hardly original.

'Oh, I've met you Ali, you just haven't met me.'

He snorted. 'I rarely meet the hired help.'

I just shrugged.

'Take him to join the boy.' He spoke to the Tweedle-dum.

'Just a minute Ali, don't you know want to know what's going on?'

Ali Mehmet turned back to me and looked me up and down incredulously. 'I say what's going on, I know everything that's going on.' He spat on the floor and turned away.

'OK have it your way.' I held up a hand. 'I just thought you might like to know what you've been doing.'

Mehmet started to turn back towards me but his attention was diverted by several cars heading through the industrial park. Two were Mercedes and I guessed he recognised them. Following was a Range Rover and a people carrier. Quite a turn out. I was impressed even though they were cutting a little fine with the timings.

The cars came to a stop in front of the unit. I was between them and Mehmet. Not a place I wanted to be. While his attention was diverted I started edging towards the hanger. Car doors started opening and large men in heavy overcoats started spilling out. One door was held open and a much older man with long silver hair stepped onto the tarmac. He strode over to Mehmet. All eyes were on the pair, so while they watched I backed towards the unit and Kash. The silver haired man spotted the movement out of the corner of his eye. He had good situational awareness. He beckoned me over. I hesitated, but the old guy fixed me in a gaze that didn't give me a lot of choice.

I joined the pair in the centre of the four ring circus. More Mercedes cars and guns surrounded us than you could shake a stick at.

From my data haul I'd taken from Mehmet's computer last night I'd finally gathered enough of a picture of his business, but more importantly his online banking details. I'd gone to the café and started transferring money out of the Cyprus accounts. I'd bought Bitcoins with the money, which I then transferred through several Bitcoin washers. OK, so I lost a fair percentage, but hell it wasn't my money. I spread the resulting money into several Bitcoin wallets. The money wasn't impossible to find, but it would be very hard, I'm sure beyond the resources of an organised crime gang, but I couldn't guarantee it would elude Jacobs for long.

The next thing I'd done was use Mehmet's email address book to contact the source of his money. Mehmet's boss effectively. I hadn't found proof Mehmet was skimming the take, but that wasn't important. He most likely was, but the thing about all criminal enterprise is that everyone is a thief. It's not hard to sow suspicion. There had been a couple of difficult phone calls to London, but when I showed them Mehmet's personal account with a vastly inflated balance it didn't take much.

Getting through to the big man had been difficult. The main function of a large gang is to provide layers of security for the big boss. When I reeled off a list of bank numbers and balances I got their attention. I was most concerned not to bring up Mehmet's name at too lower level in case I was speaking to someone with an interest in protecting him.

I had done a deal. I get Kash, they get the money back and I tell them exactly where to find Mehmet. Well they would get most of the cash back.

The pair had been talking, Mehmet leaning forward in what I read as a clear subservient pose. He suddenly straightened up and turned on me. 'This man is a liar! He is nothing more than a common nuisance.' He raised his voice at the end. I took this as a good sign, he was getting stressed. Time to have some of your own medicine motherfucker.

'Follow the money.' I said speaking to older man.

Mehmet and the older man were raising their voices now. Hand gestures were getting more expressive and all the henchmen were getting nervous. I backed further away ready to make a run to free Kash.

Mehmet's boss reached into his jacket pocket suddenly. Everyone froze. The fist came out wrapped around several sheets of paper. I was confident they were the bank statements showing a shortage in the expected balance. The papers were thrust right into Mehmet's nose. He just stood there in silence.

The first shot took me by surprise. Not by the noise, it was quieter than I expected, but rather the little angry wasp that buzzed past my ear at the same time. I ducked instinctively. The other henchmen all drew and started firing instinctively.

The larger of Mehmet's psychos seemed to catch a bullet. He jerked like he'd been punched, but recovered and continued heading towards the parked cars firing as he went. I don't think he realised he's been hit and managed to drop at least two people himself before his legs suddenly buckled beneath him and he went to his knees with a bewildered expression on his face. He didn't have long to wonder at his misfortune before a short guy with a long shotgun calmly walked round one of cars and shot at close range disintegrating the Turk's skull into a pink mist. Large chunks of skull and hair landed in arc across the tarmac.

I needed no second invitation, I sprinted for Kash's crate. The box was on it's side and the lid was off. They probably had been waiting to shove me inside as well. Kash was handcuffed but looked otherwise unharmed. I'd learned my lesson by now and had come out prepared with a handcuff key taped to my back. I ripped it off from under my shirt and freed him.

'You OK?'

'Yeah fine, well I'm hungry.' He said rubbing his wrists.

The intensity of the shooting had slackened. Kash and I remained crouched behind the crate, it wouldn't stop a bullet, but if they couldn't see us they couldn't aim at us. I wasn't confident that the big boss would honour our deal so I wanted to get as far away as possible. Harry should have made an anonymous call to the Police by now and so Armed response units would be heading towards us at a great rate of knots. I wanted to be gone long before they got here.

I propelled Kash out of the unit. As we left I saw Mehmet turn and run towards us, I've no idea what his plan was, but that became a moot point as I saw his striped shirt rupture in a bloom of red. He fell face forward onto the ground his mouth moving wordlessly as he coughed up bright frothy blood. We kept going amid the almost toy like pops of pistols and the occasional deeper boom of what I presumed was a shotgun.

We ran across the frozen turf out into the fields and towards the main road. I was just aiming for getting into the relative darkness. I was sure that Mehmet's remaining thug would soon be dealt with as he was heavily out-gunned.

Half way across the fields the shooting seemed to die down to replaced temporarily by an ominous silence, punctuated by Kash and me panting. We slowed to a jog and then a fast walk as the first wails of sirens began began in the distance and the blue strobing of the lights reflected off of the low cloud

The road was getting closer. A car slowed and stopped. According to the compromise of a plan this should be Kash's uncles to pick us up. The drivers door opened and I saw the silhouetted figure step towards us.

Kash and I advanced closer coming under the yellow pool of street lamps.

A voice called out. 'You really are a slippery bugger.'

I froze. I recognised the voice. Jacobs walked up to us.

'You've caused me a lot of trouble.'

'I try.' I conceded.

Jacobs sighed. 'I hate to get my hands dirty, but I really dislike amateurs like you.' He produced a pistol from the waist band of his jeans.

'you'd really kill both of us, your game with Mehmet is over, he's already dead? Time to move on.' I was playing for time, while I wanted to be long gone before the police arrived, their presence would make killing us very difficult for Jacobs.

The flashing blue and red got closer as the cars began pulling up around the industrial units. Even from this distance the flashing produced a disorientating stop frame effect on my vision.

Jacobs glanced down at the pistol and then into the distance at the lights. The cracks of sporadic shooting started up again. He shrugged and put the gun away. 'No, I've got a better idea. You've eluded me and evaded me all this time. I think it's fair we get a chance to finish this properly. I'm going to find you and I'm going to make your life hell. It's going to start with your young friend here. He's burned. I'll have his phone, his Internet and his home monitored. If you go near him I'll have you.'

'Why take things so personally?' I asked.

He ignored me and continued. 'And as for your girlfriend. She's burned too, was a while ago to be honest. I'll have a team permanently on her, you even get near enough to see her and I'll have you. You understand me? I'm all over you. You show up on the grid and I'll fucking bury you. You're only choice now is to run and hide, spend the rest of your miserable little life cowering in a hole somewhere.'

'You are a really sore loser.' I told him.

He glared at me. I was getting that a lot this evening. 'You're the loser. You don't seem to understand quite what I'm capable of. Well you're going to learn the hard way.'

I was tempted to stay and chat, angry as he was I felt I had a chance at making Jacobs spill more of what he knew about me. However the Police would eventually spot us here and I didn't relish trying to explain my presence here. I wasn't worried about getting shot now, he had expended too much breath talking to me now. Besides Jacobs was boring me. Over his shoulder I saw Singh's people carrier pull up. Three large turbaned figures got out. An impressive sight, I was sure they were carrying large kirpans and would only be too happy to fillet and gut Jacobs for me. I resisted the impulse to test that theory. Violence isn't my strong suit. I turned to Kash. 'Let's go Kash.' He said nothing and followed.

Kash and I silently walked past Jacobs still glowering at me. I felt his eyes on me all the way to the car.

27 Sunday 27nd January 1700 Hours.

Epilogue.

Those of the Turkish gang that hadn't been shot had been rounded up by the Police. I'd checked the news reports and I couldn't see the hand of Jacobs interfering anywhere, but I could never be sure. Besides Mehmet and the larger of his henchmen were both cooling in a mortuary somewhere. The smaller of the two monsters was breathing only with the aid of a machine and surrounded by a heavy police guard.

Jacobs words had disturbed me more than I cared to admit. Almost as chilling was Sir John's admission that he had been monitoring and playing me all along. I threw out every phone and device capable of transmitting a signal and spent fourteen hours sweeping my flat for bugs. It looked like a bomb had gone off in it, a dirty bomb at that. I never found anything, but that just made things worse.

I'd eventually fallen asleep after two days of being awake. It was a fitful sleep. I needed to go and see Clara and explain things. I couldn't call her having disposed of all my phones. I'd taken a careful stroll around her building, one block out checking for any kind of surveillance.

I'd almost completed the circuit when I saw it. It was so obvious, a van with mirrored windows, that it was clearly meant for me to find. I felt a surge in adrenaline and immediately turned off down an alley and got the hell out of the area. If I were meant to find it then there would be another better hidden OP watching the van.

I didn't know if I was more angry or sad. The whole thing struck me as ridiculous. Who the hell could afford to put surveillance teams round the clock on someone purely out of spite. No, it just wasn't tenable, not for any length of time anyway. I stayed away from everyone I knew. I took a trip to London. When I'd started moving

Mehmet's money around I'd skimmed from the skim and stuffed a few Bitcoin wallets that I didn't tell anyone about. The ones I'd set Mehmet up with also hadn't been touched so I started making use of them.

A few goes round in Bitcoin washers and some long distance transfers I started shifting the money out into a form I could use. There are several places in London where Bitcoins can be exchanged out on pre-paid credit cards. No questions asked. The only down side was that to keep it anonymous I was limited in how much I could load onto each card. I went and picked up a half dozen cards from several different outlets. It wouldn't leave me wealthy, but at least I had some working cash again.

On my return I waited till after dark and walked the box around Clara's apartment. I wondered what she must be thinking. I badly needed to talk to her and explain the hitch in our plans. It was cold and damp again and the warmth and light of Clara's flat was drawing me in. Then I saw the van again. It had moved, but was still in the same street with a good view of the doorway to the building. My heart sank. I stood in the shadows of an alleyway inspecting it. There was no way to tell from here if it was even being used or was just an elaborate decoy.

As I stood watching a taxi pulled up. Clara gracefully slid out of the back, her long legs gliding to the ground. She paid the driver and with a toss of her long dark hair walked towards the building. She stopped at the door and turned round her dark eyes checking out the van and then moving off and lingering for a few seconds over the shadows I was hiding within.

I wanted Clara more than ever. It was being denied her made me realise how much I actually needed her. I stared on sadly as she let herself in and disappeared from sight.

I slunk back into the shadows. I was going to have to find a way to deal with Mr. Jacobs.

The End.

Author's Notes.

While this is all a work of fiction and fantasy I've tried to make everything as real as I could. In recent years the topic of surveillance and intrusion have become headline news, from Phone hacking scandals to the revelation of various whistle-blowers in the security services. None of what had been revealed is really news, it's all been going on years and the information was publicly available to those who sought it out.

Unfortunately Hollywood, TV and a lot of writers have all too often used the technical aspects of surveillance as a bit of cop out to cover bad plotting. This has left the general public on the one hand with a quite unreasonable expectation of what can be done with technology, but also an astonishing naivety about how wide spread and common surveillance actually is.

Having dabbled in the trade of Surveillance myself (and barely scratched a living) a lot of the Bugman is based on personal experience. However the genesis of the character a debt is owed to one book. Quite by chance I came across a copy of *"The Basement Bugger's Bible"* by Shifty Bugman. The book is an excellent technical resources for anyone interested in learning the trade. It's a very technical book, so a good knowledge of electronics is the price of entry. However the book also contains a number of entertaining anecdotes from Shifty's career. If you can still find a copy it's well worth a read.

The whole fingerprint sequence is real and was carried out by the Kaos Komputer Klub in Germany. I've replicated the process at home and can confirm it works, however I haven't personally tested the results with a live fingerprint scanner. There is an opportunity for someone with access to a police custody area.

The night vision lens used is based on one the Author has built using the innards of an image intensifier tube that was bought on the surplus market. There are various guides on the internet showing how to box one up and add the necessary optics. For mine I built it to mate with a canon digital SLR. While it's a generation one device, and hence quite large and bulky it actually outperforms most modern, commercially available devices and costs about a tenth.

The vehicle tracking GPS device is also real and one can be built fairly cheaply at home, as the author has done. A Tellit GN862 unit was used. This comprised of a GPS receiver, and GSM unit and a control computer with a built in Python interpreter. Software can be written quite quickly and easily. Just add a battery and the relevant antenna then along with a sim card you are in business.

The section where an employee is the victim of a social engineering attack is all too real and common in the world of hacking. The greatest vulnerability of any security of computer system is the human element and this is what social engineering attacks. Anyone wishing to learn more about this can do worse that read Kevin Mitnick's *"The Art Of Deception."*

All the bugs used are practical and sample circuits can be found in the aforementioned "Basement Bugger's bible.'

The lock picking sections are again hopefully as real as I can make them. I've been picking locks for a few decades now, and while I've still not got much better, it's not that hard to open most locks, particularly if you have the right tools. Someone wishing to learn this art/science would be advised to check out http://www.lockpicking101.com you may even meet me on one of the message boards.

The method Bugman circumvents the alarm system and garage door is based on similar method used by criminal gangs for several years to steal high end cars. Their attack involved waiting in car parks and using a jammer to block the signal from key fobs and prevent the locks/immobiliser from activating. It's documented as having been used with success.

The process of putting a back-door in a computer, is again real. If you have physical access to a machine it's almost child's play. For reasons of brevity I couldn't go into too much detail in the book. Anyone wishing to do it for themselves should probably start out by learning a programming language and then progress from there, much like I and my of my friends in the hacking world did. The other thing to do is to take out a subscription to 2600 magazine. I occasionally contribute articles to this august publication. Http://www.2600.com to subscribe.

For those with an interest in the fighting arts, while I don't name it in the book, Clara is using Aikido during the confrontation outside the casino. In particular she is using a variant on the technique called *"irimi nage."* She augments that with some improvised and viscous *atemi.*

The criminal gang described here and the kind of activities they are involved in are common knowledge, the concept of globalisation and trans-national criminal organisations are very real and governments around the world are struggling to contain these entities. A good overview of the situation can be found in *"McMafia"* by Misha Glenny.

The overlap between organised crime, terrorism, multinational companies and governments is, I feel quite plausible and rational. If the kind of things I describe aren't happening I'd be very surprised.

Take care and remember you never know who's listening!

Will Conrad 2013.

14360416R00163

Printed in Great Britain
by Amazon.co.uk, Ltd.,
Marston Gate.